LOVING TOUCH

"You can't control everything, Josie." Alex leaned over and deliberately set his glass down upon the table. He returned to stand over her with a direct look. "Which ankle did you hurt?"

"The left one."

"Very well." He moved to her feet. Lifting them up, he sat down and rested them upon his lap.

"Alex!" Josie exclaimed, completely shocked.

"I only wish to examine your ankle. The doctor is going to be one busy man when he arrives." Alex very discreetly shifted the hem of her dress and slid her left slipper off. Josie started as he put his hand upon her foot. "Does this hurt?"

It did anything but hurt. "N-N-No."

"Good," Alex said. He began to rub her stockinged foot. Josie flushed deeply. "Alex?"

"Yes?" Alex asked, grinning.

"This . . . this cannot be proper," Josie stammered.

"No," Alex said. "But then, Josie, you are anything but proper, and neither am I."

"But . . . but," Josie sighed. "We are supposed to be reforming."

"We are." Alex laughed. "It stuns me how much I am reforming. But we must take it slowly, as not to traumatize ourselves."

Josie, in truth, felt slightly traumatized. Just from the pleasure. Then a thought crossed her mind and she sat up. "Alex?"

"Yes?"

"This . . . this isn't—" She halted.

"Isn't what?"

Josie flushed. "Something a . . . a mistress does?"

"No," Alex said. "You may relax."

"Thank heaven," Josie said, leaning back.

The oddest smile tipped Alex's lips. "This is something married people do."

Books by Cindy Holbrook

A SUITABLE CONNECTION
LADY MEGAN'S MASQUERADE
A DARING DECEPTION
COVINGTON'S FOLLY
A RAKE'S REFORM
LORD SAYER'S GHOST
THE ACTRESS AND THE MARQUIS
THE COUNTRY GENTLEMAN
MY LADY'S SERVANT
THE RELUCTANT BRIDE

Published by Zebra Books

THE
RELUCTANT
BRIDE

Cindy Holbrook

Zebra Books
Kensington Publishing Corp.
http://www.zebrabooks.com

ZEBRA BOOKS are published by

Kensington Publishing Corp.
850 Third Avenue
New York, NY 10022

First Printing: December, 1998
10 9 8 7 6 5 4 3 2 1

Printed in the United States of America

One

"Alexander, we have come to see you upon a matter of utmost importance," Lady Rothmier said in a die-away voice. From where she rested upon the settee, the fluttering pastel of her skirts enhanced her look of fragile femininity.

"Have you indeed?" Alexander asked, a smile twisting his lips as he surveyed his parlor, which now housed his two sisters and mother. Instinct warned him it would have been best not to have stepped foot into the room.

"The utmost," Mandy said, standing close beside her mother. She held up two vials of Heartsworn and three handkerchiefs, her eyes twinkling. It was a given sign that their frail mother intended to wage war to the highest degree. No doubt, if he did not succumb to whatever matter Lady Rothmier had decided was of the utmost importance, he would be entertained to a display of hysterics and palpitations that even the great Sarah Siddons could not perform. He sighed. He'd lay odds that within the hour he would become a serpent nursed at his mother's bosom.

"I see," Alexander said, strolling over to the bar to pour a brandy. "Permit me to ring for Biddle and have him bring some tea and cakes. Or perhaps ratafia?"

"No," Lady Rothmier said, sighing. "I cannot think to have anything to drink. You know my constitution is delicate. I dare not take anything this early in the morning."

"Of course," Alexander said in a mild tone. "Perhaps if you feel so faint this morning, you should return home and we shall have this discussion another time when you feel better."

"No, no," Lady Rothmier said, stiffening and lifting her head in emulation of a martyred saint. "Never shall it be said of Beatrice Rothmier that she denies her children anything. I shall muster all my poor strength when I know a child of mine is in need."

"Am I in need?" Alexander asked, strolling over to lower himself into a chair. "You must forgive me. I am not aware of my sad plight."

"You never are," his sister Lydia said, her tone sour as she sat ramrod straight, gazing at him with a frigid look. She was a handsome woman, with dark eyes and a full figure, dressed with the elegant propriety befitting the wife of the politically prominent Baron Southwester. Her gaze narrowed as Alexander smiled, tipped his glass of brandy to her, and then leisurely sipped from it.

"Alexander, you have turned thirty," Lady Rothmier said, her voice teary.

"Yes, so I have," Alexander said in solemn tones. "I know it is shocking and quite inconsiderate, but age, I fear, must come to us all. Please, do not permit it to throw you into the doldrums. I assure you, I do not think on it."

"That is the precise problem," Lydia said, her tone sharp.

"Yes," Lady Rothmier wailed. "You are thirty! Thirty and without wife or family."

Alex lifted a brow and looked at his mother and sisters, each in turn. "Oh, surely not without family."

"I should have grandchildren," Lady Rothmier said with a choked sob.

"But you do, my dear," Alexander said. He cast a sympathetic look upon Lydia. "You must forgive Mother. I'm sure it is just a slight memory lapse of hers. No one, I assure you, could forget your two darling children."

"She means yours," Lydia snapped, her eyes shooting fire.

"Mine?" Alexander asked. "Now it is you who are forgetting. I have none." He frowned. "None that I know of at least. If that is the urgent matter, only tell me who applied to you with a claim I have sired—"

"Oh, oh!" Lady Rothmier cried. "Mandy, quick, my Heartsworn." Mandy instantly uncapped and handed the first bottle to her mother. Lady Rothmier snatched it up and breathed deeply from it. She sighed, shaking her head. "That a son of mine would dare to talk of such matters to his mother!"

"But you came to speak to me of my children, did you not?" Alexander asked.

"No, we came to speak to you of your marriage," Lydia said.

"My marriage?" Alexander asked. He shook his head. "Now I am all at sea."

"Your marriage to dear Josephine Stanton," Lady Rothmier said, waving her Heartsworn at him as if brandishing a sword. "It is time you fulfill the promise between our families. It was your father's dying wish."

"Was it?" Alexander asked. Since his father, the late Marquis of Wyndam, had died from falling off his horse after cramming it over a fence in a steeplechase with Lord Alvany, Alexander rather imagined his dying wish was to have cleared the finish line and bested his friend.

"You should have married Josephine long before this," Lydia said. "If it were not for your callous disregard for duty and family."

"Indeed," Alexander said, his voice cold.

"Yes," Lydia said, her eyes narrowing. "All you care about is your gaming and whoring—"

"Lydia!" Lady Beatrice wheezed. Mandy immediately

handed her mother a handkerchief, even as she made a choking noise, which sounded suspiciously like a stifled laugh.

"Well, it is true," Lydia said, her face indignant. "He leads a life of disrepute and debauchery. Many are the times I have been mortified, simply mortified, to hear of his exploits. He does not consider what shame he brings upon our good name. Why, my dear Peter is perpetually shocked—"

"You are the one who wished to marry him," Alexander said. "I told you he was a pompous . . . prig, but you would not listen."

"He is not a prig!" Lydia said, her bountiful chest puffing out. " 'Tis you who are dissolute. It is past time you marry. You are now thirty and you owe it to the family."

"Yes," Lady Beatrice said. "And to the poor Stantons. Why, they have waited years for the blessed union between our families."

"Have they?" Alexander asked, raising his brow. "Why, then, haven't I even seen this girl?"

"You saw her when you were young," Lydia said, sniffing.

Alex shook his head. "I don't remember her."

"Of course not," Lydia said. "You were too busy playing with her brother. You did not care to play with any of us females."

"Ah, yes," Alex said, his lips twitching. "That was when I was young and foolish. I had not yet discovered the pleasures of playing with females."

Lydia threw up her hands with a sound of disgust. His mother moaned. Only Mandy giggled and said, "But Alex, Michael Stanton is Josephine's twin brother; they must surely look alike."

"Indeed?" He raised his brow. "I have seen young Michael about town. He is a rather pretty fellow, but I would not wish to marry him."

"You aren't marrying him," Lydia said, her gnashing teeth clearly audible. "You are marrying Josephine Stanton."

"Am I?" Alex asked in a dangerous tone.

"Yes, you are," Lydia said, glaring at him. "You have always known of the arrangement between our two families. Lord Stanton has approached Mother once more, which is his right, to ask when you intend to fulfill the promise."

"Yes," Lady Beatrice sighed, shaking her head. "I did not know what to say to the poor man."

"I am to wed merely because you did not know what to say to the poor man?" Alexander asked, quirking his brow.

"You are to wed," Lydia said, her voice stern, "because it is time for you to marry. Past time!"

"Indeed," Lady Beatrice said. "No one can deny Lord Stanton has been extremely patient, but now he grows anxious."

"Under the hatches, is he?" Alex asked dryly. "But then, when has he not been?"

"Do not be vulgar," Lydia snapped.

Alex shrugged. " 'Tis not vulgar, but a known fact. The Stantons are notorious for their excesses."

"The Stantons are a fine family," Lydia said in awe-inspiring dignity, "with blood which dates back to the Conquests. Considering the name you have created, you dare not cast stones. I doubt there is another family with such excellent lineage that would be pleased to welcome you into their midst."

"Lydia," Mandy said, "you are coming on too strong. You know Alex is still one of the finest catches on the Mart."

"Mandy," Lady Beatrice scolded, "do not use such indelicate language."

"I am sorry," Mandy apologized, "but you know it is

not true what Lydia said. She is making it sound as if Alex is a pariah."

"Well, he will become one if he continues on this course," Lydia said. "He simply must cease his reprehensible ways and take on the duties required of the Marquis of Wyndam. He owes it to the family." She glared at Alex. "Which he would know it if he weren't so selfish."

Alex smiled wryly and turned a teasing gaze upon Mandy. "What do you think?"

Mandy did not return his smile, and her eyes grew dark. "I feel sorry for Josephine Stanton."

"What?" Alex asked, stunned.

"The Stantons do expect you to marry her, Alex," Mandy said, her voice soft. "They've not even bothered to present her, most likely wishing to save the expense since they know she is to marry you. That is why you have never seen her."

Alex's smile left his face. "Then you think I am selfish as well."

"No," Mandy said, though her gaze would not meet his, and a flush rose to her cheeks. "No, I don't. But . . . but you cannot keep the Stantons in perpetual expectation. Josephine is now nineteen."

"Which means she has no more expectations," Alex said rather grimly. "But for me."

Mandy looked up, her eyes pleading. "Alex, if only you had . . . had found someone before this. If only—"

"*If only* rarely counts for much," Alex said, his smile twisting.

Mandy shook her head. "I do not think you should marry for duty, Alex—"

"Mandy," gasped Lady Beatrice. "How can you say that, you unnatural child."

Mandy's gaze did not leave Alex. "I do not. But perhaps marriage would be good for you."

"Do you really think so, dear?" Alex asked softly.

"I hope so," Mandy said, her eyes warm and caring, but with a distress lurking in the back of them.

A pain knifed through Alex. He could deny every cry and curse of his mother's and Lydia's, but he could not deny Mandy. She offered her support, but she did not think highly of him. Why should she? He had been selfish, knowing of the engagement, but never wasting a moment upon it, either to fulfill it or to deny it. He'd not thought one whit of that supposed bride, Josephine Stanton, or what the girl's life was because he had ignored his duties.

"I will think upon it," Alex said, looking at Mandy. Her eyes widened, and she nodded slightly. They both understood each other.

"What is there to think upon?" Lydia said. "It is clear and simple."

Alex rose quickly. "I said I would think upon it."

"No! You only say that to deter us," Lady Beatrice cried.

"Mother, nothing deters you," Alex said, strolling toward the door. "Now, if you will excuse me, I have an appointment with my tailor."

"You are going to leave?" Lydia exclaimed.

"Of course," Alex said. "It is my duty not to keep my tailor waiting."

"See!" Lady Beatrice cried. "He does not care. He does not care what pain he causes us." She slapped a hand to her chest. "Oh, oh, my palpitations. I . . . I think I am going to faint."

"I shall send Biddle to you," Alex said.

"Biddle!" shrieked Lady Beatrice. "You would send your butler, when it is you who should be by my side? I have nursed a serpent to my bosom!"

"Not even a half hour," Alex muttered and walked swiftly out of the room, not waiting to view his mother's final performance. He stalked across the foyer, moving with direct purpose toward the large oak entrance doors.

"Biddle," he said to the butler who hovered there, "I

am going to my club. See to my mother. She will have fainted by now."

"Yes, my lord," Biddle said in a knowing tone as he rushed to pick up Alex's hat and cane to hand him. "Is there anything else?"

"No," Alex said. "Do not expect to see me for dinner. I intend to get royally foxed." Alex rammed his hat upon his head. "Then I am going to ask for Miss Josephine Stanton's hand in marriage."

"You are, my lord?" Biddle asked, breaking into a smile. Alex stiffened and glared. *"Et tu,* Brute?"

Biddle frowned, emitted a cough, and straightened into a more dignified pose. "If you will forgive me, my lord. We, the staff and I, would be pleased to welcome a new mistress. It has been long awaited."

"Has it?" Alex asked.

"Of course, my lord," Biddle said, his gaze focused somewhere past Alex's shoulder. "Despite the low gossip from other quarters, we have always believed you would do the proper thing."

"Laying on long odds, were you?" Alex snorted.

"No, my lord," Biddle said, a red hue flushing his face. "Those other individuals, not of this house, I assure you, are not privy to the knowledge of the arrangement your family holds with the other fine house in question, my lord. We have always known the name of Rothmier will never die out." He bowed. "We live in expectation of serving your future progeny."

"Oh, God," Alex said. "I need a drink."

"Do not hesitate to take as many as you need, my lord," Biddle said, and opened the door wide, standing at attention.

"Here's your hat, go and propose," Alex said, laughing. He walked past Biddle. "Damn blighter."

"Just so, my lord," he heard Biddle say as the door shut. Alex stood upon the gracious town house stoop, ire rising in him. Damn it to hell! He was to become leg shackled for the sake of duty and family . . . and servants! He barked a laugh. He'd best be at it. His servants' coppers were laid upon him "doing the right thing." It was the way of all good men, after all. He saw Mandy's face once more, and a grim line formed at his mouth. It would be the way of one not so good man as well.

Josephine Stanton let herself into the family town house, the package of ribbons and lace securely underneath her arm. The ribbons should surely help to refurbish Mary's pink jacquard dress and give it a more current fashion.

She halted promptly. Rachel, the youngest of the Stanton girls, knelt at the closed library door, her eye scrunched to the keyhole. Leaning over and above her was her sister Mary and their governess and acting dame de companion, Miss Tellington.

"What is happening?" Josephine asked, though in a very low voice as she tiptoed across the foyer. The governess prior to Miss Tellington had often said that ladies did not eavesdrop, but no one in the Stanton household had ever believed in such impractical nonsense, except for Mary, that was. Since Mary's ear was as firmly pressed against the wood as the others were, whatever transpired behind those doors must be of the utmost importance indeed.

"What?" Miss Tellington squeaked, jerking away from the door and spinning around.

"Shh!" Rachel whispered from her crouched position.

"Oh, Josie, it is you," Miss Tellington exclaimed. Her brown eyes sparkled above her spectacles. "He has finally come!"

"Oh, dear," Josie said, slowing her pace. "Our solicitor? Father must be in a rare pucker."

"No, he came earlier," Miss Tellington said, shaking her

head until her untidy bun nearly fell loose of its pins. "It is your marquis!"

"My marquis?" Josie asked. She sucked in her breath. "Rothmier is in there?"

"Yes, dear," Mary whispered, holding out one hand toward Josie, though she kept her ear glued to the door. "He is truly here and is asking for your hand from Father."

"He is?" Josie asked. Her heart plummeted to her toes. After all these years, the marquis had actually come to propose. She walked toward the door and grasped Mary's proffered hand tightly. "I . . . I cannot believe it."

"It's him," Rachel's voice drifted up from beneath them. "And he's castaway."

"Rachel!" Miss Tellington whispered, her voice sharp. "Do not say that! Surely you are wrong."

"I am not," Rachel said, her voice indignant. "I know when a man is castaway and the marquis is castaway." Even though Rachel was fifteen, none of the elder women would think to refute her. A Stanton lady, to the very youngest, could gauge a man's level of inebriation from a bit on the go, to well to live, to shot the cat. "Though he is handling himself divinely."

"Is he?" Josie asked, a pleased flush rising to her face.

"Yes," Rachel said, her voice holding proper awe. "One almost could not tell."

A loud shout emitted from the closed door.

"What is he saying?" Josie crowded in and nestled her cheek against the door, next to Mary's.

"Father has accepted his proposal," Mary whispered urgently.

Josie heard the rumble of her father's voice and a different one. A deep, low-timbred one. A shiver tingled down her spine. So that was how the marquis's voice sounded. She had always wondered about it, sometimes dreamed of it. The only memory she had of her future husband was of a sturdy dark-haired boy, with a young voice, who spurned playing with her and her sisters. In truth, it was a rather unprepossessing if not daunting image to have of one's future mate.

Josie heard her father's bluff voice say, "W-welcome, my shon-n."

"Oh, no," Rachel said, groaning.

"What?" Josie asked quickly. "What?"

"Father is hugging him," Rachel whispered. "Got him in a clinch!"

"Oh, dear," Mary murmured. "Never say so."

"Father's been well lit ever since that mean old solicitor came. I wish he could hold his drink as well as the marquis," Rachel said. "I bet the marquis is a four-bottle man. Papa never can handle but one."

"Rachel," Mary said, her voice reproving. "You should honor your father."

"Father is kissing the marquis now," Rachel said. "He's slobbering all over him!"

Josie's gaze met Mary's. Mary flushed and her lips trembled. "Well, at least try to do so." Both girls giggled.

"Great Zeus," Rachel cried, toppling back. "They are coming!"

With no more than a concerted rustle, the ladies quickly dispersed. Josie ran and slipped behind the armor of an ancient knight whom she considered one of her oldest and dearest friends. Rachel immediately tumbled toward the large curio table upon the side wall and, flipping up its linen cloth, scrambled beneath. A bit of her blue dress peeked out. Josie bit her lip. She must remember to tell Rachel to find a new hiding place the next time. Clearly she had outgrown the table. Miss Tellington scuttled across the foyer and squeezed her small body into the corner between a grandfather clock and the wall. Only Mary, never trained in the drill, remained in the middle of the foyer, darting back and forth in obvious quandary. The library door opened, and Mary, with the smallest cry, skittered across the foyer and disappeared into the breakfast room.

"You've m-made me the h-happiest of men, my shon," Horace Stanton said, all but crying. "Th-the happiest of men."

"I can but h-hope your daughter will say the same," Rothmier's voice said.

Josie peered out from behind her knight's raised arm and sword. Her legs turned to water and she clutched at the cold armor. Rothmier, her promised fiancé, was the most splendid man she had ever seen, or imagined to see. He stood all of six feet and two. Most definitely, he had grown since a boy. His broad shoulders filled out a super-fine jacket of blue, and his buff unmentionables fitted strong-muscled calves and thighs. The raven black of his hair was shot with silver, and the deep blue of his eyes was piercing.

If that was not enough to melt a girl's heart to butter, his noble bearing while under the influence would. He held himself amazingly correct. A phenomenal feat, considering he also held Josie's shorter and portly father upright.

"We'll have the paper dr-drawn up ash fash as possible!" Horace Stanton slurred, his burly arms wrapped around the marquis's tapered waist. "Generous settlement y-you've offered. G-generous."

"We'll take care of that after I speak to your daughter," Rothmier said. Josie flushed hot.

"She'll be delighted," Horace said. "The little puss hash been waiting for yearsh for you two t-to t-tie the knot."

"So I've heard," Rothmier replied. Something in the dark timbre of his voice made Josie cringe. "I'll come and see her t-tomorrow morning."

"G-good, good," Horace said, nodding his head up and down. "N-nine o'clock?"

"Nine?" Rothmier's voice sounded shocked. Then he said, "Yes, nine o'clock. Why ever not?"

Rothmier assisted the clinging and wobbling Horace to the large double doors. Gently Alexander untangled Horace from him and propped the older man against the one door panel. Then, with a fine if not painstakingly meditative movement, he opened the other door and stepped out, closing it behind him.

Horace Stanton leaned against the door a moment, a look upon his face as if he spied the gates of heaven opening before him. Then he shoved himself from the door and roared, "Louise! Josie! Girls!" He staggered to the center of the foyer and halted. He frowned, peering around with bleary eyes. "Why ishn't anyone ever h-here when I w-want themsh to be?" He stumbled to the stairs, bellowing, "Louise! Louise! Get down here."

Josie quietly slipped out from behind her iron protector. She waited a moment while Rachel crawled out from under the table and Miss Tellington emerged from behind the grandfather clock. Casting a quick glance at them to ensure their faces were adequately composed, she said, "Father, what is it?"

Horace swung around, swaying. "Josie!" He blinked. "A-and Rachel . . . M-Miss Tellington."

"We heard you call," Josie said, widening her eyes to that of innocence. "Whatever is the matter?"

"S'matter? No, n-no, puss, everything's f-fine," Horace said, beaming. He lurched toward her and placed a smacking kiss upon her cheek. "Y-you have shaved us, my dear girl. Shaved us!"

"Father, what is it?" Mary asked, emerging from the breakfast room door. Her face was a betraying red, unlike the others.

"What is it?" Horace cried. "W-why the best newsh ever!"

"My lord," Louise Stanton's voice called, and the lady

of the house drifted down the stairs, dressed in a stunning creation of green Indian silk. Even as a matron of many years, her figure was still slim, her face unlined, and her auburn hair untraced with gray. "Whatever causes you to shout in such an unruly manner?"

"Louise! My L-Louise!" Horace cried and stumbled toward his wife just as she reached the foyer floor. "We've been shaved." He reached for her and clutched her in a bear hug, placing a loud kiss upon her lips.

"My lord!" Louise Stanton said, pushing him away. "This is improper behavior. And in front of the girls yet!"

"Oh, er, yes," Horace slurred, stepping back quickly. "F-forgive me. But . . . but got the b-best news. Rothmier's c-come up to scratch."

"He what?" Louise Stanton gasped.

Horace nodded. "Going ter ask fer J-Josie tomorrow. And . . . and in the nick of time, b'gad. O-old Barlow, damn fuss-budget sol-sol-icitor, said we'd have ter quit town, s-sell the carriage, g-get rid of the staff."

"Never!" Louise Stanton shrieked.

"D-don't have ter now," Horace slurred. "R-Rothmier is going ter marry our l-little Josie as pr-promised. H-he jusht left."

"Oh, it is marvelous news," Louise Stanton exclaimed, her eyes lighting. She appeared to see the same gates of heaven opening as Sir Horace had viewed just moments before. A sigh escaped her. "Then I can order that dress from Madame Celeste. Though I ought not to give her my patronage." She made a pretty moue of displeasure. "Do you know, she actually had the audacity to question me upon the bills?"

"Mother, those bills are nine months old," Josie said.

"What of it?" Louise said, waving a hand. "She should never have dared to be so encroaching. It is her business to wait." She sighed. "But I do want that dress. Oh, and I must have a new wardrobe befitting the mother-in-law of a marquis. And we shall entertain. Faith, we have not entertained in years, it seems."

"Yes, yes," Horace said, nodding. "Y-you can have anything y-you want m'dear. W-we'll entertain Prinny h-himself."

"But . . ." Josie made to object, but stopped as the foyer door opened.

Her brother Michael entered. He sported a lime green, slender waistcoat and yellow pantaloons. His dark hair was arranged in what he called the Windswept, and looked as if it surely had been a strong wind at that. Josie adored her brother, but she could not approve his fashion choices. Michael halted and gazed at the surrounding group. "What, ho! A family do in the foyer?"

"We've got great news, shon!" Horace bellowed. "W-we are shaved. Rothmier's c-come round. Going to ashk for Josie!"

"Is he? It's about time," Michael said, his face breaking into a brilliant smile. He glanced at Josie, his gray eyes, so very much like hers, warm. "Congratulations, dear."

Josie flushed. "Th-hank you."

"It means I can buy that prime blood I've been wanting."

"But . . . but, Michael," Josie said. "That one is so expensive."

"He's the finest piece of horseflesh I've seen, Josie," Michael said. Josie never could withstand the endearing look now creeping across his face.

"Yes," Josie said. "I-I know. But still, the cost."

"No matter!" Horace roared. "R-Rothmier said he'd shettle all our accounts. He'll shtand the nonsense."

Josie swung around, staring at her father. "W-what?"

Horace nodded. "V-very g-generous! V-very g-generous."

"Did you tell him the total sum of what we owe?" Josie asked, her chest tightening.

"C-course not," Horace said. "I ain't a bloody merchant t-to talk sh-shop wh-when a m-man's ashkin for m-my little girl's hand. But d-don't you worry your sweet h-head over it. Rothmier and me will t-talk men t-talk later."

"Men talk?" Josie asked, her heart sinking. She wondered how her father would be able to talk "men talk" since he never once glanced at the accounts. He said they made him bilious. Josie knew the accounts well, since she was the only member in the family who did them. The rest considered her quite odd in that respect, if not a little dismal, to continue to tally figures like that. Michael always said she had more bottom than sense. The total sum of their debts flashed before Josie's eyes and she swallowed. "I s-see."

"P-puss you ought to b-be happy." Horace frowned. "The marquis is g-going to shave us."

"Yes," Louise Stanton said. "And we must all buy new wardrobes. We are now attached to the grand family of Rothmier. It is a dream come true."

Josie glanced around at her starry-eyed family. She could see their minds whirling with inventive thoughts upon how to spend money, Rothmier's money. The marquis had said he would settle their debts, but that would be futile. If he settled them, there would only be new ones afresh. The image of Rothmier, tall and handsome, everything a fine nobleman should be, edged out the ledger page in Josie's mind's eye. She saw him once again, shoring up her drunken father. If he married her, he would be doing that for the rest of his life. Pain wrenched at her heart. No, it wasn't a dream come true.

Alex stood swiftly as Josephine Stanton entered the library. His brandy-beleaguered head pounded out its protest. Faith, but he had a devil of a hangover. He focused in grim determination upon the girl he would soon take to wife. She was a tall, fair girl and boyishly slim, not at all like the women he took for mistresses. He winced. He certainly was daft this morning. A wife did not need to look like a mistress.

Alex stiffened as he realized the girl was staring at him as much as he was at her, and that the moment was growing protracted.

"Hello," he said, tearing his gaze from the girl's figure to notice her face. It was a very pale face with large gray eyes, gray eyes that were dark with concern.

"Hello," Josephine Stanton said. That was all. Alex grew restive, for the girl continued to openly study him, as surely no demure miss should. Something flickered in those expressive gray eyes, and she said, "Excuse me one moment."

The girl turned and, without another word, walked back out of the door. Alex blinked. What in blazes was the girl about? Didn't she know he was here to propose to her?

Josephine returned shortly, carrying a large tray with one single glass upon it, filled with an odd-colored liquid. Alex watched in wary silence as she brought it over and set it down upon a table. "This should make the pain go away, I am sure."

Alex started. "I beg your pardon?"

Josephine Stanton looked at him, without a hint of embarrassment or censure in those large gray eyes. "I'm sure you have a devilish head . . . I mean, a severe headache, this morning. But this concoction should do the trick." Alex drew himself up to his fullest height and tried to stare the impertinent chit down. She merely gazed at him, her eyes showing inquiry as she lifted the glass and held it out to him. "It really doesn't taste all that bad. Most remedies do, I own, but I've worked on this recipe for quite some time. I cannot coax Father or Michael to drink it otherwise."

Alex's eyes widened, and then he sighed, the starch going out of him. He reached out and took the glass, then lifted it and took a cautious sip.

"No," he said, surprised. "It doesn't taste all that bad."

A wide smile crossed the girl's face. It was a rather engaging smile. "I am glad you like it. As I said, it is my own recipe." She waved her hand toward a chair. "Do let us sit down."

Alex, slightly bemused, moved to take up the proffered chair. Josephine settled upon the settee across from him. He took another quick pull of the dark liquid, attempting to regain his equilibrium.

"Rachel, my youngest sister, thinks you must be a four-bottle man," Josephine said, in the softest, politest voice, as if she had asked about the weather.

Alex sputtered and choked upon his drink. "What?"

"She said you must be a four-bottle man," Josephine Stanton repeated. An inquisitive look entered her eyes. "Are you?"

Alex stared at her, took another deep draft, and sighed. "It was six bottles."

Josephine's eyes widened. "Six bottles. Oh, dear, Father should never have asked you to arrive here so early." She flushed and lowered her gaze. "It . . . it was very kind of you to arrive on time. I know how difficult it must have been for you."

Alex smiled, his mood suddenly lightening. Whether it was from the benefit of the drink or from the unconventional conversation he could not say. "It was my pleasure."

Josephine's eyes rose to his then, twinkling. It was like sunlight flashing on deep water. "Gammon."

Alex raised a brow. "Gammon? Is that what a young lady should say when a man has come to prop—" He halted abruptly.

"Er, yes," she said, the sparkle in her eyes disappearing. She looked down again and fell silent. Alex drew in a deep breath and set his glass down. His movement drew her gaze to him once more. "Y-you may finish your drink first."

Alex smiled. "No. I thank you, but I believe I am fortified

enough." He rose and winced. He saw her wince as well. Walking over to her he studied her. She watched him with wide, cautious eyes as if she expected him to draw a pistol upon her at any moment. The thought amused him, and he suddenly had the impulse to do the thing up right. It was only fair after her kindness. Offering a crooked smile, he slowly lowered himself to one knee.

"What are . . . ?" Josephine exclaimed, her tone aghast. She reached out a staying hand to him. "No, please don't!"

"No," Alex said, restraining his groan. "I should do it properly since I've kept you waiting all these years, or so everyone tells me." He strove to gain his balance, a dizziness overtaking him at such a taxing position. He swore he'd never be a six-bottle man again. "Miss Josephine Stanton—"

"Josie," the girl said, quickly leaning forward and placing her two hands upon his shoulders in support, an unfortunately much needed support. "Everyone calls me Josie. Josephine doesn't seem right." Her face, now much closer to his, flushed a becoming pink. "It is far too—too formal."

"Josie," Alex said, secretly agreeing with her. "It has been a long-standing desire of our families to be united."

"Yes," Josie said, her voice suddenly breathless. She leaned even closer yet.

The softest scent of lilac teased at Alex. He breathed in deeply. "Yes. And I-I believe it is time for us to fulfill that . . . desire." He felt her hands jump upon his shoulders. "I mean wish. I promise to hold you in all due respect and consideration . . ." What the hell was he saying? "If you would do me the honor of becoming my wife . . ."

"Oh, dear," Josie said, her face clouding. She sighed. "I wish you hadn't mentioned that."

"What?" Alex asked, blinking.

"Honor," Josie said, drawing her hands from his shoulders. Something that looked like regret entered her eyes. "I fear I must do you the honor of rejecting your offer."

"What?" Stunned, Alex jerked backward. Without Josie's steadying hands, he swiftly lost balance and toppled to the floor.

"Oh, dear," Josie cried and rushed to kneel beside him. "Are you all right?"

Alex, cursing, righted himself and glared at her. "What do you mean by that?"

"I am doing you the honor of rejecting you," Josie said. She sighed and settled to the floor next to him. She looked at him, her face seriously intent. "And in truth, s-since I am being honest, I must advise you to bolt."

"Bolt?" Alex asked, astonished.

"Bolt," Josie said, nodding. "You don't want anything to do with my family, I assure you."

A sudden, irrational rage filled Alex. He sprung up from the floor, ignoring the dizziness. He glared down at Josie. "Madam, if you do not wish this marriage, then you have only to say so. There is no need to create excuses—"

"But they aren't excuses," Josie said. She scrambled up, appeal within her eyes. "I wish you to understand. I would like to marry you . . ." She looked down. "I-I mean it would be nice to be married, but I simply cannot do so at this time." She glanced up. "I-I know I should not have permitted you to go down on bent knee, but it might be the only proposal I receive and . . . and I did not want to miss it."

Alex, accustomed to being in control of any situation, felt terribly foolish. "You did not want to miss it?"

She hung her head. "Yes, that was rather bad of me."

"I would say so," Alex said.

"But if you would only permit me to show you, I am sure you will agree."

"Show me what?" Alex asked, narrowing his eyes.

Josie turned directly away from him and walked over to

the library desk. She flipped open a large ledger and looked at him in clear expectation. "If you would please come over and look at this, you will understand."

Alex shook his head to clear it. He, a marquis, and a much desired marquis at that, had finally proposed to a woman, and she not only did him the "honor" of rejecting him, but now wanted him to study ledgers as if he were some common shopkeeper.

"Please," Josie said.

"Very well." Alex stalked over and sat down in the large leather chair at the desk.

"Here are the family accounts," Josie said, her voice sounding weak. "Please look at them."

"Of course," Alex said dryly. He trained his gaze upon the page, forcing his aching brain to look at the neat numbers. As he began to fully take in those sums, Josie left him. Alex, with dawning astonishment, flipped sixteen pages to reach the final tally. "Good God!"

"Yes," Josie said and shoved the glass she had retrieved into his hand. Alex swiftly drank from it. It would have been better if it had been brandy. "Now you see why I think you should bolt. If you marry me, my family will bleed you dry. It is not that they would do so out of malicious intent, but because they simply cannot help themselves. It has always been their way. You wouldn't want us to batten on you for the rest of our lives, would you?"

Alex set the glass down with a thunk. He had known the Stantons were spendthrifts, but he had never imagined to what monumental degree. "How the devil could this have happened?"

"Very easily," Josie sighed as she stood next to him. Her hand came to rest upon his shoulder in what Alex knew was an unconscious movement. "Both Father and Michael have a penchant for gaming and horses. Unfortunately, neither is proficient at it. Then there is the drink. We do have one of the finest wine cellars in the country."

"At least that is an asset," Alex murmured.

"Yes," Josie said. "It would be if Father and Michael didn't drink it as quickly as they collected it. And Mama, well, she is accustomed to all the finest things in life. She is a Carlyle, you understand, and that family expects nothing but the best. Only now they will have nothing to do with us, which is quite understandable, of course." She frowned. "I fear Mother would have been wise not to marry Father. They do rub along famously, but neither has any sense of economy. I believe it was a love match between them, for Father's fortune was already waning when they married."

"Indeed," Alex murmured, a numbness invading him.

"So you see," Josie said, "I'm actually saving you."

"Yes," Alex replied, not knowing what else to say. He should certainly be grateful to the girl. Never had he thought the Stantons to be so badly dipped. Faith, they were on the brink of financial ruin. No, not on the brink, but totally mired in it. There were very few estates he knew of that could readily absorb such debts. His could, of course, but then his was one of the largest in the country. He muttered a curse. It was insanity, utter insanity, but he said it anyway. "Josie. We must marry. It is the only way out for your family that I can see."

"No," Josie said. She jerked her hand from his shoulder and walked quickly away. "No, I have thought about that." She turned and drew herself up with an odd, quaint dignity. "I-I think I can manage to pull our coals out of the fire."

"There are a bloody lot of coals there," Alex said with a sharp laugh.

Her chin lifted. "It will only take some resolution, I am sure."

"Resolution?" Alex asked, raising his brow.

"Yes," Josie said, nodding. "Up until now I see that I have not . . . not taken as many steps as I could to remedy the situation. I have tried, I assure you, but not strongly enough."

"That you are not all in the sponging house does you credit," Alex admitted.

A flush crossed Josie's face. "Thank you. But I have not made a great enough push, I fear. You see, as long as the family has had expectations of you marrying me, they have refused to consider the situation fully. Once they can no longer look to you to save them, it should help them to realize they must seek another course."

A pain shot through Alex. It felt oddly like remorse. "We should have had this talk long ago. It is my fault that we didn't." He rose and drew in his breath. "I would be pleased to marry you still."

That glint came back into Josie's eye. "Gammon."

Alex laughed, despite himself. Then he grew serious. "Are you certain that you do not wish to marry?"

"It . . . it is for the best," Josie said, flushing. She drew in a breath. "I-I wish you to know y-you are no longer under any obligation. Y-you are free to marry otherwise."

Alex smiled and shook his head. "In truth, I did not intend to marry so quickly."

Josie frowned. "But are you not already thirty?"

Alex laughed. "Why does everyone think it such an ancient age?"

Josie shrugged. "Most men marry by that time."

"I am not most men."

"No, you are not." Josie looked away. "Then you are . . . are not in love with any other woman?"

Alex laughed. "I love them all."

Josie's gaze turned back to him, her gray eyes widening. Then she nodded. "That is because you are a rake."

Alex stiffened. "I beg your pardon?"

"Rakes never care to settle down with one woman," Josie said. "Mother says a rake makes the worst kind of husband."

Alex stared. "And she married your father?"

Josie frowned and cocked her head to one side. "What do you mean? Father is not a rake."

"No, of course not," Alex said quickly. It must be his hangover that caused him to be so indiscreet. He'd best take Josie's advice and bolt as quickly as he could, before he said some other want-witted thing. He forced a smile. "Well, I had best take my leave of you now."

"Of course," Josie said, nodding. She looked hesitant. "Only . . . would you mind it very much if I told Father this w-was your notion as w-well as mine?"

"Of course not," Alex said. "I assure you, no man likes to admit he was rejected."

"But I've rejected you for your own good," Josie said.

"Yes," Alex agreed with a solemnness.

She appeared to turn shy. "I-I wish to thank you for your proposal. It was . . . was very nice."

"It was nothing," Alex said, a twinge of self-disgust flicking him. He had come to propose to her so hungover that it had been patently obvious, and the girl still thought it wonderful of him. Shaking his head, he walked over to her. "Your rejection was far more gracious." He reached out and took up her hand. Bending over, he kissed it in a courtly manner. He felt her hand tremble and he glanced up. Her eyes were large upon him. "What is the matter?"

"Nothing," Josie said. "Only I've never had a man kiss my hand before."

"Never?" Alex asked, stunned.

"No, I-I do not go out into society much."

"Of course." Alex cursed himself. That could be laid at his door as well.

"Could you do it again?" Josie asked in a soft voice.

"No," Alex said, the slightest smile upon his lips. "For I can do even better than that." He leaned over and gently kissed her lips. They were innocently pursed together, and yet they clung to his in a warm, sweet way. Alex, feeling the oddest jolt, pulled back swiftly. Josie's eyes were closed, a stunned look upon her face.

She opened her eyes. The look in them was dazed. "Yes, that . . . that was better." Her body swayed toward him.

"Was it?" Alex said, finding his voice husky. He leaned toward her, and Josie lifted her head, her eyes closing, her lips naively pursed again. Alex froze. What the devil was he doing? He shook his head to clear it. "Er, we really should tell your father now."

Josie's eyes opened. Honest disappointment showed within them. The child had no guile, no protective deception. "Oh."

"Come," Alex said with what he hoped was a voice of authority.

She hesitated. "P-perhaps I should tell him without you there."

Alex stiffened. He was not that much of a cad. "No. I will not leave you to do this alone."

"Very well." Josie drew in a deep breath. "If you are sure. He and the family are waiting in the parlor. I made Mary promise to keep them all there."

"You did?" Alex asked.

"Yes," Josie said, nodding. "So do not fear. We were not overheard."

Alex blinked. In truth, it had never been a consideration of his. "That is nice, I assume."

"Mary can be depended upon," Josie said, her voice confident. A dark shadow passed through her eyes. "A-are you certain you wish t-to do this with me? Y-you don't have to do so."

"I am positive." Alex smiled.

"Truly?" She acted as he were offering to enter the fiery pit with her.

"I insist," Alex said firmly now.

"Very well," Josie said. She turned and led him from the library and into the foyer. She halted as did Alex. The

Stantons' butler, silver-haired and ramrod stiff, stood positioned at the closed parlor door, a cart before him. "Do you have everything prepared, Musgrave?"

"Yes, Miss Josie," Musgrave replied. He nodded and winked in a fatherly fashion, his stateliness totally destroyed.

"Then, let us do it," Josie said, drawing in a deep breath. Astonishingly, her hand crept into Alex's. Alex felt a jolt shoot through him, but clasped it up, a protectiveness overcoming him.

Musgrave nodded and, opening the door, took hold of the laden cart and pushed it through. Silently, Josie and Alex followed. Josie's hand tightened upon his, or perhaps it was an equal, convulsive grip. The entire Stanton family was indeed entrenched within the parlor. Horace sat in one large chair; Louise Stanton and the older daughter sat upon the settee. Michael Stanton, whom Alex could easily recognize as twin to Josie, stood by the fire. The youngest daughter and a lady who clearly must be the governess sat close by.

"Well, well," Horace boomed, a grin splitting his face as his gaze took in Alex's and Josie's entwined hands. "Lovebirds already!"

"No, Father," Josie exclaimed. She ripped her hand from Alex's, a deep blush rising to her cheeks.

"Horace," Louise said. "Do not tease Josie. Where are your manners?"

Horace flushed. "Er, yes. Only meant . . . well, they are going to be married after all."

"Yes," Louise said. "But it does not mean they can . . ."

"But we aren't . . . ," Josie said, her voice shaky.

". . . act in an uncircumspect manner," Louise continued.

"Louise," Horace said. "Let the children be, they are . . ."

". . . going to be married," Josie finished as quickly as possible.

"Exactly," Horace said. "So if they hold hands . . ."

"I said we aren't . . ." Josie started once more.

"See," Louise said. "She is my daughter. She knows proper behavior."

". . . going to be married," Josie repeated.

"Holding hands ain't that improper," Horace said. "And I didn't raise my daughter to be some pinched-up prude."

"Of course not," Louise said. "But she is not fast or . . ."

"Father," Josie said, her voice imploring. "Mother . . ."

Alex had suffered enough. His head was starting to pound. He roared, "We aren't going to be married!"

Silence reigned for one blissful moment. The entire family froze, as if they were a scene in a painting, though it would have been difficult for a portrait artist to have captured the looks of shock, astonishment and horror properly.

"What?" Horace finally gasped.

"We aren't going to be married," Josie repeated in a much smaller voice.

The painting came to vibrant if not vicious life, assaulting Alex's every beleaguered sense. The cries, curses, shrieks and moans were so intertwined as to be a solid block of sound, one deafening, heavy block. The Stanton family vocalized their emotions as loudly as any charging barbarian horde.

"Now, Musgrave!" Josie shouted, and rushed over to the cart. Musgrave, despite his years, moved swiftly. He snatched up what Alex could determine was a full shot glass and moved promptly to Horace Stanton, shoving it into his master's wildly gesticulating hand. Josie snatched up a wad of handkerchiefs, which Alex recognized as his own mother's staple, but she also snatched up a large box of chocolates.

"We've decided we won't suit," Josie explained loudly and rushed over to shower her mother with both handkerchiefs and chocolate.

"Won't suit?" Louise moaned, spraying the handkerchiefs off her as she tore open the box and immediately stuffed a confection into her mouth.

"I'm so sorry, Josie," the daughter beside her said, snatching up one fallen handkerchief to hold tightly.

"Won't suit?" Horace cried. He shot the glass back. His face twisted and he coughed. "God, what is this?"

"Oh," Josie exclaimed. "Wrong glass, Musgrave."

"Yes, Miss Josie," Musgrave said. He quickly snatched up a shot glass of a different color from the cart, while Josie took another and walked over to Michael, who stood, wide-eyed, as if he had been shot. "Here, Michael."

"Th-thank you," Michael said in a mechanical tone.

Musgrave had given Horace the new glass by this time, and Horace shot that back. He expelled a shuttering breath and glared at Alex. "What's wrong with my little girl? Heh?"

"Nothing," Alex said. "Nothing at all."

"She's wonderful," the governess said. "Anyone would be proud of her!"

"Thank you, Pansy," Josie said, and to date, took from the cart the strangest of items. They were two dice which she moved to gently place into Pansy's trembling hands.

"If anything is wrong with Josie," Pansy said, slowly rubbing the dice together like worry stones, "it is my fault, all my fault."

"No, it isn't," Josie said firmly, patting her on the shoulder. "It's not your fault at all."

"Of course not," Alex said. Faith, it was a nightmare. He considered himself a brave man, but he had to force himself not to turn and run.

"It was a mutual decision," Josie said. She returned to the cart to pick up two more shot glasses.

"But, Josie," the youngest daughter exclaimed. "He's perfect for you. He's a four-bottle man!"

"I know, dearest," Josie said, walking directly up to Alex. Her gray eyes were warm and concerned. "One's blue ruin, and one's whisky."

Alex automatically reached for the whisky. Then his hand froze in shock. The girl was reading and understanding him, just as she was doing with her family. And taking care of him, just as she was her family. Blast! None of them deserved her consideration, including him. He jerked his hand back and glared at them all. "Josie and I are not going to marry. It was a mutual decision. Do not dare to place the blame upon her. If there is any blame, it is mine."

"No," Josie said. "You don't have to say that."

"The blame is mine," Alex said more firmly. "And not because she is deficient or anything else. It is simply the way it is going to be. And I don't want any one of you to make her feel uncomfortable about it, or dare to harangue her."

Josie's eyes widened, and then with a dazed look, so very similar to when he had first kissed her, she whispered, "Thank you."

"Here, here," Michael said, lifting his empty glass.

"We ain't haranguing her," Horace objected.

"It's time for you to go now," Josie said, and grabbed up his arm. Alex stiffened. "Please?"

"Very well," Alex said curtly. He cast her family one more stern look and strode out. Josie chased after him into the foyer.

"I am sorry if they upset you," Josie said.

He spun, glaring at her. "Do not apologize for them. They behaved abominably."

Josie stared back. That winsome smile crossed her face. "I thought they took it rather well."

It was Alex's turn to stare back. Then it struck him. Knowing their finances and how they had pinned all their hopes upon him, and had for years, her family had indeed taken it well. A sudden chuckle escaped him. Come to think of it, he doubted his family was going to take it any better. "You are right."

"Thank you again," Josie said.

Alex laughed wryly and picked up her hand. "Don't thank me. I've done nothing."

Josie gazed up at him, the oddest look in her eyes. Suddenly Alex wanted to kiss her again. Clenching his teeth, he dropped her hand and opened the door. He charged down the steps, throwing over his shoulder a swift goodbye. He thought he heard a whispered farewell.

Alex kept on walking. His mind roiled. What a family! Ramshackle and abominable. His pace increased. Sixteen ledger pages of debts. They all should be in a sponging house by now. He walked even faster. God, what a close call that had been.

Alex suddenly rammed into a passerby.

"Hey! Watch what you are doing," the man said.

"Sorry," Alex murmured.

The man moved on, but Alex stood frozen as an unfelicitous thought occurred to him. He was doing exactly what Josie had told him to do. He was bolting. Literally. He drew in a deep breath and proceeded at a slower pace. What did it matter, after all? There was nothing he could do. He had done his duty and proposed. He'd been rejected. That was the end of it.

Still, he couldn't help but wonder. What was his now unpromised bride going to do to try and save her family from destitution?

Two

Josie held her candle high and walked down the hall toward her room. She had survived the day and so had her family. Her father was four sheets to the wind and had become morosely resigned. Her mother had devoured the whole box of bonbons and, with the soothing comforts of the excellent chocolates, was already determining which dress she should buy to help her through the terrible crisis.

Mary had finally dried her tears. Those had been the hardest for Josie to accept. Mary cried not for herself, but for Josie. Deep, deep down, perhaps Josie cried a little for Josie, too. If a girl could marry, Rothmier would certainly be the one. He was not only the handsomest man in the world, with the looks that struck to a girl's very heart, but there was something else about him that struck to her very soul. And his kiss! Josie flushed. To be kissed like that every day for the rest of her life would be heaven.

Josie frowned and reprimanded herself sharply. She was not a girl who could marry. Not while her family was in such a condition. She had her honor. She needed to stop her air-dreaming and settle down to devising a plan to save her family. It had been her decision to reject Rothmier, and now it was her responsibility to make sure her family did not suffer because of it. She also shoved the terribly selfish, pitiful thought from her mind that if she could bring her family about, she would then be a girl who could marry Alex. She flushed. Or someone like Alex. She had rejected him, and at the pace he had pelted from the house, it was obvious he held no regrets in that quarter.

She halted as she heard a familiar voice singing out a slurred song. Soon a weaving, bobbing candle flame appeared. Then a weaving, bobbing Michael himself appeared.

"Michael?" Josie gasped. He looked terrible. It wasn't unusual for Michael to be drunk, but normally he was a happy-go-lucky drunk. Tonight, even though he sang, his face appeared haggard, the shadows etching across his cheekbones almost ominous. "Are you all right?"

"F-fit as a f-fiddle," Michael said, staggering up to her. "S'why?"

"I don't know," Josie said, quickly blowing out his candle which was listing severely downward. "Y-you don't look well."

"Don't I?" Michael asked. He chuckled low in his throat. It wasn't a pleasant sound. He wrapped one brotherly arm across her shoulder. "D-don't y-you f-f-fret about me. H-how do you feel?"

Josie slipped her arm about his waist in support and sisterly affection. She unobtrusively directed him down the hall toward his room. "I'm fine."

"So-o-o am I." Michael nodded.

They both stopped a moment and looked at each other.

"Gammon," Josie said.

"P-pop-pycock," Michael retorted.

They both broke into laughter. Josie was still chuckling as they reached Michael's bedroom door. She expertly propped him up against the wall beside it. Her laughter faded as she noticed Michael gazing at her, his eyes solemn. "Been a devil of a day for you, hasn't it?"

"Oh, no," Josie staunchly lied as she opened the door. "I'm all right."

"What happened?" Michael asked. "Really?"

"Nothing," Josie said, leading him into the room. "I . . . I mean we . . . that is Rothmier and I . . . together . . . simply agreed . . . that w-we wouldn't suit."

Michael shook his head. "Too m-many we's there, Josie."

"No," Josie said. "Truly . . ."

"Y-you can tell me the truth," Michael said. "Didn't want him, did you?"

Josie flushed. Never would she tell him she had rejected Alex because of the family's excessive, spendthrift ways. "Very well. You are right."

"Shame," Michael said. "I thought he'd be capital for you."

"Yes, I know," Josie sighed and went to set her candle firmly on the bedside table. Then she started. "I mean, no!"

Michael scrunched his face up as he attempted to take off his jacket. "I know he's got a rackety reputation, but you ain't a girl to hold it against a fellow. I wouldn't want to see you with a high st-st-ickler. You're too sweet for one of th-them."

"Thank you," Josie said.

"He's also handsome," Michael said, frowning as he became totally entangled within his sleeves. "Leastw-ways, m-most women think he is. But if y-you d-didn't find him that w-way . . ."

It was sheer torture to Josie. "I-I'd rather not talk about it anymore."

"C-course, c-course. Wouldn't want you to m-marry a man you don't l-like, don't want." Michael sighed, a deep, heavy sigh, and stopped his struggles, totally bound by his jacket. "N-no matter wh-what, I want you happy."

"You are in trouble," Josie said, the knowledge blooming in her. "Aren't you?"

"N-o, no such thing," Michael said. "I'll get this jacket off yet. Won't b-beat me."

"That isn't what I meant," Josie said, walking over to tug and jerk the jacket free from Michael. "Tell me the truth."

"How'd you do that?" Michael asked, blinking at the jacket in her hands as if it had betrayed him.

"Michael," Josie said, "are you in trouble?"

"Course not," Michael denied, drawing himself up into a stiff pose. Josie stared steadily at him. He slumped. "B-blast! Might as well tell you."

"Yes," Josie urged, taking him by the hand and leading him over to his bed.

Michael crumpled down upon it. He shook his head. "I mean, it ain't as if you won't find out. Not when Desuex c-comes round for me."

"Who is Desuex?" Josie asked.

Michael laughed as he reached to struggle with his cravat. He choked then. Whether it was from self-imposed strangulation or from his thoughts Josie couldn't tell. "He's a c-card sharp and ch-cheat."

"Oh," Josie said, dropping his jacket and quickly pulling his hands from the cravat. "Let me. You'll kill yourself."

"Y-you'll want to kill me y-yourself," Michael stammered, "w-when you f-find out w-what I did."

"How much did you lose?" Josie asked, working at his cravat.

Michael blinked. "D-did I tell you that?"

"Yes," Josie said. "You said this Desuex was a card sharp and cheat. Of course you lost to him. You don't cheat."

"I should have," Michael said, his face glum.

"No," Josie said, unraveling the cravat from around his neck. "You don't play well enough to cheat."

"You're right." Michael laughed. Finally, a real humor entered his eyes. "Gads. I wish it had been you there last night ins-t-tead of me. You would have fl-fleeced the blighter. Given him a dose of his own medicine."

"Yes," Josie said without conceit as she bent down to

reach for Michael's booted foot. She knew cards inside and out. Miss Tellington's father had been a famous game-ster. Not that it had ever appeared upon her references, of course. Yet over the years, it was one of the odd and various talents she had taught Josie. Unfortunately, no mat-ter her efforts or Josie's, Michael had never acquired the same talent. Frowning, Josie tugged at Michael's recalci-trant boot. "Just how much did you lose?"

"F-five thousand pounds," Michael muttered.

The boot gave, or perhaps merely accompanied Josie, as she squeaked and toppled. The contact of her backside with the threadbare carpet was painful, but not as painful as Michael's confession. Josie hugged the boot to her. "Five thousand pounds? In one night?"

"The play there is deep, very deep," Michael said, red washing his face. "I w-wouldn't have gone. I m-mean, not before. O-only th-the highest *ton* allowed. B-but . . . well, I knew Rothmier w-went there, and . . . and I just dropped in t-to see if I could meet my future brother-in-law." He flushed even more deeply. "Or who I thought was my—"

"I understand," Josie sighed.

"I'm sorry, Josie," Michael said, his gray eyes regretful. "I'm in the suds again. I sh-should just r-run off and join the military, that's what I should do."

"You don't mean that," Josie said quickly. She crawled back up and attacked the other boot.

"T-to tell the truth, Josie," Michael said, "I th-think I'd like it."

"Truly?" Josie asked, astonished.

"It would g-give me s-something t-to do," Michael said. "Other than wh-what I'm doing. It'd k-keep me out of tr-trouble. I would like that. But I would n-need a set of colors." He barked a laugh. "God. I j-just lost that last night."

"But the man cheated you," Josie said fiercely. Michael's boot received the same fierce treatment. It came off swiftly.

"What a damn . . . er, darn fool I am. I sh-should have known Desuex was out of my l-league. B-but h-he just kept taking m-my vows." Michael hiccuped. "A-and taking them. And taking them . . ."

"That's enough, I understand," Josie said, cringing. "But why would he do that? Why would he trust you so?"

"I didn't see any harm in telling him about you and R-Rothmier getting sh-ackled. S'truth, I-I was celebrating." He hung his head. "I w-was telling q-quite a few chaps th-that night."

"Oh, dear," Josie sighed. "I'm sorry."

"He said any friend of Rothmier's was a friend of his."

"With friends like that, you do not need any enemies," Josie muttered. She collected both boots. "When does he want the money?"

Michael looked dismayed. "He said he'd give me a week, since I was a fr-friend . . ."

"I know, of Rothmier." Josie rose, her mind roiling. Desuex hadn't only fleeced Michael. He knew if Michael didn't pay, Rothmier would. She blanched. Heavens, she couldn't permit that. "D-don't worry, Michael. We'll think of something. We must."

"Will we?" Michael asked with a snort.

"Yes, we will," Josie said, numbly picking up the jacket and cravat. "Now go to sleep."

"No, Josie." Michael shook his head. "Thish is my problem. We're twins, but w-we ain't the s-same and one."

"I know," Josie said, forcing a grin. "I can play cards better than you."

"Ha! And I'm more handsome than you." Michael laughed.

Josie stared at Michael. Her heart jumped as an idea streaked through her mind. It had been an old joke between them. Yet now she wondered. She really wondered. "Go to sleep. There's nothing that can be done tonight."

"Guess you're right." Michael sighed and fell back upon the mattress. "S'good night."

"Good night," Josie said softly. She heard the first snore from Michael as she silently left the room, taking his clothes and boots with her.

"Well, am I as handsome as Michael?" Josie asked, strutting in front of a mirror and smiling.

Pansy cocked her head to one side. "Yes, dear, I do believe you are." Josie laughed and Pansy frowned. "But remember your voice."

"Yes, Miss Tellington," Josie said, lowering her voice a few octaves.

"Better." Pansy nodded. Then she sighed. "I don't know, dearest. We both think you look like Michael, and after all these years, you know his every action, but what if we are wrong?"

Josie shook her head. "We won't be wrong. Michael said he only went to Desuex's once and only played cards with him once. I do not see why I cannot fool him."

"Yes, but . . ."

"Pansy," Josie said, earnestly, "we've got to help Michael. You know he must pay within the week, and I don't know where else we will get the money otherwise. And . . . and we can't have Desuex going to Rothmier."

"No," Pansy said. "That would be completely mortifying. But what if something goes wrong?"

Josie bit her lip. She couldn't see what else could go wrong. It already had. "Nothing will go wrong."

"I hope not," Pansy said, her voice dubious.

Josie felt a moment's qualm. She shook it off with grim determination. She had told Rothmier that it was time for her to make a push to save the family fortunes. Well, push she would, even if it were done in her brother's boots. "It won't. Besides, it isn't right this man cheated Michael."

Pansy's face stiffened. "That it isn't. You will teach that sharp a lesson. I've never seen a more perfect sleight of hand than yours."

"Thank you," Josie said, warming inside. She looked down. "And thank you for giving me your money. I know it is all you have saved."

"Fiddlesticks," Pansy said. Her eyes gleamed and were suspiciously wet. "I'd stake you anytime, my dear. I'm so very proud of you."

Josie hastened over and hugged Pansy. "Wish me luck."

"I do." Pansy reached into her pocket and with a sniff drew out two dice. "Here, I want you to have these."

"Thank you." Josie drew in a breath. "I'll only use them if I lose at cards."

"You won't," Pansy said, her tone vehement. "I don't worry about your play; I only worry you'll be discovered."

"I won't be. Now, are you certain you can keep Michael home tonight? If he's seen on the town as well, we'll really be in the briars."

"I can keep him here," Pansy said. "Poor boy. He is so depressed, it was no trouble asking him to remain home for the evening and play chess with me."

"Good. Don't wait up for me." Josie hugged Pansy once more. Then straightening, she strolled from the room with a jaunt to her step she'd seen her brother employ for the greater part of their lives together.

Josie strode as manishly as she could through Paul Desuex's establishment. She feigned a nonchalance, though she wanted to stop and gawk. No lady should ever be caught in a gaming hell, but if a lady must, Paul Desuex's would certainly be a favored choice. The furnishings were of the finest, and the wine and champagne offered were of the best vintage. She listened carefully to the bets called at faro and studied the tables to judge what stakes were

being set. Heavens! Michael wasn't bamming her. The play
was deep, very deep.

Her gaze finally settled upon the man who she had discovered from a servant was Paul Desuex. Here was the
card sharp she must out-sharp. He sat alone at a table, his
French origins clearly defined in his dark hair and skin.
A glass of wine beside him, his hands riffled through a
deck of cards in a careless caress. Josie plucked up her
courage. She would win all of Michael's money back. They
certainly needed it far more than this man did.

She threw back her shoulders and forced an added swag-
ger to her step as she approached him. She cleared her
throat and lowered her voice. "Desuex."

Desuex glanced up. His eyes, which were astonishingly
light brown, glinted in amusement. "Ah, Stanton. You've
come to redeem your vowels?"

"No," Josie said, her tone curt. "I'd rather try my hand
at cards with you again."

Desuex's eyes widened and he frowned. Something flickered in his gaze, something like astonishment. *Mon Dieu.*"

"Surprised?" Josie asked, nettled. He clearly didn't
think much of her brother.

"No," Paul Desuex said. A broad, friendly smile crossed
his lips. "Charmed, rather. Quite charmed. But are you
sure you wish to try, er, again? You already owe me a great
sum."

"I know," Josie said. "But I have my head about me
tonight. The other night I was ape drunk."

Desuex choked. "Were you now?"

"Yes," Josie said firmly. "And Mic . . . er, my abilities
are never good then. But when I do not drink, I am the
very devil with the cards."

"Are you?" Paul asked.

"Yes." Josie nodded. She caught her breath. "In fact,
you might even think me a different man."

"Indeed," Paul said. He raised his brow. "And this is all due to the drink?"

"Yes," Josie said eagerly. "It changes me frightfully. But I'm not drinking tonight, so you should take care."

Paul Desuex laughed. "You frighten me."

"You are bamming me." Josie suddenly grinned. She couldn't help herself. She had expected to hate this man, but somehow could not. Then remembering herself, she schooled her expression back to serious. "But I do think it only fair to warn you. You'll not find me an easy mark . . . er, I mean as easy to beat as last time."

"Thank you for the advice," Paul Desuex said, his tone appropriately solemn, though his eyes twinkled. "You are indeed a . . . man of honor."

"I try to be."

"Very well." Paul glanced about. "Let us go to a private room, Machelle."

Josie frowned. "It is Michael."

"Machelle is the French version," Paul said, laughing. He stood promptly and led her into a small room. Josie sat down at the lone table with a sigh. It would be much nicer to play quietly, without fear of interruption or recognition, though she doubted any of Michael's friends haunted this establishment.

Paul set a new pack of cards upon the table. Josie's eyes lighted. She might be here upon the serious and righteous mission of winning Michael's money back, but it didn't mean she could not enjoy the challenge of it.

As they began their game, Josie grew even more thrilled. Desuex was indeed a fine card player. He forced Josie to remain on her toes, especially when, after Paul lost the first few hands, he began to perform some of the finest sleight of hand tricks known to man, or Miss Tellington.

Josie responded properly to suit. Every time Paul cheated, she would counter with a different trick to offset the damage. In truth, she no longer tallied her winnings, so intent was she. It was a chess game of devious tricks more than anything else.

Suddenly, Paul threw down his cards. His gaze was stern. "I'll play no more with you, Machelle."

Josie looked up from her cards, her face falling. "What? Why not?"

"You just cheated," Paul said, shaking a finger at her.

Josie smiled in delight. "You just now noticed?"

Paul's eyes shuttered open in surprise. "You mean you have been cheating all along?"

"No," Josie said, shaking her head. "Not until you started cheating in the third hand."

Paul stared at her and then barked a laugh. "I thought you must be cheating, but could not believe it."

"Then, you truly didn't know?" Josie asked. A tingle of pride coursed through her.

"No," Paul said. He frowned severely. "I thought you said you were a . . . man of honor."

"I said I try to be." Josie grinned impishly. "Besides, I am honorable. I only cheat when someone else cheats. Otherwise it is not fair." She cast him a frown. "Which is more than I can say for you."

Paul shrugged. "I did not say I was a man of honor."

"Which you shouldn't," Josie replied, still severe.

"Those very well could be dueling words," Paul said, his tone stiff.

"Why? It is only the truth," Josie said, cocking her head. "You fleeced Mi . . . me the other night. Out of money I could ill afford, I might add."

Paul chuckled. "You won it back tonight."

"I did?" Josie asked. She looked down at the mound of chips before her in bemusement. "Heavens, I had not noticed."

"Ah," Paul said, nodding. "A true gamester. Never watch the money, or you will lose."

"Are you sure you don't want to play anymore?" Josie asked.

"No," Paul said. "You have won back what you owed me, but that is where I draw the line."

"Very well," Josie said. The taste of winning pulsed through her veins. "I'll go and find someone else to play."

Paul frowned. "Are you certain you want to do that?"

"Yes, why ever not?" Josie asked, her mind already focused upon finding another card game. The butcher's bill and the servants' wages had suddenly mingled with the gamester fire.

Paul cast her an odd look. He shrugged. "Very well, I am no nursemaid. But do not cheat any of my customers." He grinned. "Only I am permitted to do that."

Josie stood, scooping up her chips. "I told you, I only cheat those who cheat."

"No," Paul said. "I do not want you to do that either."

Josie sighed. The man had the right. It was his establishment. Also, she had seen a huge, fearsome man at the door who obviously did Paul's bidding. "Very well."

Paul rose, still frowning. "I do not normally give advice, but if you were wise, you would draw back now. Go home while you are still . . . ahead."

"No," Josie said. Perhaps even one or two of the dressmaker bills. "I need the money."

"For what?" Paul asked.

Josie blinked. "You do not know us Stantons if you must ask that."

"Forgive me. That was foolish of me," Paul said, chuckling. He raised his brow. "But surely your fortunes are secure now that . . . er, your sister is to marry Rothmier."

Josie flushed a deep red. "I-I was mistaken that night. I . . . my sister and Rothmier are not going to marry."

Paul whistled lowly. "That is bad."

"Yes," Josie said, flushing.

"What did Alex do?" Paul asked. "Isn't he in breach of promise?"

"No. Oh, no! The decision was totally mutual between . . . between my sister and him." Josie found herself shifting and twitching under his gaze. "So, you see. I really do need the money."

Paul nodded. "If you wish to take your chances, then do."

Josie smiled and started to depart the room. Paul called after her. "Mis . . . Machelle. Do you play faro?"

Josie stopped. "Yes, I do."

"You will not tonight," Paul said. "I'll not have my bank broken."

Josie sighed. She had Pansy's lucky dice burning a hole in her pocket. It was a shame. "Very well."

Alex arrived late to Desuex's establishment. He had gone to the opera with Cybil and then dropped her off at her town house. She had expected him to stay, he knew, but for some reason he was not in the mood. He smiled wryly. He must be growing old. That or the past few days, after he had almost stepped into the parson's mousetrap, had offset him.

He winced. He had thought the Stanton family had taken it poorly, and had behaved poorly, but the scene within his own family had been just as frightful. His mother had fainted and taken to her bed to wail about serpents at her bosom. She had not believed the decision between Alex and Josie was mutual. She placed the blame squarely upon him. He had purposely destroyed his chances. Lydia had turned cold and biting, declaring he was determined to remain on the path to perdition, and she wiped her hands clean of him. Only Mandy had taken the news in a calm way, saying that what was not meant to be, would not be.

Alex chuckled. It most certainly was not to be. Still, a small voice nagged at him. If he were on the path to perdition, just what path was Josie Stanton on? She had sounded so positive that she could do something to help her family. Yet she was only a young girl. What could she do? She had no prospects whatsoever. In rejecting him, she had thrown her last chance away. She had saved him, but now she would have no life herself. The image of Josie, a lonely destitute spinster, sitting at home day after day with her sixteen pages of ledgers, arose in his mind.

Alex shook his head, trying to clear it. He must forget all this. They may have been promised to each other for years, but he'd only met Josie once. It was ridiculous to feel guilt or anything else over the matter. She had made her decision. He was in no way responsible.

This settled, he determined to put Josie from his mind. That decision went a-begging when Alex scanned the room for likely company, only to view Michael Stanton at a table, just then laying down a hand of cards. Instant anger welled within Alex. The young fool. His family was swimming down the river tick, and here he was squandering away their nonexistent funds. His sister would become a lonely, destitute spinster because of him.

Alex growled and headed toward the table. He'd only advanced a few steps before he faltered. He sucked in his breath. It couldn't be. It simply couldn't. He narrowed his eyes, telling himself he was insane. Young Stanton leaned over to pick up the chips. Blast and damn! He wasn't crazy. That was definitely the wrong Stanton playing at the table. Alex knew it more in his gut than anything else.

"Good evening, Alex," Paul Desuex's voice sounded next to his ear.

Alex swung around. Paul stood close beside him. "Good evening."

"It is a pleasure to see you here tonight," Paul said, his brown eyes glinting.

"Is it?" Alex asked, turning his fulminating gaze back to Josie.

"Indeed," Paul said. He chuckled. "I see you are watching young Stanton. He is doing amazingly well tonight. You might enjoy playing a hand with him."

"I wouldn't," Alex said, gritting his teeth. "Sh-she shouldn't be here."

"No, I suppose she shouldn't," Paul said quietly. "But she is."

Alex turned a narrowed gaze upon him. "You know."

"But of course," Paul said. He shook his head, wonderment upon his face. "It appears that we are the only two men of any understanding present. Understanding of women, that is."

"If you say so," Alex said. At the moment he didn't feel particularly understanding.

"Do not worry, my friend. I have watched her all evening," Paul said. "No one else suspects, that I can tell."

"Blast it, Paul," Alex said, clenching his hands. "How could you let her stay, knowing she was . . . a she?"

Paul shrugged. "I respect bravery. Whether in a man or a woman."

"Bravery?" Alex asked. "You mean stupidity."

"She came to win back the five thousand pounds her brother lost to me the other evening. I call that brave," Paul said. He laughed. "Especially since she succeeded. She is a devil with the cards, you know?"

"I don't give a damn how she plays."

"Of course not," Paul said. "You are not going to marry her after all. What does it matter her talents or faults?"

Alex glared at Paul. "She told you?"

"Yes." Paul nodded. He quirked a brow. "She said it was a mutual decision."

"No," Alex said. "She rejected me."

"I cannot believe it," Paul said, his eyes widening.

"She doesn't wish to marry," Alex said, his jaw clenching, "until she has repaired her family fortune. She says she'll not have them batten on a husband of hers."

Paul laughed. "Well, she is making a good . . . er, stab at repairing her fortunes tonight."

"She can't do it in a bloody gaming hell." Alex seethed while he watched Josie shuffle the cards with smooth, sure fingers. The chit acted as if she belonged at that infernal table with those men!

"Actually, *mon ami,* she can," Paul said, his tone rueful. "I told you she's already won five thousand from me. And now she is cleaning out Darwood, Sheridan, and Trent."

"She's a woman for God's sake," Alex said, rage flaring high. She was supposed to be at home, alone and destitute with her ledgers, not brazenly wearing her brother's clothes and inhabiting a gaming den. "No, a girl in fact. A naive, foolish girl."

"That naive, foolish girl is winning," Paul pointed out.

"I don't give a damn if she is winning," Alex muttered. "She shouldn't be here."

"Spoken like a well-heeled gentleman who is not in need of money," Paul said. "Gaming is still one of the more honorable professions. Especially for a woman."

Alex glared at him. "Don't be crass. Josie is a lady."

"Ah," Paul said, his lips twitching. "A moment ago she was a foolish girl. Do make up your mind."

Alex's hand clenched into a fist. "Damn you, Desuex." He halted as a shout arose from the table.

"You cheat, Stanton," Lord Darwood cried out, springing up from the table. He was drawn up to the fullest of his medium height, his balding pate as red as his face.

"Fiend seize it," Alex muttered, even as the crowded room silenced.

"No," Josie said, her tone frightfully calm, reasonable in fact. "I didn't need to cheat. Not with you."

"Then you admit you cheat!" Darwood shouted.

"I said I didn't with you," Josie reiterated, frowning. "I'm sorry, but you are abominable at cards."

"Oh, no," Alex groaned. Clearly Sheridan and Trent thought the same as he, for both silently rose from the table and backed away.

Only Josie remained sitting. She looked at the angry Darwood in a stern manner, that of headmistress of the harshest of finishing schools. "You really shouldn't be playing at all. But I did not cheat. It wouldn't be fair. It would be like taking a rattle from a baby."

"Mon Dieu," Paul said, shaking his head. "She does not fawn, does she?"

"Baby! You take that back," Lord Darwood cried. His stubby hand shot out. He clutched Josie's cravat and dragged her up from the chair. The height difference would have been ludicrous if Darwood hadn't been so enraged, or Josie a slim, defenseless girl. "Admit you cheat. Admit I'm not a baby!"

"Damn," Alex said, attempting to head toward the table without much success. The increasing ring of onlookers was too thick.

"No, you are a poor sport and a bully," Josie choked out. "Let me go!"

"Poor sport! Take that back!" Darwood cried, rattling Josie like a terrier with a firm grip on a Great Dane. "Take it all back."

"That's a long list," Paul said from behind.

Evidently Josie thought the same thing. She vibrated a "n-n-o." Then the "slim, defenseless girl" balled up her fist and popped Darwood directly in the jaw.

Darwood stiffened, very much as if Josie had struck him with a lightning bolt, rather than an amateur punch. He groaned and toppled backward, his frozen fist still clenched to Josie's cravat. Josie let out a shout as she was dragged down with him. Cursing, Alex shoved the men aside, and bolted over to the fallen couple.

A singeing string of swear words drifted up from the entrapped Josie. The real Michael Stanton could not have done better. Alex halted, stunned as he watched Josie wrest her cravat from Darwood's hand and scrabble off of him. She made it to her feet. Her face brightened when she spied him. "Alex, hello." Then she frowned and looked down at Darwood. His one hand was still crooked up, frozen just as he fell. "What on earth is the matter with him?"

"Matter with him?" Alex gulped, his gaze not upon Darwood, but upon Josie. Or her chest rather. In her efforts to break free, the buttons on her shirt had broken free. A camisole with pink ribbon and French lace shined through. He thought he could even see the curve and shadow of. . . . Alex moved. He jumped in front of Josie.

"Alex!" Josie squeaked. "What are you doing?"

"We are going," Alex said, ramming his back up to her and glaring at the onlookers for added measure.

"But I didn't hit him that hard," Josie said, trying to step around him. "How could I have hurt him?"

"He's got a glass jaw," Alex gritted. His own was sure to shatter, he clenched it so tightly. "Come on."

"But I . . ."

"Now," Alex barked. He said it with such command that the men all muttered and backed away.

Only Josie did not respond with equal respect. "But, Alex, I am winning . . ."

"Mr. Stanton," Paul Desuex said, coming to flank her as well as Alex. "I will not tolerate any more disturbances in my establishment. I fear I must ask you to leave."

"But you know I wasn't cheating," Josie objected as Alex, with the aid of Paul, started crowding her back away from the table.

"I understand that," Paul said. "But you have caused a brawl. You must leave."

"Very well," Josie said. She attempted to squeeze

through the two men. "Only let me collect my winnings . . ."

"No, you don't," Alex said, grabbing hold of her. He
half shoved and half carried her from the room.

"But my money," Josie wailed.

"I'll bring it to you," Alex heard Paul shout. He could
also hear the men's laughter, exclamations and mutters.
God only knew what they thought. He refused to think
about it and didn't stop until he had dragged Josie into
the foyer.

"Alex," Josie exclaimed, finally breaking free. "Stop
mauling me!"

"Stow it," Alex muttered, once again jerking her full to
him as a large, burly man appeared.

The man stopped. He goggled. "Excuse me. Didn't
mean to . . . er, interrupt?"

Alex recognized Paul's henchman. His name was Mike.
"Get me a cape."

"A cape?" Josie asked, struggling in his arms.

"A cape?" Mike asked, just as slow-witted.

"Yes, a cape," Alex said.

"But . . . ," the footman said.

"Now!" Alex roared.

"Yes, my lord," Mike said, his large frame jerking to
attention.

"I do not need a cape," Josie objected as Mike disappeared. "I want my winnings."

"You want a cape," Alex said curtly. He looked swiftly
about to ensure they were alone. "Look at your front."

"What about my front?" Josie frowned. She pulled away
from him and looked down. "Oh, heavens!"

"Here you are, my lord," Mike's voice said again.

"Oh, no!" Josie squeaked. She promptly jumped back
into Alex's arms, hiding her face in his shoulder.

"Blimey," Mike exclaimed.

"It's not what you think, damn you," Alex said. Unfortunately Josie burrowed even closer at that moment.

"No, my lord," Mike said. His face flushed to a bright red. "Whatever y-you say, my lord."

"Well, I say it," Alex growled. "Now give me the damn cloak."

"C-certainly, my lord," Mike stammered. He approached cautiously and held the cloak out stiff-armed, as if frightened to be any closer to the embracing Alex and Josie than absolutely necessary.

Alex snatched the proffered cape from Mike and wrapped it around the now trembling Josie. He whispered, "For God's sake, act like a man."

"What? Oh! Oh, yes," Josie said. She straightened, struggling into the cape. "Sorry." She turned to Mike. "Thank you, I shall have the cloak returned tomorrow. It was very kind of you . . ."

"Stanton, come on," Alex breathed, shoving her toward the door. "I'm taking you home."

"But I want to play some more," Josie exclaimed.

"No more playing," Alex said, opening the door. "I'm taking you home and you are going to bed."

"Very well, Alex," Josie said. "You can take me home. But you don't have to be so impatient and demanding about it."

"Gore," Mike breathed.

Alex clenched his jaw and, grabbing Josie, dragged her through the door and down the steps. He cursed as he looked about. He didn't see his carriage. Benson must have taken it for a turn, not expecting to be needed for the next few hours. "Where's your carriage?"

"I took a hack," Josie said. "For secrecy."

"Famous." Alex glanced over his shoulder. Mike still held the door open, watching. Alex took up Josie's arm and directed her down the street. He'd not stand waiting, especially when Darwood came, to. "We'll walk for the nonce."

"Yes," Josie said, snuggling into her cloak and strolling beside him. She drew in a deep breath, looking up at the sky. "It is a lovely evening."

"Lovely evening?" Alex stared at her. "I can't believe it!"

"Neither can I," Josie said. She almost skipped. "Alex, I won almost seven thousand pounds tonight. Why, if I can continue playing like that—"

"You aren't going to," Alex interrupted with a growl.

Josie sighed. "No, I understand I can't be a winner every time. Lady Luck is fickle, after all. But if I am judicious . . ."

"Judicious!" Alex barked a laugh. "You are anything but judicious!"

"But I am," Josie said, frowning. "A good gambler must be judicious. Else, they are . . . well, like Michael or Papa. Always losing. It is not only skill, it is—"

"I'm not talking about cards." Alex grabbed Josie by the shoulder and swung her around, forcing her to look at him. "I'm talking about you masquerading as your brother!"

"Oh, that."

"Yes, that," Alex said. "Do you realize you would have been ruined if they had discovered your masquerade tonight?"

Josie had the grace to blush. "Yes, but . . . but I wasn't. No one knew."

"Desuex knew."

"He did?" Josie's eyes widened. "Heavens, he is sharp."

"And I noticed."

"But you know me," Josie said. "None of the others do."

"I assure you, all of the others would have in very short order," Alex said bitterly, "if we hadn't gotten you out of there in time."

Josie shrank into her cape. "Perhaps."

"There is no perhaps about it," Alex said. "God, I don't want to even think about what might have happened."

"But nothing did," Josie said, her tone hopeful.

"This time," Alex growled. "You cannot do it, Josie. You cannot masquerade as your brother again. Do you hear me?"

Josie's chin lifted in defiance. "But I could win so much money! Perhaps this is the way to help my family."

"No," Alex said. "You must think of something else. Masquerading as your brother is pure lunacy. You were just fortunate Darwood can't take a punch."

"But . . ."

"No." Alex gripped her shoulders more tightly. "You must promise me, Josie!"

"Alex . . ."

"I want your promise." Alex was determined, so determined he didn't notice as another couple bumped into them.

"Excuse me, love." A low voice laughed.

Alex glanced up, irritated at the interruption. A redheaded strumpet, clearly drunk and enveloped in the familiar hold of her escort, grinned at him. "Think nothing of it," Alex muttered in a semblance of politeness.

"So-o-o kind, "the lady trilled and cast him a flirtatious look, even as her burly escort growled and dragged her away.

Alex turned his attention back to the infuriating girl in his grasp. "Josie, you heard me. I want your promise."

"What?" Josie asked. She looked past him, her gaze focused upon the retreating couple.

"You aren't listening," Alex gritted. "I want your promise."

"Who is she?" Josie asked, frowning.

"Who is she?" Alex rolled his eyes in exasperation.

"How should I know? She's just some . . . er, lady of the evening. Now will you—?"

"Lady of the evening?" Josie asked, her gray eyes widening.

"Yes," Alex said. "A prostitute in other words."

"Is that what she is," Josie exclaimed. "I know of them. They make men pay for their company."

"Yes," Alex said. "Exactly."

"I've never seen one before, though," Josie said, blinking. "At least, I didn't think I had."

"I should hope not." Alex frowned.

Josie shook her head, a look of confusion upon her face. "I don't understand. She is very well dressed."

"No she isn't," Alex said, distracted a moment. "She is dressed exactly for what she is, a low-class strumpet."

"Low-class?" Josie asked.

"Very low class," Alex said briskly. "We are digressing . . ."

"Then there are high-class strumpets as well?"

"Yes." Alex was totally exasperated. The woman's mind flitted about like a butterfly. "Would you pay attention to me . . ."

"Just what is high-class?" Josie asked. Her gray gaze finally turned to him, intent and totally riveted.

Alex groaned. Now she paid attention! "Josie, this is not a subject we should be discussing. I apologize—"

"Please, don't apologize," Josie interrupted. "I told you, I am not one to stand upon ceremony."

Alex looked at Josie, dressed as her brother. He laughed bitterly. "That is an understatement."

"What is a high-class strumpet?" Josie asked again.

Alex sighed. "They are the mistresses and courtesans. The women kept by gentlemen—"

"Kept?"

"Er, employed as it were," Alex said. "For long-term relationships."

"I see," Josie said. "Mistresses are employed long-term and dress even better than strumpets."

"Yes," Alex said, eager to change the subject. "Now, can we return to the matter at hand?"

"How much does it cost for a gentleman to 'keep' a mistress?"

"Josie, I told you. We shouldn't be discussing this."

"Is it a goodly sum?" Josie persisted.

"Sometimes," Alex said, shifting.

"And do you pay them quarterly?" Josie asked, her voice rather odd.

"Sometimes," Alex said. A strange, nervous tingle chased down his spine. "Why are you asking? You aren't thinking about raising money that way?"

Josie looked at him, her eyes widening. "Oh, no. At least, I hadn't considered it. Miss Tellington told me that it is something no respectable woman would ever do."

"She is right," Alex said full-heartedly. "Good for Miss Tellington."

"But she also said that it didn't pay." Josie sounded confused.

"It doesn't," Alex said firmly.

Josie looked at him. "It is very hard work, then?"

"Yes, very hard." Alex blinked, and actually felt a flush rising to his face. "I mean, very difficult work. It takes much . . . er, training and study."

"Oh, dear," Josie said. "What am I to do?"

Alex felt that nervous tingle again. "What do you mean, what are you to do?"

Josie looked directly at him, her eyes dark. "I think my father is keeping a mistress."

Alex groaned. "Oh, Josie."

"He is, isn't he?" Josie asked, her gaze steady. "There's always been a quarterly sum taken out which he refuses to talk about. And I saw him with a lady once who reminded me of that woman who went past us. He is keeping a mistress, isn't he?"

Alex debated a moment. Yet Josie's open, questing look forced him to be honest. "Yes, I think he is. But you shouldn't let it overset you. Most men have them."

Josie frowned. "Miss Tellington told me only single men did."

"She was mistaken. Married men do as well." Josie looked so distressed, Alex added quickly, "Not all of them of course, but some of them. It doesn't mean they do not love their wives. You mustn't think that. It only means . . . well, it is just something they do. It does not affect their heart or anything."

"It doesn't?" Josie said, her eyes wide upon his.

"It doesn't."

Josie appeared to mull it over. She suddenly gave a swift nod of her head. "Then Father shouldn't keep his mistress."

"What do you mean?" Alex asked nervously.

"If he is keeping this woman, but . . . but it does not affect him, then that is an expenditure he should curtail."

"Josie!" Alex exclaimed.

"You can't imagine the sums he is laying out." She frowned. "But we must think of the lady as well. If she is working so very hard, it isn't fair to end her employment without thinking of her."

"I-I suppose not," Alex said weakly.

She looked at him, a rather considering look. "Would you be so kind as to employ her instead?"

Alex stared. "What?"

"Would you employ her instead?" Josie asked in a reasonable tone. "You can afford her. Father cannot."

For some reason, Alex found himself totally insulted. It was obvious that Josie wasn't the most common of young ladies, but for her to ask him to take her father's mistress over went well beyond the mark. First she rejected his suit, and now she wanted him to take on a mistress. Not only was she indelicate, but she did not have any sense of the proper emotions that passed between a man and woman. "I cannot believe you are asking me this."

"Why not?" Josie said. "Is it presumptuous?"

"Yes," Alex said. "Most ladies do not wish for men to have mistresses."

"Why?" Josie asked. "Because of the expense?"

"No, damn it," Alex said. "Because they are supposed to be jealous of mistresses."

"Jealous?" Josie asked. "Why?"

"Why?" Alex exclaimed. He'd had women threaten to kill themselves if he so much as looked at another. He'd had women tear each other's hair out over him! "Here is why."

He hauled Josie into his arms and kissed her. He didn't hold back. A thunderbolt shot through him, though, for Josie did not hold back either. She gasped only once, then melted into his embrace, her arms sliding up to cling to his neck. Her lips were all accepting, tasting of eagerness and awakening fire.

Alex, startled by the heat flashing through him, attempted to draw back, but Josie held to him. Her lips followed his, wildly questing. Alex groaned, and deepened the kiss, answering her desire. His hands moved over her, shaking at the feel of her supple body, her delicate curves. Her height was perfect, matching his own length, only female, all warm and willing female. God, she would feel the same beneath him.

The need tormented him. Shocked him. Appalled, he jerked his lips from Josie's and pulled her hands from around his neck.

"That is what a man does with a mistress," he muttered. He said it as much as a reminder to himself as for an explanation.

"H-he does?" Josie asked. She stood staring at him, her eyes passion-dazed, her lips showing the ravages of his kiss.

"Yes," he said, his breath ragged.

"I-I see."

The words hung in the air. What she exactly saw, Alex didn't know. He only knew that if she continued to stare at him like that, he would kiss her again. Rage, and an unknown fear, welled within him. "And I don't want your father's mistress. I have one of my own."

"Oh," Josie said. Something painful flashed through her eyes. Then disappeared. She squared her shoulders. "Th-that is all you would have had to say. I would have understood."

A vicious self-loathing ripped through Alex. That was all he would have had to say. He looked away. "We need to find a damn hack."

As if on cue, he heard the sound of horse and vehicle approaching. He glanced to the street. A hack trundled toward them. Expelling a relieved breath, he sprinted out and hailed it down. He gave the driver the address and tossed him the coins. He turned to discover Josie standing close beside him, quietly.

"H-he'll take you home," Alex said, his voice sounding rough.

"Yes," Josie said. Without another word, she went to the door and opened it. Climbing in, she closed the door.

Alex walked over and looked through the window. "Josie . . ."

"Yes?" Josie asked, her voice small.

"I want you—" Alex stopped.

"What?" Josie asked after a moment.

Lord, what had he intended to say? He didn't know. "I . . . I want you to promise me you won't masquerade as your brother again."

Josie looked at him a moment and then nodded. "I promise."

Alex, feeling at a loss for words, waved the driver on. The hack started up, and Alex stared after it, feeling stupid. What the devil could he have said? He groaned. His body was still tense and wanting. It was as if it still felt, against his will, the impression of Josie's body against his, the taste of Josie's lips upon his.

He cursed. He knew what to do. He had a damn mistress, after all.

Three

"Josie, dear, wake up." Pansy's voice drifted through Josie's dreams, dreams of Alex and heated kisses. "Josie?"

Josie groaned and opened her eyes. Pansy bent over her, a look of both eagerness and fear upon her face. "G-good morning, Pansy."

Those were the only words necessary. Pansy immediately plopped down upon the bed. "You must tell me! Tell me all!"

"Pansy, really," Josie said, embarrassment mingling with the fog of sleep. One didn't tell her governess about heated kisses. "I-I cannot talk about it."

"Oh, dear," Pansy gasped. "How much did you lose?"

"Lose?" Josie asked, blinking.

"Yes, you can tell me," Pansy said.

"Oh, no," Josie gasped, sitting up quickly. She had totally forgotten for a moment the thing Pansy would really want to know. How could the memory of Alex's kiss make her forget she had won seven thousand pounds? "No. I won seven thousand pounds."

"Seven thousand pounds," Pansy gasped. "Gracious. Why wouldn't you want to tell me that?"

"I-I er, wanted to build up to it?" Josie said hesitantly.

"You sweet dear," Pansy patted her hand. "Now you can tell me. Each and every detail."

"Yes," Josie said, swallowing. She was right back where

she started. Fortunately, a knock sounded at the door. Josie
sighed in relief. "Come in!"

The door opened and Mary entered. "Josie, how do you
feel this morning, dear? I've been worried about you."

Josie paused. She made a hesitant guess. "I feel fine?"

"Do you?" Mary looked at her with deep, concerned
eyes.

"Er, very fine?" Josie asked.

"No, but you feel much better," Pansy said with a steady
look at Josie. "You are over that terrible migraine you suffered last night. Aren't you, dear?"

"I am?" Josie asked, staring at Pansy.

"Yes," Pansy said in a firm tone. "The one which kept
you in your room all last night. The one which wouldn't
permit you to see Mary."

"Oh, *that* migraine," Josie said, nodding in understanding. She looked to her sister. "Yes, Mary. I feel better, much
better. Fit as a fiddle, in fact."

"I am glad," Mary said, smiling. "I was quite worried.
You've never suffered from a migraine in your life."

"I-I think you can grow into them," Josie murmured. A
sudden thought occurred to her. Mary would have come
to see her far past ten o'clock. Mary religiously retired at
nine. It was Josie's turn to be concerned. "Why were you
awake past ten? Is something wrong?"

Mary sighed, coming to sit upon the other side of the
bed. "Oh, Josie, I know you are going to tell me I should
not worry, but I cannot help it."

"What is it?" Josie asked.

"It's Father," Mary said, twisting her hands in her lap.
"H-he called me down to see him in the library last evening. H-he's thought of a plan t-to save the family."

"He did?" Josie asked, stunned. Her father bending his
mind to financial matters was always astonishing. Then she
swallowed hard. On the rare occasion that he did, his no-

tions were generally so farfetched as to be frightening. "Wh-what did he think to do?"

"S–since you aren't going to make a match of it with Rothmier, h-he has decided that it should be me who should marry instead."

"What?" She had never thought of Mary wedding. Why hadn't she?

"Oh, Josie," Mary said, her brown eyes tearing. "He says that the Earl of Canton would be a good match."

"Canton!" Josie gasped. "But he is . . . old!"

"And has wooden teeth," Pansy exclaimed.

"I know," Mary said. "But he is very rich, and Father says th-that the earl has always had a *tendre* for me."

"*Tendre* or not," Josie said, her chin jutting out, "you cannot marry that man. Why h-he's . . ."

"A loose fish," Pansy finished. She shook her head. "Which has always confused me. How a man who looks like that can still have—" She halted. "Well, still have a reputation with the ladies is beyond me."

Josie stared at Pansy. Suddenly she knew exactly what Pansy had meant to say. Before last night, she would have taken Miss Tellington's statement in a totally different manner. This was today, however, and she now understood Pansy's delicate phrasing. Anger rushed through her. Mary could never wed a man like Canton. She needed a different kind of man. She, out of all the Stantons, would require the most upstanding and respectable of men.

"No," Josie said firmly. "You won't marry Canton. I will see to it."

"But, Josie, if Father is determined, h-how will I gainsay him?" Mary asked, her voice panicked.

"You simply tell him no," Josie said stoutly. "Or I will tell him no."

Mary looked down. "But . . . but to save the family, I w-would marry."

Josie flushed. Unlike Mary, she had refused Rothmier,

regardless of the family. Now it had thrown poor Mary into this predicament. Her lips pressed into a firm line. She had refused to sacrifice Rothmier on the family financial pyre; she would not permit Mary to throw herself upon that flame either. She thought a moment. "How drunk was Father?"

Mary flushed. "It was late. He was drunk."

"Just well to live?" Josie asked, intent. "Or shot the cat?"

Mary thought a moment. "Shot the cat, I would say."

"Good." Josie smiled. "Odds are three to one he doesn't even remember it today."

"Of course." Pansy grinned in return. "You know your father. He always has those 'ideas' when he's befuddled."

"Thank heaven he never remembers them," Josie said. She recalled the time her father became taken with the notion of migrating to the Americas and starting his own wine vineyard. That inspiration had lasted only through one bottle. Or the time he thought to get a patent for Josie's morning-after concoction. He intended to title it Stanton's Secret Sauce. In truth, that notion had stuck for four days, until he'd imbibed too much of it and came down with hives. "If none of us mention it, I am sure he will forget."

"Yes," Mary said, relief crossing her face. "What a goose I am. I-I hadn't thought of that."

"Just put it from your mind," Josie said. "I'm sure it is far from Father's this morning."

"You are right. I am fretting over nothing," Mary said, her face clearing. She rose. "I will leave you. I am sorry to trouble you when you have been so ill."

"No," Josie said. "I-I feel fine now."

"I will go with you, Mary." Pansy stood. She cast Josie a conspiratorial look and then herded Mary from the bedroom.

Josie gazed after them. She had told Mary to put it from her mind, but Josie intended to keep it firmly planted within her own. In truth, her father in his castaway state had hit upon a portion of a fine idea. Mary should have a husband. Her father had only lost his mooring with whom he had chosen. She jumped from her bed and scurried to dress, rolling the notion over and over in her mind. It was astonishing how many things she could do to help her family, but had never considered attempting before now. She had barely finished when another knock sounded at the door. "Yes?"

"Miss Josie," Musgrave's voice came through the wood. "You have a . . . gentleman who wishes to speak to you."

"A gentleman?" Josie asked. "Who is he?"

"He did not choose to give me his name," Musgrave replied. "But I believe he is French. He said he has come to pay a debt."

"Desuex," Josie whispered. She dashed to the door and swung it wide. "I'll see him."

"Are you sure, Miss Josie?" Musgrave asked, frowning.

"Yes," Josie said, already halfway down the hall. "Where did you leave him?"

"In the small salon, miss," Musgrave said. "The ladies are in the parlor."

"Good work, Musgrave." Josie vaulted down the stairs.

"I suspected so, miss," Musgrave said, amazingly keeping pace with her. "If I may be so bold as to ask, what kind of rig are you running?"

"Nothing," Josie said, lying blithely. "Nothing at all. Only don't let anyone know he's here."

"Just what debt does he owe you?" Musgrave panted.

"Money, Musgrave," Josie exclaimed. "A bundle!"

"Excellent, Miss Josie," Musgrave said. "But how . . ."

"Don't ask, Musgrave," Josie said, hastening through the house toward the small salon.

"No, miss," Musgrave said, following. "When do I ever? I assure you, I see many things in this house, none of which I divulge to the wrong parties. I am not one to blow the gaff as it were. Only, as a longtime retainer, it is not unusual that I have grown fond of you. I have only raised you since you were in leading strings. I would not wish to see you troubled, or engaged in any activity harmful . . ."

Josie halted before the door to the salon. She turned to grin at Musgrave. "I am not doing anything dangerous. Anything outside of the law. Or anything harmful. Only something you wouldn't like."

"Very well, Miss Josie," Musgrave sniffed. "That is all I needed to know."

"And I'll have this month's wages for you," Josie whispered, closing the door on Musgrave's properly astounded face. She turned to discover Paul Desuex sitting upon the settee, beaver hat and cane resting negligently beside him. He looked very much at ease. "I am so pleased you came," she greeted.

"Did you fear I would not?" Paul Desuex asked, frowning. He rose. "I do pay my debts."

"Oh, no, I never thought that." Josie smiled. "But I worried that you would not know who . . . I mean my direction."

The tension disappeared from Paul's face, and he laughed. "How could I not?" He cast her a roguish glance. "May I say, I like you better as Josephine, than as Michael."

"Thank you," Josie said, flushing. "And you may call me Josie. Everyone does."

"Josie, then." He reached into his pocket, pulling out a large purse. "Here are your winnings, Josie. All of them."

"Thank you." Josie rushed over to take the purse. It was gloriously heavy. Pure exhilaration shot through her. Then she sighed. "It is a shame."

"What is a shame?" Paul asked, his eyes twinkling. "Is that not enough?"

"In my family, no," Josie admitted. "But it will have to suffice, I suppose."

"Why?" Paul asked. "You are a talented gamester. There will be more from where that came from, if you choose."

"No." Josie blushed. "Rothmier has made me promise not to masquerade as my brother again."

"He made you promise?" Paul asked. He lifted his brow. "I was under the impression he was not your fiancé."

"He isn't," Josie said. "Not at all."

"Then, why must you listen to him?" Paul asked in a reasonable tone.

"I don't have to." Josie lifted her chin defiantly. Then the wind went out of her sails, and she sighed. "But I did promise him, and I keep my promises."

"A sad failing. You handicap yourself, *cheri,*" Paul said, shaking his head. His look turned speculative. "However, there is still a way I could arrange for you to play, and keep your promise."

"How?" Josie asked, frowning.

"You promised not to masquerade as your brother. But what if you masqueraded as someone else."

"S-someone else?"

"Yes, someone like . . ." Paul shrugged. "Someone like my cousin, perhaps. Who has come from abroad, yes? The, er, effeminate mode is the fashion in France at this time. And if I introduce you myself, they will believe me. Men see what they expect to see, just as they did last night."

Josie stared at him. "I wouldn't be lying to Alex then. I only promised him not to masquerade as my brother."

"Yes." Paul nodded. "And your personality would be so exacting that you would only engage in the personal and private games I arrange for you."

"You . . . you would do this for me?" Josie asked, eyes wide.

"Of course." He grinned. "For sixty percent of your winnings."

"Sixty percent!" Josie exclaimed. "That is outrageous."

"Why?" Paul said. "I would be taking on great risks. I

would be making all the arrangements to ensure you play only the proper persons. None like Darwood. I could have warned you he was not the man to lose gracefully. I can ensure your safety as well. It is only fair I am allowed compensation."

"But sixty percent?" Josie asked, frowning severely at him. "That is not fair."

"I think it is," Paul countered.

"No," Josie said, shaking her head. She smiled. "Now, forty percent would be fair."

Paul stared at her. "Forty percent?"

"Yes," Josie said. "Regardless, it would be my reputation which is ruined if discovered, whereas you can always claim I fooled you, which lowers your risk."

Paul's eyes lighted. "Ah yes. I could."

"And as for setting up the games," Josie said, imitating his shrug, "I am sure you do that for yourself often enough."

"I see," Paul said, pursing his lips.

"It would be an easy forty percent," Josie said, eagerness slipping into her tones.

"Very well," Paul sighed. "You draw a hard bargain, but I accept."

"Good!" Josie exclaimed, holding out her hand. "Then that is settled."

Paul took her hand and shook it. "I can foresee a long and profitable partnership."

"And totally secret?" Josie asked, a sudden fear tracing through her. The Stantons were a ramshackle lot, but Josie would not care for the scandal. Worse, she would not care to think of Alex's reaction.

"Totally," Paul said. His lips twitched. "I have a fine understanding of secrecy. It is what makes life intriguing."

"Intriguing?" Josie asked, frowning. "In truth, I do not consider it so."

"That is because your nature is far too open and honest." He smiled. "But do not worry, that will be my job."

A relief flooded Josie. "I have complete faith in you."

"Don't," Paul said, his eyes turning serious a moment.

Josie frowned. "But—"

"Miss Josie," Musgrave's voice called out. The door swung open, and he rushed into the room. "The marquis is here to see you."

"Alex?" Josie exclaimed. Her heart beat faster. "Oh, dear."

"He requests a private word with you," Musgrave said, giving her a steady look.

"I see." Josie flushed. "Wh-where is he now?"

"I've left him in the hall," Musgrave said.

"I'd best take my leave," Paul said, strolling toward the door.

"No," Josie exclaimed, and clamped a staying hand upon him. "You can't go out that way. He will see you."

"What does it matter if he sees me?"

"He will start asking questions," Josie said. "And I might make a mistake. And then . . ."

Paul shook his head. "What do you propose to do? Shall I hide under the settee, perhaps?"

"I don't know," Josie said, looking desperately about. Then she smiled. "What on earth was I thinking?"

"I don't know," Paul said in a mild tone.

Josie pointed in triumph at a door on the other side of the room. "There! It leads to the ante room, which leads to the picture gallery and . . ."

"Ah," Paul said. He grinned and moved directly toward the door. "Do not worry, I shall find my way out."

"Good," Josie said. Then she gasped. "How shall we make arrangements for . . ." She halted and then glanced at Musgrave. ". . . for you know what."

"I shall take care of it," Paul said, "and send a message when all is prepared."

"Yes, thank you," Josie said.

"Do not fret so, *cheri.*" Paul laughed as he opened the door. "Be calm."

"Calm," Josie murmured, feeling anything but that particular emotion as Paul disappeared. She looked at Musgrave. "You may show Alex in now."

"Yes, Miss Josie." Musgrave nodded.

Josie drew in a deep breath as Musgrave left. She strode to the settee and sat down. "Be calm," she repeated quietly, clutching the pouch of money in her hands tightly. "Be calm. It doesn't matter what Alex thinks. I am not exactly lying to him. Even so, it does not matt—what?" Josie exclaimed, her gaze falling upon a beaver hat beside her. She stared at it as if it were still a living animal, and one baring its teeth at that. "No! No!" She grabbed it up and dashed madly toward the connecting door. "Paul! Are you there?"

"Yes," a muffled voice came through the wood.

"Your hat," Josie hissed and cracked open the door. She saw a hand rather than Paul and shoved the betraying beaver into its outstretched fingers.

"Thank you," Paul's voice said as she closed the door.

"You're welcome," Josie replied, remembering her manners. She spun and dashed to take up her position upon the settee once more. She settled and drew in a steadying breath. Which blew out with a choke. A man's gold and ebony cane lay at her feet.

"Paul!" Josie exclaimed.

"What now?" Paul's disembodied voice drifted to her, a tremor of laughter in it.

"Your dratted cane," Josie hissed, bending to snatch it up. She bolted over to the connecting door, cracked it open, and rammed the cane through.

"Ouch!"

"Sorry!" Josie closed the door. "Gracious!" she breathed, gripping the money pouch to her. Her heart stopped short. She had been tossing out every suspicious item, but one. That one she had unconsciously clung on to for dear life.

Voices sounded directly outside the room. Alex's deep tones were clearly defined. Josie looked quickly about her person. Today of all days she must choose to wear a dress with nary a pocket sewn into it. Desperate, she lifted the pouch and shoved it into her bodice. Her mother often hid her handkerchiefs there. Josie groaned as she looked at her handiwork. The pouch was certainly no piece of lace, nor, alas, did she possess near the bounty her mother did. She looked positively deformed.

She delved into her bodice again and pulled it out. Though it pained her greatly, she turned around and opened the door again.

"Good morning, Josie!" Alex's voice said from behind. Josie tossed the pouch through the door.

"Caught it," Paul's voice came softly.

Now *that* he would catch! Josie grimaced as she jerked the door shut.

"Josie, what are you doing?" Alex's voice came again.

Josie pinned a smile upon her face and turned. "Nothing. J-just closing this door, in order that we may be private."

Alex's eyes widened, and he raised them to the ceiling. "Ah, Josie?"

"Yes?" Josie asked.

"Look at your front," Alex said.

"My front?" Josie looked down. She had unwittingly mauled her neckline until it was quite low and revealing. "Oh, dear. Not again.

"Excuse me, what are you doing?" a woman's voice asked quietly from behind.

Paul started. The cane, hat, and pouch which he had

been aptly juggling, flew into the air and rained down to the ground. *"Sacre bleu!"*

"I beg your pardon?" the voice asked.

He turned swiftly. His eyes widened. A woman with large brown eyes was watching him. He grimaced. "Pardon, mademoiselle. I was just taking these things for Josie."

"Josie?" The woman's eyes widened even further.

"Er, Mademoiselle Josephine?" Paul hazarded quickly.

"Why?" the woman asked, a frown wrinkling her delicate brow.

"I . . . I . . . am . . ." Paul bent quickly to pick up all his items, thinking hard. When he rose, he smiled in deep satisfaction. "The footman. Yes. The new footman!"

"Footman?" She studied him carefully. Pure confusion and, yes, nervousness flashed through her eyes. "You don't look like a f-footman."

The woman was delightful. Such a reserve, a sweet politeness. It was the shy wariness in her eyes, however, that Paul could not resist. He smiled devilishly at her. "And who are you, mademoiselle?"

"Mary."

"Mary who?" Paul persisted.

"Mary Stanton," the woman answered, without any hautiness or indignity.

"Ah, Mary, sweet Mary."

Mary blinked. "I beg pardon?"

"I mean, Mary is a sweet name." Paul chuckled. "You are Mademoiselle Josie's sister, yes?"

"Yes." Mary nodded.

"Ah, then I am your servant as well." Paul strolled toward her. "Can I be of service to you, sweet Mary? I would be delighted to do anything for you that you . . . desired."

She flushed. Aha! She was not so unaware as to mistake his meaning. She shook her head quickly. "Oh, no. No, thank you."

Paul laughed. "No thank you?"

"No, thank you."

"Surely you must have something I can do for you?" Paul gazed down at her in mischief. "Some little errands for me to run? I can carry your billet-doux to your lover, perhaps?"

Mary gasped. "Oh, no."

"I would be very discreet," Paul continued to tease. "I would keep all your secrets safe, mademoiselle."

"I have no secrets," Mary said, shaking her head quickly.

"No secrets?" Paul asked. "All women have secrets. It is their charm."

Mary flushed. "I-I do not."

Paul knew he should not toy with her. It was surely beneath him. Yet he could not help himself. She drew him, drew him in an unusual way. "Then you openly send your letters to your lover?"

"I have no lover."

"None?" Paul asked, smiling. He had guessed the answer, but it pleased him to hear it from her, pleased him greatly.

"None," Mary repeated.

"A beau, then," Paul said, though this time he doubted the answer. His jaw clenched. "Someone who courts you? Sends you flowers and trinkets? And verses to your beautiful eyes?"

Mary looked down. "No, no, I do not."

"I see." His jaw relaxed. Then clenched again. "But you have a man you dream of, *non*? Someone you wish was your beau, your lover?"

Mary's gaze flew to his in shock. She looked down. "Y-you ask very personal questions f-for a f-footman."

"Do you?" Paul repeated.

"You . . . you should not ask."

"You said you had no secrets."

"I don't," Mary said, her gaze rising to his in hurt. "I don't have a beau, or . . . or a lover . . . or even know of

a man I-I dream of." Her voice lowered. "I have no secrets."

Paul cursed. He, one of the wisest of men in the ways
of women, realized that in his strange need to know this
woman's heart, he had forced her to admit what could
only humiliate her.

He smiled. "Ah, but you do."

"D-do what?" Mary asked innocently.

"Have a secret . . . now," Paul said. He gently placed
his hands upon her shoulders and, just as gently, leaned
down and kissed her. She remained still, not frozen or
cold, just breathlessly still. Paul stole one more soft kiss
and then drew back. He flushed. He was acting like a veritable schoolboy. Yet this woman was not one to be treated
without respect.

Mary gazed at him, stunned and vulnerable. Paul
laughed a shaky laugh. "Ah, *cherie.* Do not look at me that
way, or you will have far more secrets."

Mary blinked. "Oh."

"Yes, oh," Paul said, fighting the urge to touch her
again. Smiling, he offered her the purse. "Please give this
to Mademoiselle Josephine. She will want it."

"What is it?" Mary asked.

"Ah, that is another secret," Paul said. "I trust you will
not look?"

"No, of course not."

He laughed. The sisters were not alike in any fashion.
"I-I must be about my duties." He bowed. *"Adieu."* He
walked past her, not knowing where he was going, but certain he would find his way out. It was his talent. Yet at the
next connecting door, he stopped. He turned. Mary was
gazing at him wide-eyed. "Perhaps, you could dream of
me, *cheri?"*

He turned swiftly, before she could speak, before he
could see what might be in her eyes, or might not be in
her eyes. His jaw clenched. If he was not careful, he would

not find his way out. He didn't mean from the house either.

"Forgive me," Josie said, quickly setting her neckline straight. "I . . . I . . . I just . . . just didn't notice. I mean, I . . . I mustn't have paid attention when I dressed this morning. I was tired . . ." She petered out, flushing.

Alex finally looked at her, his gaze solemn. "I understand."

Surely he could see the guilt in her eyes, read her every intention. Her nerves taut, she walked haltingly over to the sofa, now gratefully void of any telling articles. She sat down, unable to look at Alex.

"Josie," Alex said, walking over to sit down beside her.

"Yes?" It came out a squeak.

"Look at me," Alex said, rather gently.

Josie steeled herself and looked at him. "Yes?"

His smile was tilted. "Do you know what I admired the most about you the first time we met?"

"What?" Josie asked.

"Your honesty." His gaze darkened. "I always want you to be honest with me."

Josie's heart sank. "Very well."

"Now I want you to tell me what you are thinking about," Alex said, still very gently. Josie's eyes widened. She didn't know what to say. Alex sighed. "No, you don't have to tell me."

"I don't?" Josie asked, feeling a reprieve.

"No," Alex said. "For I know."

"You do?" Josie's mouth went dry. Alex was an intelligent man, but she hadn't known he was omnipotent.

"Yes," he said. "You are embarrassed because of last night."

"Last night?" Josie asked. The memory engulfed her.

His kisses. This time she did flame red. They had been such wonderful, earthshaking kisses. "Oh, yes."

"I'm sorry, Josie," Alex said. "I should not have kissed you in that manner."

"You shouldn't have?" Josie asked. She had thought he had kissed her perfectly. She couldn't imagine any other manner being better. Of course, if he had another way of kissing her. . . .

"No," Alex said. "I used you abominably. I promise it won't happen again."

"It won't?" Josie asked. Evidently, he wasn't going to satisfy her curiosity. For a moment she debated being honest like he'd suggested. However, Alex's face held such a grim, determined look, she decided against it. If he didn't wish to kiss her, then she must accept it.

"You will forgive me for kissing you?" Alex said.

"Yes," Josie said. At least she could be very honest about that. "Most certainly."

"Thank you." Alex smiled. It seemed rather strained. "And you do understand why you cannot masquerade as your brother anymore?"

"Indeed." Josie nodded and squirmed at the same time. A change of subject was definitely in order. The subject immediately came to Josie. It would serve two purposes very well. "Alex, may I ask you a question?"

"Yes." Alex smiled. "Certainly."

"Do you know any rich, unmarried men?"

"I do," Alex said slowly. His gaze narrowed. "Why? You aren't still trying to find someone to take over your father's mistress, are you?"

"No," Josie said, frowning. "I've decided to let that lay for the nonce."

Alex choked. When she looked at him, his gaze was solemn. "I am glad to hear that."

"Yes," Josie said. "However, another coil has cropped up."

Alex groaned. "I am almost afraid to ask."

"Oh, no. This is very proper and respectable, or at least that is what I am hoping it will be."

"Proper and respectable?" Alex asked, raising his brow in obvious disbelief. "Do tell."

"I need to find a husband for Mary," Josie said, worrying her lip. "Which of course makes it of the utmost importance that it is proper."

"You don't say?" Alex said, his voice rife with amusement.

"Yes." Josie nodded. "Because Mary is extremely proper."

"I see."

"And I must be quick about it, just in case Father does remember."

"Remembers what?" Alex asked, frowning.

Josie flushed. "Father has decided that since I will not marry you, it is Mary who should wed and save the family. Which, now that I think about it, has some merits. I mean, not that she should marry to save the family fortunes, but that she should marry. But most certainly not to the Earl of Canton."

"Canton!" Alex exclaimed. "Good God, no."

Josie smiled in deep satisfaction. "I am glad you agree with me. We simply must find Mary the right husband. I would like him to be respectable, and well situated, but not terribly rich like you."

"Why not?" Alex asked.

"Because then Father will think he can live off of him," Josie said reasonably.

"Josie, your father would try to live off of a coal heaver if he thought he could."

Josie's face fell. "Oh, no. Never say so."

Alex grimaced. "No, do not listen to me. If this is something you feel you should do, so be it. It is better than any of your other plans."

There was no need to let him she still cherished hopes for those other plans. "Do tell me about the eligible men you know."

Alex frowned. "Let me see. I think the Earl of Anton very eligible."

"How does he look?" Josie asked eagerly. "Is he handsome?"

Alex's brow rose. "How should I know? What women consider handsome or not is out of my realm."

"Oh," Josie said, disappointed. "Well, describe him to me. How tall is he? What color of eyes does he have? What is his smile like?"

Alex stared at her. "How would I know all that?"

"Well, it would be nice if you did."

Alex began to laugh. "No, no. I see the trap already. I am not about to give you descriptions. You are sure to disagree. What I suggest is that you see for yourself."

"How?"

"Let me take you for a ride in Hyde Park this afternoon."

"Would you?" Josie asked breathlessly.

"Most certainly," Alex said, rising. "It will be better you see for yourself than you questioning me upon every eligible bachelor in town."

"But wouldn't it be an . . . an imposition?" Josie asked, even as eagerness ran rampant through her.

"It will be far less an imposition than last night was," Alex said, his gaze pointed.

Josie flushed. "Oh, er, yes."

He chuckled, walking to the door. "I will take my leave of you now. Until this afternoon."

"Until this afternoon." Josie wrapped her arms about her, hugging herself in delight. She was going to go for a ride with Alex. She could look for Mary's future husband. Paul would arrange for her to play cards. Heavens, it had been a very productive morning. Things couldn't be going better.

"Josie?" Mary's voice called hesitantly from the doorway.

Josie quickly pulled her arms from about her, flushing. "Hello, Mary."

Mary entered the room, the oddest look upon her face. She held out a pouch. "This is for you."

Josie's eyes widened and she swallowed. "Where . . . how did you get that?"

"The footman gave it to me."

"Footman?" Josie asked. "What footman?"

"Our footman."

"But we don't have a footman." Josie frowned. "Oh, lud, did Mother hire a footman?"

Mary's eyes widened in alarm. "Josie, he said you hired him."

Josie froze. Everything tumbled into place. "Oh, so I did. How . . . how skitterwitted of me. Yes, yes I did hire him."

"You did?" Mary asked.

"Yes," Josie said, springing up. "I . . . I thought it might be a wise idea, b-but now I'm not so certain."

"He's very . . . er, different," Mary said hesitantly.

"Yes. That is what I thought. I don't think we should employ him after all."

Mary's face showed alarm. "Josie, you can't just hire and fire him. And certainly n-not because of wh-what I said."

"We'll just have to see." Josie walked over to take the pouch from Mary. "Thank you."

"What is in it?" Mary asked.

"You didn't look?"

"No, of course not."

"Good," sighed Josie. She blushed. "I mean, it is nothing much."

"I see."

Josie bit her lip. Mary was now blushing as much as she. Josie felt as small as an ant. Not knowing what else to say, Josie hastened from the room. Indeed, it had been a productive morning, but not a very honest one, she feared. The verse about tangled webs and deception ran through Josie's head. She forced it from her mind. The Stanton family web was already so entangled, surely a few more skeins judiciously misdirected couldn't hurt.

Four

Michael Stanton sat at Whites, sharing a bumper of brandy, well, actually three or four, with his favorite crony, Winston St. James. It was rather early in the afternoon, but a celebration was in order. His eyes flicked to the card table where a group of men played. He turned his glance away, steeling his resolve. He was feeling within the Grace of God for the moment, and did not wish to appear ungrateful. Miraculously, Paul Desuex had sent a message around that very morning saying he'd had an attack of remorse. He knew he had taken advantage of Michael when he was too intoxicated to play and therefore released him from his debt.

A voice whispered inside Michael that that was odd, very odd. Michael drowned that nagging little fellow with his very next swallow of brandy. Never look a gift horse in the mouth was his motto, and he intended to stay as far away from this particular horse's molars as possible.

"I'll lay you odds," Winston exclaimed, "that Thunder and Turf will win the race."

"What kind of odds?" Michael asked, his interest piqued. His friend Winston was one of the poorest judges of horseflesh known to English kind. Since Michael was within Grace, certainly now would be a good time to look at the track. It would help him stay clear of the card tables.

"Aha! Here you are," an unfamiliar voice growled.

Michael looked up. A medium-height, balding man stood before him. The stranger wore an unaccountably angry expression upon his face, but Michael was an easygoing chap. "Good afternoon. How do?"

"I demand satisfaction, Stanton," the stranger said, clenching his fists.

Michael blinked. "Satisfaction?"

"Yes," the man growled. "I'm calling you out."

"What for?" Michael asked, shaking his head. He'd only had two brandies, so he knew it couldn't be him who was castaway. A bit on the go, yes, but not castaway. "I don't even know you."

"That's Lord Darwood," whispered Winston beneath his hand. He jerked his head toward Darwood as if he were well across the room rather than within inches of them.

"Ah," Michael said, nodding. He'd heard of the fellow. "The nabob."

"Don't know me?" Darwood exclaimed. "You cheated me at cards last night! And called me a baby, and a poor sport, and a bully!"

"I say! All that?" Winston exclaimed. He looked at Michael and whistled. "That's a long list, old man. I didn't know you had such a way with words."

"I don't," Michael said, shaking his head. "I'm clear it wasn't me. Besides, I stayed at home last night. I remember it well. A quiet evening. I played chess with my governess."

"What kind of story is this?" Darwood cried out. "Don't insult me."

"Ain't insulting you," Michael said, indignant.

"It does sound suspicious, Michael," Winston said, his look dubious. "Your governess? It don't hold together. Best say you was with your mistress."

"It's Tellington, you dolt."

"Oh," Winston nodded. "That explains it. I forgot she was your governess once. She trounce you?"

"Yes, confound it," Michael said. "Almost had her on the third game, but—"

"Damn it, Stanton!" Darwood shouted. "You can't fool me. You cheated me at Paul Desuex's."

"Now I know you're castaway," Michael said. "I swore I wouldn't go there again, and I haven't. The man cheated me out of a bundle."

Darwood seemed to shake in an apoplexy. "Like you did me! I demand satisfaction."

"Well, you ain't going to get it," Michael said. "I don't go out with drunken strangers—"

"You did with Sanderson," Winston said.

"Yes, but he wasn't a stranger," Michael objected. "He was a friend. There's a difference."

"I demand satisfaction!" Darwood shouted. "On the field. You aren't going to get a chance to knock me out again."

"Knock you out?" Michael asked, stunned.

Darwood flushed. "You caught me off guard. And just because you have a strong left—"

"You say I knocked you out?" Michael repeated. "With my left?"

"Now we know he's got the wrong man," Winston said, nodding. "You don't knock anyone out. Never with your left. You've got a decent right, but no left."

"See," Michael said. "Winston knows it. Everyone knows it. I am a peaceable man. I don't go knocking people out. And I don't go out dueling either."

"But for—" Winston said.

"But for Sanderson," Michael said. "And I was tap-hacket. Ain't tap-hacket now. He is, but I ain't."

"Damn you to hell," Darwood said, clenching his hands. "I want satisfaction! Name the time and place—"

"Time!" Michael exclaimed. He jumped up. "Blast. I almost forgot. Here we sit talking, and the auction's about to start."

"Gads!" Winston said, horror in his voice. He bolted from his chair. "You're right."

"Sorry, old chap," Michael said to Darwood, who stood gaping at him. "I don't have time to chat. I advise you to go home and sleep it off. You have the wrong man. I don't know who did that to you; sounds like a rotter, but it wasn't me."

Without further ado, Michael and Winston hastened toward the exit doors, shouting to the footman for their coats. Darwood chased after them, shouting for Michael's blood. His wrath was only increased when he rammed into a waiter, who swiftly lost hold of his tray of brandies, which directly toppled into old Lord Willowby's lap. Darwood's demands for satisfaction were quickly intermingled with Lord Willowby's threats to thrash Darwood a good one, if he could but rise on his gouty foot.

"Persistent fellow," Winston observed as he received his three-caped coat from John, the awaiting and prepared footman. "Thank you, Thomas. You're a good man."

"You're welcome, my lord," John said with a nod, promptly holding out Michael's five-caped coat.

"Queer, is what I say," Michael said, snatching it up and struggling into it. "But he's a nabob. They're always queer. Too much money. Rattles up the bone box."

"Stanton!" Darwood finally broke free of his entanglements and charged directly toward Michael, fists clenched, face mottled to purple.

At that moment Michael shot his arm through his left sleeve. It contacted directly with Darwood's jaw. Darwood gurgled, stiffened, and toppled back.

"Now, if I had that kind of money," Michael said, his words muffled as one of his capes flapped up over his face. "I'd make sure—"

"My lord," John said.

"What?" Michael asked, shaking off the material.

John coughed and pointed.

Michael looked down. His eyes widened as he spied the prostrate Darwood. "Well, I'll be hanged. Would you look at that."

Winston peered down as well. "Passed out, b'gads."

"Bound to happen," Michael said, his tone sympathetic. "Dipped too deeply."

"Can't hold his liquor," Winston added, shaking his head.

"Well, best thing for him," Michael said. "It'll keep him from approaching other chaps with his ravings. He might not find them as amiable as me." Michael looked at the footman. "Better bundle him up and send him home, Thomas. Name is Darwood."

"A nabob," Winston provided helpfully.

"Yes, my lord," John said. The slightest sigh escaped his lips.

"I have to leave," Michael said, now successfully coated and forging ahead. "I'll miss the auction otherwise. I have to see Sherwood's breakdown. I've heard the bay is a sweet goer."

"S'true," Winston said, following behind.

John, with the help of two other footmen, sent Darwood, the inert nabob, home in a hack.

"Gracious," Josie exclaimed, as she sat next to Alex in his carriage, her face a mobile display of interest and amazement. "You know so many people."

"Yes." Alex smiled. The *ton* was flocking to their side to discover just who Josie was. He could see first their curiosity, then their knowing looks, and then whatever opinion they divined of Josie. The play was all the more amusing, for Josie greeted them all with an open, friendly manner, never once giving them a chance to do anything but accept her, whether they intended to or not.

"And the lady who just left us," Josie said, her gaze following Letitia Farthingate's retreating carriage. "Who was she? I fear I missed her name."

"She's just a friend," Alex said, his amusement dispersing. Josie had missed the "lady's" name because he hadn't given it. He and Letitia, the lovely widow, had shared a brief liaison a year ago. He had found her enticing for all of three weeks. It was not a liaison in which he took pride. To make matters worse, Letitia made it obvious she wished to rekindle that quenched-out flame.

"I see," Josie said, nodding. "I thought she might be your mistress."

"What?" Alex exclaimed. "No, no she isn't."

"Oh." Josie gazed at him, her mind definitely debating something.

"What is it?" Alex asked, before he could stop himself.

Josie shook her head. "I don't know. It's just something in her behavior seemed . . . well, I don't know how to explain it."

Alex sighed. He did. Letitia had thrown out lures the size of anchors. "Letitia is a very flirtatious woman, that is all."

"Flirtatious?" Josie asked, cocking her head to one side.

"Yes, flirtatious." Josie wasn't looking at him in accusation, just open interest. He sighed. Just how did one explain to a girl as direct as Josie the art of flirtation? Or how did he overlook the fact that though Josie didn't understand flirtation, she instinctively knew there had been something between Alex and Letitia.

"It is nothing you need to concern yourself with, I assure you," he added.

Josie studied him a moment and then nodded. "Very well."

Alex sighed as Josie dutifully turned her gaze back to the crowd. Perhaps it hadn't been such a wise notion to bring Josie to the park after all. There were more pitfalls in introducing her to society, and his past, than he had expected. He'd always associated with knowledgeable women, who never needed explanations. He was swiftly discovering that having to explain his, life was not a comfortable matter.

He heard Josie gasp. She was looking across the park. She pointed. "Who is that man?"

Alex turned his gaze to where she directed him. He stiffened. He was well acquainted with the man she pointed to. Indeed, the two of them had spent many a fine and rowdy evening together. "That is Torvel Seeton."

"He is very handsome," Josie said, gazing at Seeton in what appeared inane awe.

"Most women think so," Alex said, his tone clipped.

"I like his eyes," Josie said, her gaze still infuriatingly riveted upon Alex's friend. "And his smile."

"Do you?" Alex asked, not smiling.

"Yes." Josie nodded. "Tell me more about him."

Jealousy shot through Alex. "There isn't anything you need to know."

Josie frowned. At last, her gaze returned to him. "But how will I know if he would be a good husband for Mary if you won't tell me about him?"

"I see," Alex said. The tension drained from him. "I'm sorry. But Torvel would never make a good husband for Mary. Or for anyone else for that matter."

"That is a shame." Josie sighed. "He is very handsome."

"Yes," Alex said. "But he would never do for Mary."

"How about that man?" Josie's face brightened. She nodded her head to the left.

Alex looked and groaned. The Marquis of Alvany. He was a premier rake. "No, not him. Most definitely not him."

"Very well." Josie's gaze moved on, scanning the crowd. When it halted again, Alex didn't even need to ask which man she considered. It was another friend of his. "No, Josie, no!"

"Not him either?" Josie asked.

"Not him either." Faith, Josie possessed an in-built divining rod for every rake and rogue present. He had been insane to bring her here. With her attraction to such men, she was a positive danger to herself. She would be a mere lamb for the fleecing. It didn't sit well that some of those men were his best friends. Friends of his they might be, but friends of Josie's he would never permit.

"Then just who is a good and decent man?" Josie asked. Her expression held as much exasperation as Alex felt.

Alex laughed ruefully. "That is a deep question. I really can't say. But I can show you which men are well thought of and considered respectable." He scanned the crowd. Nodding in satisfaction, he pointed. "There, the Viscount Applebee. He is the type of man you want."

Josie peered eagerly to where he directed her. Her face fell. "He has no chin."

Alex chuckled, both at the look on her face and her comment. "Josie, he is a good man."

Josie peeked at him and giggled. "He may be, but I refuse to have Mary wed a man with no chin."

"That would be frightful," Alex said with mock seriousness. He quickly reviewed the crowd once more. Eyes twinkling, he waved his hand. "How about the Earl of Stanhope? He is well-situated and possesses a spotless reputation."

Josie leaned forward and studied him. "He is mounted on the most spavined horse I have ever seen. Michael and Father would disown him immediately."

"No doubt," Alex said, his tips twitching.

Josie laughed. Her gray eyes were bright, sparkling water as she peered around. She almost crowed as she pointed to a man. "Him. I'll lay odds he is respectable."

Alex looked. "Ah, the Baron Lathanham. Utterly respectable. Can talk the ear off of an elephant."

"I'm getting the knack," Josie said. "It was his dress

which gave me a clue. Mother would think him an undertaker."

"I'm sure he'd die himself if he knew the expense of your mother's wardrobe."

"No doubt." Josie's lips curved into a wry smile. "This is going to be more difficult than I thought. Finding a respectable man who will find suit with the Stanton family. I fear we don't lean toward them."

"No, you don't." Suddenly Alex's good humor returned to him. Of course, she didn't lean toward respectable men. She leaned toward rakes and rogues. Men like him. "It merely will take more time. I'm sure we can spy one out sooner or later. We'll just have to go farther afield. We'll most likely bag our quarry at one of the dances or other."

He heard Josie's intake of breath. "But would you mind taking me . . . so that I could look?"

Alex gazed down at Josie. He told himself it was the least he could do for her. She was trying so very hard to help her family. Granted, her methods were sometimes shocking, but totally innocent. "I wouldn't mind at all."

Josie's eyes grew starry, and her smile brilliant. Alex ignored the warmth that flooded through him. He'd just have to watch and protect her. A penchant for rakes she may have, but he intended to be the only rake of his acquaintance she would know.

"You look lovely," Alex said to Josie as he assisted her out of the carriage.

"Thank you," Josie said, flushing with pleasure. The silver dress she wore had cost her counterpart, Joseph Landril, two nights of play at Paul's, but to hear Alex's praise made it all worthwhile. She looked forward to the evening with anticipation. Her only worry was that she knew she must leave at twelve. She'd promised Paul she'd play tonight. She hadn't planned to do so, but Paul had sent

round a message that he'd set up a game for the evening
that should prove to be most lucrative for her. Since Josie
had suffered two rare evenings in a row where she had
lost, she was determined to recoup.

"It was rather expensive, wasn't it?" Alex asked in a lowered voice.

"Yes," Josie said, flushing. "But it is for a good cause."

Alex laughed. "Of course. Though I think you should
permit me to assist you in that matter."

"No!" Josie said. She looked down. "You are already
doing too much for me."

"What have I done?" Alex asked, his brow rising.

"Y-you keep squiring me to all these balls."

"Josie, that is a pleasure," Alex said softly. "Not a duty."

Josie gazed at him, her heart pounding. Every moment
she spent with Alex was a pleasure to her, but she couldn't
believe it was so for Alex. "Oh."

"Alex," a voice called out.

Josie started and looked toward the voice. Marcus Tre-
main, a friend of Alex's, was strolling toward them. She
smiled. Marcus always made her laugh. "Hello, my lord."

"Josie," Marcus said, his eyes gleaming. "You will be the
most beautiful woman in the room tonight."

"You are just being kind," Josie said, coloring.

"Marcus is never just being kind," Alex said, taking
Josie's arm and leading her up the steps.

"I was just about to say that." Marcus laughed, falling
into step with them. "Dare I ask if I may have a dance with
you this evening, Josie?"

"Dare?" Josie asked, wrinkling her brow. Then she
laughed. "Of course you may dare."

Marcus cast an odd look at Alex. "Oh, I don't know."

"Just one dance, old man," Alex said, returning a look
just as odd. "Josie's card is already full."

"No, it isn't," Josie said, blinking. "I've only just arrived."

Marcus cracked a laugh. "Your lack of guile, my dear,

is delightful." He raised his brow to Alex. "Is she always this honest?"

"Always," Alex said, his tone rueful.

"No," Josie said, guilt covering her. "I am not always very honest, I fear. I-I try to be, but there are always circumstances that seem to arise that push one to be dishonest."

Marcus chuckled. "I see why you guard her, my friend."

"Yes," Alex said. It was all he said.

Josie frowned. "Alex doesn't guard me."

"Ah," Marcus said. "This is definitely my cue to leave. Sorry, old fellow." He bowed and left, still chuckling.

"Do you?" Josie persisted as they entered the ballroom.

"From the likes of him, I do," Alex replied.

"But he is your friend," Josie exclaimed.

"Exactly," Alex said, his tone dry.

Josie shook her head. "I don't understand."

"I know you don't."

"But I like Marcus," Josie tried again.

"Josie," Alex sighed, a tone of exasperation in his voice. "You like every wolf there is to like. None of them are proper candidates for Mary, I assure you."

"Perhaps I will do better tonight." Josie cast a look around.

Alex laughed. "Perhaps. They are starting the first set. Let us dance. You can keep an eye out for the man of Mary's dreams."

"I will," Josie said. She permitted Alex to lead her to the dance floor. That she was a frightfully deceitful woman struck Josie. In truth, whenever she danced with Alex, she forgot to look for Mary's future spouse. Indeed, she forgot to look at anyone but Alex.

And it happened again. They danced and talked, and danced again. It wasn't until they left the floor that Josie halted with a gasp, staring at a man who sat next to a matron. He was tall, well built, with golden hair. Though he wore a conservative jacket, it might as well have been polished armor, for he appeared a gallant knight to Josie. He also had a chin, a nice, square chin. Josie clutched tightly to Alex's arm. She could swear she saw a light shining down upon the man, a light showing that he was the one.

"What is it?" Alex asked, frowning.

Josie, unable to speak, held out a finger and pointed.

Alex looked to where she directed him. "Good Lord!"

"Wh-who is he?" Josie asked breathlessly.

"The Baron Lexing," Alex said.

"Please," Josie asked. "Is h-he . . . ?"

"One of the most upright and honorable men known in England," Alex said, his tone rueful.

A satisfied thrill shot through her. "He is handsome, isn't he?"

"If you care for fair looks," Alex said, his tone neutral.

"Mary would," Josie said. "I am sure she would. What is his income?"

"Healthy, but not obscene."

"Oh, Alex," Josie sighed. "We have found Mary's husband. They will be perfect together."

"Josie," Alex replied gently, "don't be so positive."

"But I am," Josie said. This was no time to talk about the light shining down. "I just know he is right for Mary."

"What if Mary isn't right for him?" Alex asked.

Josie tore her gaze away from the vision and stared at Alex. "But she is. Everyone loves Mary. Could you introduce me to him?"

"I don't think I should." Alex shook his head.

"Why not?" Josie asked, frowning.

"The lady beside him is his mother," Alex said, an odd tone to his voice. "She is a friend of my mother's."

"That makes it all the better," Josie said eagerly. She looked at the woman who would be Mary's mother-in-law. She appeared a most proper lady. "Please, Alex."

Alex sighed. "Very well. But you must remember, they are the highest sticklers in the *ton.*"

"Yes," Josie said, nodding vehemently. "That is good."

"I wouldn't be too sure," Alex said softly. "Come."

The closer they drew to the Baron Lexing, the more eager Josie became. She all but clung to Alex's arm in anticipation. Alex cast her a warning look before he bowed and said, "Good evening, Lady Lexing." He nodded to the knight. "Gerard, how do you do?"

Lady Lexing smiled. "Ah, Alex, I am so pleased to see you again. How is your dear mother?"

"She fares well," Alex said.

"I mean to see her the minute I am settled in," Lady Lexing said. "She and I have been corresponding, but it will be so nice to have a pleasant coze with her in person again."

"You've just arrived in town, I assume?" Alex asked.

"We have come up for the season," Gerard said. His voice was deep, well modulated.

"Good," Josie breathed, before she could stop herself.

All eyes turned to her. Josie flushed and offered a weak smile. Alex cleared his throat. "May I be permitted to introduce you to Josie, I mean, Josephine Stanton?"

Lady Lexing's eyes widened. "Stanton? Is she not the one you—"

This time the baron cleared his throat and looked at Josie with solemn brown eyes. Mary's and his children would definitely have brown eyes. "I believe I know your brother then, Miss Stanton."

"Do you?" Josie asked. She drew in her breath. "Then w-would you care to come to dinner this Saturday? It . . . it will be a small affair." The baron's face stiffened. Lady Lexing made a sound like a huff. "Of very good people," Josie added. She looked at Alex with a pleading look. "Alex will be there."

"Er, I am sorry . . . ," Gerard said.

"We are otherwise engaged," Lady Lexing's tone was cool.

"Having just arrived in town . . ." Gerard added.

"Of course." Josie flushed. "Perhaps later."

"I do believe it is about time for the dinner buffet," Lady Lexing said, rising. "Come, Gerard. You know I like to be settled before everyone else."

"Yes, Mother." Gerard stood and bowed. "It was a pleasure to meet you, Miss Stanton."

The baron and his mother walked away. Josie stood, numb and completely embarrassed. "I-I made a mistake, didn't I?"

"Don't worry about it," Alex said, his tone gruff. "Lady Lexing is a harridan. And Gerard is no better. You don't need a pompous ass like that."

"No," Josie said. "I'm sure it's just because of our family difficulties. But Mary is sweet, and very respectable. It . . . it isn't fair that Mary will be stopped from wedding a good man because of us."

"Josie," Alex said in exasperation. "If he is truly a good man, he would overlook your family 'difficulties.' "

Overlooking just how badly dipped the Stanton family was, was not an easy thing, Josie thought sadly, even for a good man. Then she gasped. "Oh, dear. Lady Lexing said it was time for the buffet. It cannot be that late, surely?"

"It is close to twelve," Alex said.

Josie flushed. How had she mistaken the time so? No, she knew the answer. When she was with Alex there was no time. She must hurry if she meant to make the card game. Fresh determination welled within her. She wasn't about to miss this game. Money was what she needed. "I have to go now."

"Now?" Alex frowned.

"Yes," Josie said. "I . . . I have a headache."

"Josie," Alex said. "You shouldn't let this upset you . . ."

"I-I won't." Josie hastened toward the exit doors. "But I must go."

"Very well." Alex followed her. "I shall escort you."

"No," Josie said quickly. She generally changed into her other clothes at her own house, but tonight she would go directly to Paul's. She had a set there as well. "No, I don't wish to ruin your night. I-I will take a hack home."

"Josie," Alex objected.

"Please, Alex," Josie said, halting. "I-I must leave. Y-you do not . . . there is no need to follow."

"Very well," Alex said, nodding.

Josie smiled gratefully and, turning, hastened away. Her only thought was of winning tonight like she had never won before. Someday the Stantons wouldn't have any difficulties. They would be so well situated that the Baron would be pleased to have Mary as a wife. After all, except for money, or the lack thereof, Mary was perfectly respectable and good.

"No need to follow," Alex gritted, as he sat in his coach and stared at the back of Paul Desuex's establishment. He laughed bitterly. He'd actually followed Josie, worried that she had been devastated by Lady Lexing and Gerard. Instead the little minx had torn out to go to Paul's. Anger surged through him. He knew this wasn't a romantic rendezvous, only a rendezvous with the card table.

He clenched his teeth. She had promised him she wouldn't masquerade or game, and here she was, going behind his back and doing it. Well, two could play at that game. The little idiot didn't even know what she was about. She needed to be stopped for her own good. He shook his head. There wouldn't be any more talking to her, however, or trying to reason. He knew who he'd talk to on the morrow, and he wouldn't reason with him either.

Mary heard the noise. She had been sleeping much too lightly of late. It must be Josie coming home. Suddenly,

Mary wanted to talk to Josie. It seemed as if she never saw her sister anymore. She rose swiftly and pulled on her wrapper. She quietly padded to the door and opened it. She was just about to call out, when her breath wheezed out in a gasp. It wasn't Josie moving down the hall, but a man. She stood frozen, her mind numb. The man moved with confidence, not stealth. His demeanor was anything but that of a thief.

Mary squelched her first instinct to scream. The second instinct of discretion overrode it. In the Stanton family one learned not to overreact without complete information. She slipped into the hall and followed the man. Perhaps it was a friend of Michael's. Yet what was a friend of Michael's doing here so late, strolling down the halls?

She skittered to a halt. The man had stopped at Josie's door and, without a knock or by your leave, entered. Mary's heart pounded. She couldn't believe it. A man had just entered her sister's bedroom. She shook her head. Her sister would never entertain a gentleman this late. Suddenly the remembrance of the Frenchman, the one who had claimed to be Josie's footman and then disappeared, entered her mind.

Her heart fell. Poor Josie. There was a man who could lead anyone astray. Ire for the devil who could sway her poor sister rose within her. It mattered not that the man had not looked anything like the Frenchman as she remembered him, Mary knew it must be him. Who else could it be?

She drew in her breath and stalked down the hall. She shoved open the door with no further by your leave than the man had done before.

"How dare you enter my sister's bedroom!" Mary's eyes widened. The man had his back to her. His jacket was already off and he was stripping off his shirt. "No!" Mary gasped, covering her eyes. Her worst fears had been realized.

"Mary!" Josie's voice exclaimed, somewhere close to the man's vicinity.

"Josie," Mary said, still hiding her eyes. She feared to discover the state of her sister's dress, or undress. "I-I, please, don't do this. I-I can understand, at least, I-I am trying to understand . . ."

"Understand what?" Josie said, her voice sounding odd.

Mary stiffened. "If I could talk to you in private, please."

"We are in private," Josie said.

"Private!" Mary's hand flew down in ire. "How can you say . . ." She blinked. The man had turned around. It was Josie. Unmistakably Josie, dressed in men's clothing. "Josie! What . . . what?"

"I'm sorry, Mary," Josie said, rushing up to her. "I didn't mean to give you a fright. Now you know my secret."

"Your secret?" Mary asked.

"I've been dressing as a man."

"I see that." Mary flushed. "But why?"

"So that I can play cards at Paul's," Josie said. "You wouldn't imagine how much money I have won."

Mary swayed. She tottered over to the chair and fell into it, staring at her sister, whose camisole was glimpsing out of a fine lawn shirt and hanging cravat. Mary sat still, her mind working through it slowly. Josie stood patiently, almost sympathetically, allowing her time.

"Who is Paul?" Mary finally asked.

Josie's eyes widened. She laughed. "That is the question you ask?"

Mary blinked. It wasn't hard to imagine Josie masquerading as a man. At least, now it wasn't. But the piece to the puzzle was the man who would aid and abet her. "Yes."

"Very well," Josie said. "Paul Desuex is the owner of a gaming hell."

"I thought as much," Mary almost groaned. The last piece chinked into place. "H-he wasn't the footman, was he?"

"Yes," Josie said. "He came to bring me my earnings from the night before."

Mary's chest tightened. "You have been playing cards w-with that man?"

"No, not since the first night," Josie said. "Now we play together and split the profits."

"Josie," Mary groaned. "You cannot mean it. It is far too dangerous."

"Oh, no," Josie said, smiling. "Paul makes sure they are select groups, and we play privately. I will not be recognized."

Mary shook her head. "Even so. That man . . . he is dangerous."

"Paul?" Josie laughed. "Oh, no. Paul is not dangerous at all. He takes very good care of me."

"Josie," Mary said urgently. "Y-you are too innocent. You must stop this. Please, dearest, stop this before that man . . . before it is too late."

"Mary, please do not worry," Josie said, coming to sit on the arm of the chair and hug her sister close. "That is why I did not tell you. But honestly, I am quite safe. Paul and I have worked it out perfectly. Please, don't worry."

Mary bit her tongue. Josie could be hanging over a cliff and holding on by one hand and she would blithely tell Mary not to worry for she had it all worked out. She sighed. She also knew from long experience if Josie liked hanging over the cliff, there would be no reasoning with her. Merely for politeness sake, Mary said, "There is no way I will be able to talk you out of this?"

"No," Josie said, her tone firm. "I am earning far too much. It is amazing. If Father and Michael could play that way, our family would be in fine fettle."

Mary bit back a laugh, imagining that was impossible. Only dear Josie could be such an inveterate dreamer. Mary nodded and pinned a serene smile upon her face. "Very well."

Josie's eyes widened. "Y-you are not going to try and stop me?"

Mary chose her words carefully. "It is clear you are set on this course. Stopping you would be well nigh impossible." She rose and hugged Josie. "Only be careful."

"Oh, I am," Josie said, hugging her back. "Paul really does take care of me."

"I hope he does," Mary said. "I am sure you are tired. I will leave you."

Josie smiled. Indeed, a very sleepy smile. "Thank you, Mary."

"For what?" Mary asked.

"For not ringing a peal over my head. I-I *am* rather tired tonight."

"Then go to sleep." She hugged her sister once more and slipped out of the room.

Mary walked down the hall, running through her choices. She had told Josie that to try and stop her would be well nigh impossible, but she had not said she would not do it. She considered telling her father. She shook her head. It wouldn't serve. Not only was it totally ingrained in every Stanton lady not to inform upon the other, but she was not certain Horace Stanton wouldn't approve of Josie's endeavors.

Mary drew in a deep breath. She knew very well who could stop Josie from this ruinous course. Indeed, it was the man who had clearly set her upon the primrose path. Her heart pounded. Josie believed this Paul was not a dangerous man. Mary knew the case to be very different. She would do anything, anything at all, to save her sister from the clutches of such a man.

Five

"So, Alex," Paul said, leaning back in his chair and smiling at Rothmier across the card table in his private room. The game at hand required no cards. "I wondered how long it would take you before you tumbled to it. Our Josie is—"

"Our?" Rothmier raised a brow.

"I mean that in only the most brotherly fashion," Paul said with a chuckle. He raised his own brow. "As I am sure you do."

"Yes," Alex said after a moment. "And I do not want my *sister* playing in your den anymore."

"I am sorry, I see nothing wrong with *my sister* playing in my club. Well, actually she is my cousin here, or he is, I mean." He grinned. "It grows confusing, *non?*"

"Not very," Alex said. "Either way, Josie should not be playing here."

"Why? We take every precaution possible, and she is an excellent player." His lips tightened. "Josie must make money. This I can understand."

"Not this way," Alex agreed.

"Why not this way?" Paul retorted. "Josie has a rare talent; why should she not use it?"

"She is a lady."

"Yes, a lady who can make money by playing cards." Paul laughed bitterly. "Men have gained entire fortunes by play, but a lady must not do so. Rather she should marry a man who can give her that fortune." His eyes narrowed and he smiled grimly. "Ah, forgive me, I forgot. Josie lost that option, did she not? You would not marry her, but now you wish to stop her from this?"

"It was she who rejected me," Alex said in clipped tones.

"Ah, yes." Paul nodded. "But you were quick to accept her rejection. You, who by report, can talk any woman into doing whatever you desire?"

"Not Josie," Alex said.

Paul nodded. "So now you wish to, as the saying goes, put a spoke in her wheel?"

"Do not try to make me out the villain here," Alex said. "You supporting her in this folly is the villainy. She is a total innocent and doesn't realize the scandal if she is ever discovered masquerading as a man in a gaming hell."

"Does she not?" Paul asked. "You and I both live with scandal. Me, because I am a gamester and have chosen to survive by my wits rather than . . . bend to the will of society. You, because you have the power and the means to do exactly what you wish, and do not give a damn about convention. We are permitted this, but not Josie, because she is a lady."

"Do not try to fool me," Alex said. "None of that matters to you. The truth is you are gaining a share of Josie's profits and that is why you support her."

Paul shrugged. "I am a businessman, after all."

Alex growled and was across the table before Paul knew it. He received a crashing fist to his jaw, the force of which sent him and his chair toppling back. The pain searing through his face immobilized him. Alex dragged him up, glaring.

"As a businessman I am sure you can appreciate this offer. You are going to tell Josie you no longer want her to come here. You no longer wish to take the risk. The risk being me killing you the next time."

Paul chuckled, even through the pain. "A very generous offer."

"Yes," Alex said, releasing him. "I thought so."

Paul barely maintained his feet. "Very well. But Josie isn't going to like this."

"I don't care if she likes it or not," Alex said, the tendon along his neck jerking. "Only tell her she cannot play here anymore."

Paul stared and then laughed. "I will, *mon ami*. I assure you, I will."

"You will tell her tonight," Rothmier ordered.

Ire rose in Paul, but he stifled it. "But of course. This is your business now."

"I'm glad you understand." Without another comment Alex strode from the room.

Paul moved slowly to the chair and sat down. He thought a moment. A slow smile crossed his lips. Oh, yes, he most certainly would tell Josie tonight. Alex had said it mattered not to him whether Josie liked it or not. Paul would take him at his word.

A knock sounded at the door, and Mike entered. "Mr. Paul?"

Paul looked up. Mike's ugly face held a concerned look upon it. "What is it?"

"There is a lady who wishes to speak with you."

"A lady?" Paul asked, his brow rising.

"Yes, sir," Mike said. "She's got all these drapes on, but I's can tell. She's a lady. She shouldn't be here, I don't thinks."

"Indeed?" Paul asked, intrigued. "Do bring her here."

"Yes, Mr. Paul." Mike hesitated. "But wouldn't you . . . er . . ."

"Wouldn't I what?" Paul asked.

"Like to clean up maybe," Mike said. "You've got a mighty shiner there."

"I know," Paul said. "But *if* she is a real lady, we cannot keep her waiting."

Mike nodded, and left, clearly concerned. Paul negligently straightened himself, all the while attempting to guess the woman's identity. He held reservations to Mike's claim she was a lady. He rarely received visits from that kind these days.

When the lady entered the room, Paul still didn't know her identity. She was indeed covered in black veils. However, his respect for Mike rose significantly. His henchman had called the cards correctly. Despite the profuse amount of draperies, it was obvious a *real* lady lay buried beneath them. Yet, Paul had been raised to recognize a lady. How Mike, a retired prizefighter who had been punched in the head so many times as to forget his own name, had understood the same astounded Paul. The bruiser upon occasion showed rare insights and a rarer personality.

"Now you just calls me when you're done with Mr. Paul," Mike said in a gentle, gruff voice. "You don't need to go running around without me escort."

"Thank you, Mr. Mike," a voice said softly.

A shiver ran through Paul. He knew that voice. He had heard it only once, but he remembered it. It was a voice he had determined he would not hear again. He was a bounder, but in that one respect he was honorable. He had not once asked Josie about her sister. Now here she stood, within his establishment.

He walked slowly over and lifted the veil. It felt as if his very heart sighed. "Mademoiselle Mary."

"Y-yes," Mary said. Her brown eyes widened, and then darkened with concern. "You are hurt."

Paul winced. He should have taken more time to straighten himself and perhaps employ the use of a hefty beefsteak to cut the swelling. The worry in Mary's eyes hurt him more than the bruise. "It is nothing. Only a minor altercation with a . . . customer."

"I see," Mary said, looking down.

"Why?" Paul asked softly. "Why have you come here?"

Mary colored the sweetest rose. "I-I have come here . . ."

"Because I am the man of your dreams?" Paul had meant to tease, but found his voice sincere.

"No," Mary said quickly. She stepped back and turned from him. "I-I have found out the truth about you."

Paul instinctively tensed. Then he relaxed. She couldn't know the truth about him. No one did anymore. "What do you mean?"

"That—that Josie comes here," Mary said, her voice low. "And . . . and you help her play cards."

"Ah," Paul said, nodding. Josie's indiscretions last night were multiple. "Yes, we have an arrangement."

Mary spun. Her face was pale. She clasped her hands before her. "Please, I-I ask you to release my sister and leave her alone."

Paul stiffened. She had the look of a martyr pleading with the devil. "Why should I?"

"She is an innocent."

Paul laughed. "And you are not?"

"Josie is different," Mary said, shaking her head. "Sh-she trusts too much. She believes all is good. Sh-she doesn't always understand things."

"But you do," Paul said, anger searing him. It was the second time within minutes he had been painted as the villain in the piece. That Alex had thought it of him did not matter. That this woman thought it, did. His eyes narrowed. If she wanted a villain, then he would play the part for her. "Since you understand so much more than Josie, then tell me, why should I release her? Our 'arrangement' is very profitable to me."

"Because . . ." Mary began. "Because . . . because it would be the right thing to do."

Paul barked a laugh. "Now who is the innocent? It is

clear you recognize I am wicked. Then why should I release Josie simply because it is the right thing to do? You must give me a better reason."

"I-I have none," Mary said weakly.

"Do you not?" Paul asked. He smiled. "Then let me think of one for you. I will release your sister . . ."

Mary gasped. "You will?"

"I will. Only if . . ." He halted. His pause was as good as any dastard upon the boards at Drury Lane.

"What?" Mary asked.

Her face was so alarmed, Paul almost resisted, but a shard of anger still pierced him. "If you will promise to have . . . a late dinner with me tomorrow night."

"I-I couldn't!" Mary exclaimed.

Paul shrugged. "You understand these things. If you want to save your poor, innocent sister from my clutches, you will come. And you will make a promise."

"A promise?" Mary asked. Her face whitened to the color of new-fallen snow.

"Yes. A promise. That you will continue to see me." Paul grinned in true amusement. A gambler always raised the stakes. The lady wanted to play the martyr; he would make certain she was not bluffing and would stay in the game.

Mary's eyes widened. Her lashes fluttered down. "Very well. I-I promise."

Paul fought the surge of respect that coursed through him. The woman hadn't folded. He forced a gruff tone. "You will come here tomorrow evening at midnight."

"Yes," Mary said. Tears shimmered in her eyes. "But— but you must promise to turn Josie away. You must tell her she cannot come here again."

Paul stifled a laugh. Perhaps he was a villain. "I will promise, as long as you keep *your* promise."

"I will." Mary nodded.

"Very well," Paul said. He walked to the door, opened

it wide, and grinned at Mike, who hovered in the hall. "Mike, you may escort the lady to her carriage."

"Yes, Mr. Paul," Mike said.

Mary stood one long moment. Then she left without another word. Paul gazed after her, anger, pride and anticipation warring within him. "Ah, *ma belle.*"

Suddenly, he laughed. Everyone sought to protect Josie. It was humorous. She, out of them all, at least knew what she wanted and what she was doing. His lips curved. Other than himself, that was.

"Paul, what is it?" Josie asked as Mike led her into a private room. "Isn't it time for us to play the baron and earl. I hope they did not cancel."

"No," Paul said, his voice solemn. *"They* did not cancel."

Josie noticed the bruise under his eye, and a cut upon his lip. She gasped. "Paul, what happened to you?"

"I-I should not tell you, *cherie,*" Paul said, turning his face away. "Do not ask."

"But you must tell me," Josie said, concerned. "If you are in trouble, perhaps I can help."

Paul looked at her. His eyes darkened and he shook his head. "Almost, almost you make me want to not tell you. But I think I shall. You should not have to play this hand blind. Rothmier did it."

"Alex?" Josie exclaimed, flabbergasted. "B-but . . . why?"

"He discovered you still play here," Paul said.

"Oh, no!" Josie cried.

"Oh, yes," Paul said. He shook his head, looking terribly sad. "I'm sorry, Josie, but you are not permitted to come here anymore. Rothmier has forbidden it."

"He has what?" Josie gasped.

Paul sighed. "I tried to tell him this was an important source of income for you, that you needed the money, but he would not listen. He says there are too many risks." He rubbed his cheek slightly. "He has added one more I cannot deny. I value my life."

"Paul," Josie exclaimed, anguished. "Y-you cannot do this. I-I was just now beginning to . . . to . . ."

"I know," Paul said, his tone sympathetic. "But Rothmier was adamant. He is rich and powerful, far too powerful to fight."

"Is he?" Josie asked, a cold numbness overtaking her.

Paul shook his head. "Here you seek with your best will to save your family, and he destroys your every chance."

"Yes," Josie said.

"What does he care?" Paul continued. "He did not even see you. He saw me!"

"Why?" Josie whispered. "W-why didn't he come to see me?"

"It is a betrayal," Paul said. "He is the puppet master pulling the strings. You are but his puppet."

"I-I am not his puppet," Josie said, finally firing up. The rage fueling into her blazed away the cold numbness. It was a welcome relief. "How dare he! How dare he do this!"

"I-I fear for you, *cherie.*"

"Fear for me?" Josie yelped.

Paul shrugged. "If you permit him this. If you do not stop him from toying with your life . . ."

"Toying with my life!"

"What else can it be?" Paul asked. "If you do not stop him now, where will it end?"

"Yes, it must end," Josie said, her teeth on edge. "And I will tell him so. See if I do not!"

"Do you wish for Mike to take you to his house?" Paul asked quickly.

"I certainly do," Josie exclaimed, hot flames of rage licking at her.

"Very well," Paul said. "Mike!" Mike entered as if he

had been waiting outside the door. "You know Rothmier, do you not?"

"Yes, Mr. Paul. I remembers him from the last time. He's the one that, er . . . is a particular like friend to that Stanton lad."

Josie started at her own name. Paul cast her a warning look. Even now, with all Josie's comings and goings, Mike was blithely ignorant. "He is the one. I want you to drive my cousin to his house. It is 17 Mayflower."

"Yes, Mr. Paul." Mike shifted on his feet.

"Thank you, Paul," Josie said, sincerely.

"Do not consider it. It is the least I can do," Paul said, his lips twitching. "I am only sorry for you. He should not have treated you this way."

"No," Josie said, sucking in her breath. "B-but he will not toy with me anymore!"

Mike's mouth fell open. "Gore, you, too?"

"He has betrayed me," Josie said.

"Blimey," Mike muttered. "He's worse than a real man."

Josie blinked. It was she who was furious with Alex. Paul's face showed equal bewilderment, but he shrugged. Then his eyes darkened. "Farewell. I regret it has come to this end. I will miss you."

"We will see about that," Josie said, her chin jutting out.

Paul shook his head. "No. I would like to help, but I'll not chance Rothmier calling me out. You can no longer come here. Ever."

"I understand." Josie's sense of fairness forced her to agree. She would miss Paul as well, and it was all Alex's fault. She turned to Mike, the light of battle blazing in her eyes. "Take me to Alex."

"I am sorry, sir," Biddle said, standing tall and straight. "My lord is not at home."

"Then where is he?" Josie asked, her fingernails clenching into her fist. "I wish to talk to him."

"Yeh, where is he?" Mike said from behind. "He wants ter talk to him."

"I do not know of my lord's whereabouts," Biddle said stiffly.

"But you must." Josie's eyes narrowed. "I can tell that you do."

Biddle's face did not change one whit. "Sir, I am merely the butler. I am not privy to all my lord's activities."

"Who'd want ter be," Mike muttered. "Would curdle a man's stomach."

Biddle glared coolly at Mike. "If you will excuse me now."

"No," Josie said, determined. Biddle looked just like Musgrave did when he was covering for her. "You do know where Alex is. Tell me."

"I said I do not," Biddle stated, beginning to close the door.

"Step aside, sir," Mike said. Josie hadn't a moment to obey, for Mike took her in large hands and literally picked her up and set her aside. Biddle had even less time to consider than Josie, for Mike's ham-sized fist wrapped about a goodly amount of the butler's jacket and jerked him forward. "Now, the lad here wants to talk to yer lord, so you just tell us where he be."

"Mike!" Josie exclaimed.

"I-I will not tell you," Biddle said.

"I think yer trying ter protect yer lord," Mike said. "But don't you think he can take care of himself with this here poor lad . . . better than you can take care of yerself with me?"

Biddle's eyes flicked to Josie and then back to Mike. It took a hair's breath. "He's at Miss Cybil Benton's."

"That high-flyer?" Mike asked, scrunching up his face. "Whot's he doing there?"

Biddle choked. "What do you think he's doing there?"

"Nothing much." Mike grinned.

"Don't you insult the master that way," Biddle said, starting to struggle. "You . . ."

"Hey," Mike said. "I understands, he's got to make people think he's a regular toff." He pushed Biddle away. "Now whot's the address."

Biddle stiffened, turning steely-eyed. "It is 932 Cruzon Street. But my lord does not wish to be disturbed. And I assure you, you will be disturbing him."

"From whot? Playing old maid?" Mike laughed. "Or maybes ducks and drakes, without the drakes."

"He'll be playing something else," Biddle said, appearing riled. If he were a porcupine, his quills would have been straight on end.

"Oh," Josie fumed, taking in the part of the conversation she did understand. "He's allowed to play cards, but I am not. It's not right."

"No, it ain't," Mike said, snorting. He turned. "Come along, sir, we'll be going to see my lord, the queer duck."

He turned and barreled down the steps. Biddle was saying something heated about Alex and what sounded like his virility. Flushing, Josie turned in retreat, and chased after Mike. She was panting when she caught up with him at the coach. "I want to thank you, Mike."

"Ain't a problem," Mike said. "I can't say I hold with yer type, but it still ain't right that high-and-mighty lord playing you that way, no matter whot's you are."

Josie blinked. Evidently Mike had divined she was female after all. She debated what to say, but Mike bundled her into the coach so quickly she didn't have a moment. Josie sat back as it jerked forward. First Paul was right. Now Mike was right. Alex shouldn't be permitted to treat her like this.

The coach finally stopped. Josie had whipped herself into a fine lather, as fine a lather as Mike's horses no doubt, so fast had they driven. She sprung from the coach, a militant tilt to her chin. The town house before her was small, but its edifice quite elegant. It also appeared dark. Josie hesitated until she spied a light in the upper window.

"Here we go, then," Mike said and stomped up the steps.

"Yes, here we go." Josie followed him with just as good of a stomp.

Mike pounded his large fist upon the door. He received no answer, so he pounded again.

"I hope we have the correct address," Josie said, adding her smaller fist to the door in a counter tattoo.

"We's got it," Mike said, snorting.

Finally, the door cracked open. The white face of a maid in a mob cap peeked out. "What do you want?"

"We want to see Alex," Josie said.

"Alex?" the maid stammered.

"Lord Rothmier," Josie said impatiently.

The maid's eyes, even in the dim street light, widened. Or perhaps it was merely the whites showed. "H-he can't be disturbed."

"He's going ter be disturbed," Mike said, pushing the door, and the little maid attached to it, inward.

The maid screeched loudly. "You can't come in here!"

"We are already in." Mike grinned.

The maid cowered back. Her next screech rose two octaves higher.

"Please don't," Josie said, her plea a very small voice of reason beneath the furor. "We just want to see Alex."

"Stop your blithering, woman," Mike said, clasping his hands to his ears.

The woman only blithered more.

"What the devil is going on!" Alex's voice shouted out. A candle's light appeared. Bathed within its glow was Alex himself. Indeed, far more of Alex himself than Josie would have ever imagined. He wore nothing but pantaloons. As if to make up for the lack of any other clothing, he held an officious-looking Manton in his free hand.

"Heavens, yes," a blond woman with another candle asked from behind. She was fully dressed. Or at least the dressing gown she wore was full length. However, it was very diaphanous, and Josie could only stare. There was surely enough material to be proper, but for the purpose of coverage, it was well nigh non-existent. "What is the matter?"

Josie choked, and her gaze turned to Alex. A heat suffused her cheeks even as the oddest pangs shot through her body. His chest was broad and furred and . . . and beautiful.

Mike stared, too, though definitely at the woman. "Gore, he weren't just playing cards."

Those words acted as a pure tonic, snapping Josie back into cold reality. Anger gratefully replaced the strange tingles and shivers dancing along her skin. "Neither am I. And that is what is the matter!"

"My God! Josie!" Alex exclaimed. He appeared to dislike reality just as much as she. He turned and bolted. His words drifted in the air. "I'll be back."

Everyone stared at each other. Finally, the blonde smiled. "Alex will be back in a moment. W-won't you come in?" She giggled. "Well, you are already in, aren't you? Let us go to the salon. By the way, my name is Cybil." She looked to the cowering maid, who sobbed and whimpered. "Betty, we shall need the candles lit."

"Y-yes, madam," Betty said. With a wail, she scurried away.

"More candles?" Mike cracked a grin.

"We don't want to sit in the dark, do we?" Cybil said, sounding confused.

"No, ma'am," Mike said, his voice fervent. "The more light the better, I's say."

"Do come this way," Cybil invited, smiling. She turned and drifted before them, looking like an angel, a scantily clad angel. Josie and Mike dutifully trooped behind. As they entered the room, Josie's eyes widened. Betty, with a sob and hiccup, was lighting a large candelabrum, shedding light on an elegantly arranged room of varying shades of mauve, accented with gold.

"Wh-what a lovely room, madam," Josie said in awe. Even the little pillows on the settee were lined with dark rose lace.

The blonde gazed at her a moment and then smiled. "You may call me Cybil." Her lashes fluttered in a strange manner. "It isn't often a man recognizes the finer tastes."

Josie suddenly remembered her masculinity. She coughed and lowered her voice. "Er, yes. Just have the knack, b'gads."

"But it's pink!" Mike said. He sounded as if spiders crawled up the beautiful walls.

"It's mauve," Josie and Cybil said together.

Cybil laughed and waved a hand. "Do have a seat, dear sir."

Josie sat down upon the settee and picked up the pillow to finger the delicate lace.

"Betty, some brandy," Cybil said. In a whoosh of diaphanous draperies, she sat down next to Josie, very close. Her lashes fluttered madly. She apparently had something in her eye. "Now, what does a fine young man like you want with Alex?"

Josie leaned back as Cybil leaned forward. Evidently Cybil was myopic as well. "I have an argument with him."

"Do you? Why not tell me all about it?" Cybil said in a soothing tone. She placed her hand upon Josie's knee. And squeezed it.

Mike coughed. "Barking up the wrong tree, Miss Cybil."

Cybil turned the largest blue eyes upon Mike. "What?"

Mike looked down. "Er, nothing."

"Alex called you Josie," Cybil said, turning those blue flames back upon Josie. "Is that short for Joseph?"

"Er, y-yes," Josie stammered. Cybil inched even closer. Just then Betty appeared at her side with a tray and a glass of brandy. Josie grabbed it desperately, trying to ignore Cybil, who sounded as if she were purring. "Thank you," she muttered and drank it down fast.

"Cybil," Alex's voice cracked from the entrance of the room. "Stop that. And Josie, don't drink that!"

"Oh, Alex," Cybil said, drawing back. The slightest pout puckered her lips. "You know I didn't mean anything by it. I was only flirting."

"Josie's not a man, Cybil," Alex growled.

"Here now," Mike exploded. "You're a fine one to be talking. You ain't a real man either."

"Who are you?" Alex asked, his eyes narrowing. A low growl arose from him. "You're Desuex's man. You brought Josie here."

Mike puffed out his barrel chest and lumbered toward him. "I's sure did. He's got a right ter talk to you, yer queer, bloody blighter."

"Watch your language! He's a she!" Alex shouted. His fist shot out and punched Mike in the stomach.

Mike merely sucked in his breath, his face flaring red. "Played him false, ye did. And you with a ladybird, too!" His ham-sized fist whizzed out, shying Alex's jaw.

Neither man's language bore scrutiny as they closed in on each other, wrestling.

"Ladybird?" Josie gasped. She stared at Cybil. "Y-you're Alex's mistress?"

"She?" Cybil asked breathlessly. "She? You're a girl?"

"Yes." Josie took a big swallow of brandy. It gratefully bit as it ran down her throat.

"Oh, my God," Cybil said. She snatched the glass from Josie and gulped. Wheezing from it, she shifted noticeably farther away. "Why are you pretending to be a man?"

The two real men grunted, delivering equally strong blows upon each other.

"Because I play cards." Josie impolitely took the glass back. Sipping from it, she sighed heavily. "Or I did. But now Alex has put paid to that. He doesn't think I should masquerade as a man."

"I see." Cybil retrieved the glass and took another sip. Her brow wrinkled. "Or I think I do."

"It's difficult to make money," Josie said. She grabbed the glass back, watching as the men careened about the room. They crashed into a fine French table, knocking it over and sending the delicate china curios upon it flying into the air. She quaffed the remainder of the brandy and coughed. "Th-they just broke your table."

"I know." Cybil took the glass from Josie's numbing fingers and lifted it, only to lower it in clear disappointment.

Josie flushed. "Sorry."

Cybil merely tossed the glass to the side. "Betty, stop sniveling and bring more brandy."

Betty, who was huddled in the corner, and sniveling indeed, skittered over to them with the brandy decanter.

"Sh-shouldn't we stop them?" Josie asked. "They are destroying everything."

"No," Cybil said, taking the decanter from Betty's shaking hands. "It's one thing I've learned. You cannot stop men from fighting, not without getting hurt yourself."

"I suppose not," Josie sighed.

"It's a man's world," Cybil sighed as well. She took a healthy swig straight from the decanter and handed it to Josie.

"Thank you," Josie said. She took a sip, observing Alex and Mike. They rammed into the fire irons which clattered and clanked to the floor. Betty squeaked and jumped. Josie held out the decanter. "Here."

Betty didn't say a word, but snatched the decanter up and downed a hearty swig. She choked and crumpled onto the settee beside Josie. "Gore, ain't it just a man's world."

"Problem is," Josie said, retrieving the brandy from Betty, "they make very little sense."

"That they don't," Cybil said, waiting for Josie to take her draft and then reaching for the decanter. She drank swiftly and lowered it. A grin crossed her lips, even as Mike and Alex knocked over a chair. "But sometimes, you just have to love them."

"You do?" Betty asked. She leaned over and pulled the decanter from her employer's hands. She swallowed deeply from it.

"You do," Josie sighed. Her heart wrenched as Alex received a leveler from Mike, and she held out her hand. Betty obligingly shoved the decanter into it.

"Well, I do," Cybil said, laughing. "I don't intend to be dest-tit-tute in my old age."

"Really?" Josie asked. At this moment, her vision of old age was unpleasantly blurred. "Then you like your occupation?"

"Yes, I do," Cybil said. The two men knocked into an ancient grandfather clock. Josie groaned and Betty moaned. Cybil shrugged. "I can buy another."

The other two looked at her, totally impressed. "You can?"

Cybil's smile was smug. "Yes, I can."

Josie hiccuped. "I think we sh-should talk."

The two men came together in what should have been a clinch, but looked more like a mutual shoring up of each other.

"Had enough, gov?" Mike asked, his voice weak.

"Don't know," Alex said. He actually laughed.

Mike chuckled. "Wells, I have."

Josie shook her head. "They make no sense."

Mike grinned through his nicely coloring bruises. "Guess you're a real man when's it comes to fighting."

"I'm a real man in every way," Alex said. "It's only Josie who's not. He truly is a she."

"Gore!" Mike backed away. He staggered without Alex's support. Swinging his head, he peered at Josie. "That true?"

Josie blushed. "Yes, yes it is."

Indignation crossed Mike's face. "Whys didn't you tell me?"

"I did," Alex said. His face darkened. "That's why she shouldn't be playing at Paul's. She'll be discovered sooner or later."

Mike scratched his head and then winced. "She fooled me."

"Me, too," Cybil said, giggling.

"She doesn't fool me," Alex growled, glaring at Josie.

Josie lifted her chin and glared back. "I do not care if I fool you. You had no right to go behind my back and hit Paul and . . . and stop me from playing cards."

"I did it for your own good," Alex said. "And do not talk to me of honesty. It was you who went behind my back. You'd promised me you wouldn't play anymore."

"I promised I wouldn't masquerade as Michael anymore," Josie said, pushed to defend herself. "And I didn't. I masqueraded as Paul's cousin."

"Gracious," Cybil said. "You do like to masquerade. You should become an actress."

"No!" Alex roared. He glared at Cybil. "Don't put any more ideas into the little idiot's head."

"Idiot!" Josie exclaimed. A strong desire to try and add one more bruise to Alex's face filled her. "I'm not an idiot. And I'm not a . . . a puppet!"

"Puppet?" Alex asked. "What the devil are you talking about?"

"I'm talking about the fact you are toying with my life," Josie said. "You have no right to do so. Especially behind my back."

"I was only trying to save you from yourself," Alex said.

"Well, I won't have it anymore." Josie stamped her foot. "Do you hear?"

Alex stiffened. His voice was ice. "Very well. Do whatever you wish. I assure you, I don't give a damn."

Josie drew herself up. "Good!"

"Fine," Alex said.

"Very well," Josie said.

"Indeed," Alex said.

Josie stood a moment. Cybil watched them with wide blue eyes, and Mike's battered face displayed an embarrassing amount of sympathy. Josie fought the sting of tears. "We are going now."

"Do," Alex said. "Cybil and I wish to retire."

"Of course," Josie said. Spinning on her heel, she walked directly from the house.

Mike silently followed her. His blackened eyes reflected regret. "Guess I shouldn't have brought you here."

"No," Josie assured, her chin wobbling slightly, "I'm glad you did."

"He's a mean customer, he is," Mike said. "Routed us both."

"Yes," Josie choked out and crawled into the coach. She sighed in relief as Mike closed the door.

However, he peered through the window. "Are you going to be all right, Miss . . . er, Josie?"

"I will be fine," Josie said.

"Where am I to take you?" Mike asked.

Josie gave her address. Mike nodded and finally disappeared. Josie leaned back against the seat and permitted the tears to fall. She was not the crying type, but the tears rolled down her cheeks nevertheless. She brushed them away.

"I will be fine," she said to herself in determination. She forced herself to think upon her future. She was free to do whatever she wanted. The dreadful tears only increased. She shook her head. She didn't know why she cried. Tonight she had learned of an avenue to a rich life. One where she wouldn't be destitute in her old age. Cybil enjoyed being a mistress excessively. She could even go out and buy another grandfather clock without blinking.

Josie sniffed. She was sure she would enjoy being a mistress as well.

Six

"Thank you for seeing me," Josie said, once again sinking down upon the settee in Cybil's salon. The room in the light of day was even more lovely. Josie sighed and fingered her notebook and pencil.

"It is my pleasure," Cybil said, rustling forward in an emerald satin gown. It seemed more appropriate for evening wear than day, but that was what Josie was here to learn. "Only why did you come?"

"I-I would greatly appreciate it," Josie said, drawing in a breath, "if you would tell me how to become a mistress."

Cybil's blue eyes widened and she sat down swiftly. "Goodness."

"Please," Josie pleaded.

"I don't know if I should," Cybil said, her brow furrowed.

"I really would like to know," Josie insisted. "And if you are worried about Alex, you shouldn't be. He did say it didn't matter to him what I did."

"Yes, he did say that." Cybil nodded, the frown disappearing.

"And . . . and I truly do need to make money," Josie said. "Now that I cannot play at Paul's anymore."

"Very well," Cybil said. "I'm sure masquerading as a man must be very confusing and difficult. I know I wouldn't enjoy it."

"Yes." Josie refrained from saying that with Cybil's endowments, no matter what she did, she would never be mistaken for anything but a woman.

Cybil thought a moment, her eyes almost crossing with the effort. They finally cleared. She leaned forward, her look severe. "The first and most important thing . . ."

"Yes?" Josie asked eagerly, gripping her pencil.

"Is to remember to make the men pay for your services."

Josie blinked. She had expected something far more earth-shattering. "That is it?"

Cybil shook her head, her blue eyes bewildered. "You would be surprised how many women forget to do that."

"They do?" Josie asked.

"They do." A look of horror crossed Cybil's face. "They become mistresses for free."

"And that is bad," Josie said.

"Very bad," Cybil stated. "And so . . . wasteful. I've always found men happy to pay. All you need to do is ask. In fact, the more you make them pay, the better they seem to like it."

"Truly?" Josie asked, astonished.

"Yes." Cybil nodded with all sincerity. "They respect you for it."

"I see," Josie said, tangling with the concept. She wrote "Never undercharge!"

"Of course, in return, you should try to be very good."

"Good?" Josie asked. She thought a moment. As a whole she was a nice person, or endeavored to be. No one ever called her shrewish or anything like that.

"Yes, and learn what they like and don't like. Their every little taste." Cybil giggled. "If you know what I mean."

"Know every taste," Josie wrote down. Beside it she wrote "Favorite pastimes?" "Favorite wine?" "Favorite cigar?" She smiled. That wouldn't be difficult. Her father always said she had a talent for knowing just what people needed. "I can do that easily."

"True." Cybil nodded. "Most men are all the same. I myself prefer them to be that way. Though I've had one or two patrons that were . . . odd."

"Odd?" Josie asked, frowning.

"To me they were," Cybil said. "I am rather conventional. I don't like being tied up one whit."

"I can understand that," Josie said sincerely. "One's freedom is very important."

"And as for the man with the feather duster," Cybil said, appearing as ruffled as a kitten with wet paws, "I refuse to be furniture."

"Indeed," Josie said. She wrote down, "No servants," and looked up. "He probably couldn't pay well anyway."

"You are right," Cybil said, her eyes widening. "You catch on very fast."

"Thank you," Josie said, beaming.

Cybil mused a moment. Josie waited patiently. "I think being particular in who you choose makes the difference between being successful or not. If you don't enjoy your job, you won't last in the business."

"Be very particular," Josie wrote down.

"Some women choose their patrons willy-nilly, or worse, let their patrons choose them."

"This is wrong?" Josie asked, attempting to appear sage.

"Definitely," Cybil said. "Every man should be an advancement in your career. Alex is a marquis. My last patron was only an earl."

"Really?" Josie asked.

"Yes," Cybil said proudly. "All it takes is knowing where you want to go. And being careful. You must always have protection."

"Protection." Josie wrote it down. Beside it she drew an arrow and added, "Hire someone like Mike."

"The last thing you want is children," Cybil said.

"Good heavens, no!" Josie exclaimed. How could a child protect you? That would be ridiculous. She looked eagerly at Cybil. "What else?"

Cybil blinked. "Let me see, I think I've told you everything that is important."

Josie bit her lip. "W-would you mind telling me, er . . . how do you attract a . . . patron?"

"I'm not sure." Cybil frowned. "I've never really thought about it until now. I-I think, though, it is an individual thing or something."

"Oh," Josie said, nonplused. "Well, how do you do it?"

Cybil's lips pursed. "I know you should never be serious and you shouldn't talk too much."

"I see," Josie said, slightly shaken. She was in a territory that would require work. The family always said she took things too seriously.

"Men must always believe they are more intelligent than you are." Cybil smiled. "I'm very fortunate in that. I never have to pretend. Almost everyone is more intelligent than me. But I do know of ladies who must act it. And—" Cybil looked at Josie in gentle stricture—"you should never fight with a man."

Josie flushed. "Like I did last night?"

"Yes, like last night." Cybil frowned. "I think men are so busy fighting every day with everyone else that they are just too tired to fight with you at the end of it. And if you do fight with them, do it only for so long, until they feel guilty enough to buy you a diamond necklace or something. In fact, now that I think about it—that is a very good rule. If you aren't going to get a necklace for it, do not fight. It makes life much easier."

"Yes," Josie said. "That makes sense."

"And . . ." Cybil's blue eyes studied Josie. "You might like to change your style of dress."

"I would?" Josie asked.

"Men like colors and . . . and pretty things," Cybil said.

She added quickly, "Please don't take me wrong. What you are wearing today is much better than what you were wearing last night. At least you are dressed as a woman. But you might want to add more, er . . . dash."

"Dash?" Josie asked, frowning.

Cybil's face brightened and she sprung up. "Let me show you. And I want you to see my boudoir; it is divine."

"I would enjoy that," Josie exclaimed, standing.

Cybil led her swiftly through the house and into a bedroom of satined purple and gold. The accents were fuchsia. Josie blinked.

"Isn't it divine?" Cybil asked.

"Yes?" Josie said. Evidently this was what she needed to learn. Dash.

Cybil strode over to a lengthy row of armoires, swinging wide the doors. More brilliant colors of satin and silks bedazzled Josie's already straining eyes. Josie tilted her chin and set herself to assimilate as much as she could.

One hour later, Josie returned home, armed with a veritable book of notes. Her head reeled.

By late afternoon Josie had perused her notes avidly. She bundled them up, prepared to search out her next reference source. She'd debated the ethics of seeking free information from her father's mistress, but shoved the niggling worry from her mind. Once she had realized the purpose of the mysterious funds, Josie had easily chased down the funneling of those monies and to which address they finally were applied. In truth, she had sought out the information with no real notion of what she intended to do with it. Now she knew.

She commandeered a hack and ordered the driver to take her to an unprepossessing neighborhood, and to a town house which was much smaller than Cybil's. She asked the driver to wait without, climbed three small steps and knocked on the door.

It was opened by an older lady. Her hair was a brilliant red, and her figure could only be considered well-upholstered. Her dress was pleasant, but just as conservative as Josie's own. Josie blinked. "Mrs. Margaret Cranston?"

"Yes?" The woman smiled a warm smile. Her green eyes were just as welcoming. Everything about this woman seemed to comfort.

"I-I am Josephine Stanton," Josie stammered.

The woman's eyes widened. "Coor, so you're little Josie"

Josie flushed. "Yes, yes I am."

The woman laughed, a deep, hearty laugh. "What brings you here, love? I doubt your father sent you."

"Well, I . . ." Josie stopped. It was more difficult to initiate the conversation than she had expected.

Margaret chuckled. "Just spit it out, dearie. I've found it's the only way."

"Well," Josie said. "I know it might be an imposition, but since you *are* my father's mistress, I wonder if you would mind very much telling me how to become one."

"One what?" Margaret asked.

"Why, a mistress," Josie said. "A good one."

"Saints alive!" Margaret exclaimed.

Josie held up her papers. "I've already taken notes from Cybil . . ."

"Cybil?" Margaret asked, blinking.

"Yes, she is Alex's mistress . . ."

"Alex who?" Margaret asked.

"The Marquis of Rothmier."

"My, my," Margaret said. "She must be a real high-flyer."

"She is very serious about her career, I believe," Josie said. "She gave me very good advice on many things."

"Did she now?" Margaret's gaze drifted to the pages in Josie's hand. Curiosity glowed within her eyes. "Like what?"

"Like how to choose the right patron. Every man should

be an advancement for you," Josie said from memory. She flushed then. Judging by the difference in establishments, she doubted Cybil would consider her father a wise career choice.

"You don't say?" Margaret Cranston shook her head. "I really shouldn't be talking to you . . ."

"I-I understand," Josie said, her heart sinking.

A broad smile crossed Margaret's face. "But since you've already talked to this here Cybil, I can't see the harm in exchanging notes, as it were. Come in, dear."

Josie's heart lifted, and she returned an eager smile as she entered.

Josie sat in her bed later that evening, her notes strewn across the quilt, mulling over the wealth of information she had acquired that day. She had talked to two mistresses and found them totally different. Margaret's best advice was that a man liked a cozy place to come to, a warm armful upon his lap, and a sympathetic ear. Men needed to be able to talk about their troubles. A good mistress should listen to a man's woes for as long as she could stand, and then she was to take his mind off those woes. When asked how to do that, Margaret had said blowing in his ear always did the trick for her. It seemed very odd advice to Josie, but she was positive that was what Margaret had said.

She shook her head. The conversation had drifted after that. Margaret was far more interested in hearing Cybil's advice than anything else. A pang of guilt shot through Josie. Clearly Margaret was not as financially successful as Cybil. Which, once again, could be laid at the Stantons' thriftless doorstep. In truth, Josie had wanted her father to cut the expenditure, but since she had met Margaret, she feared the dear lady wasn't receiving enough.

A knock sounded at the door. Josie quickly shuffled her papers together, burying them beneath her pillow. "Yes?"

"Josie, it's me," Mary's voice called.

Josie smiled. "Come in, Mary."

The door opened and Mary entered. She halted as she saw Josie in bed. Something like relief entered her eyes. "You are in bed. Good. I mean . . . I just came to say good night."

"Come," Josie said, patting the quilt. "We can have a chat."

"N-no," Mary said. "I can't stay. I mean, I am going to bed directly myself."

"Oh." Josie frowned.

Mary looked away. "You . . . you are not going out to play cards, I see."

"No." Josie shifted uncomfortably. "And I won't be."

"Indeed?" Mary asked. Her voice was odd, and breathless.

"No," Josie said bitterly.

"I'm sorry."

Josie blinked and then laughed. "I thought you would be pleased."

Mary appeared to jump. "I am. I mean, well . . . I don't know what I mean. I guess I am tired, that is all."

"Yes, I suppose I am, too," Josie said. All of Mary's talk about sleep was making her so.

"Well," Mary said quickly, "I will leave you to your sleep. I-I am going to go to sleep now as well."

"Good night," Josie said. "Sweet dreams."

"You, too." Mary hastened from the room.

Josie stared after Mary a moment, frowning. Her sister's behavior seemed peculiar. She yawned and shook her head. She was tired and merely imagining things. This was always the time Mary went to bed.

Leaning over, Josie blew out her candle and lay back. She heard the crackle of paper. Remembering, she pulled out her notes and dropped them to the side of the bed. There would be time enough for that tomorrow. She burrowed back down with a sigh. Tonight she could rest.

Josie fell asleep immediately. Indeed, very peacefully.

"You have not touched your food," Paul said softly.

"I-I know." Mary twisted the crisp linen napkin on her lap. The private sitting room was romantically lit. A simple silver candelabra rested upon the equally crisp damask tablecloth. China and silver place settings glistened within its glow. Dishes of food arrayed every inch of the table. Each one appeared perfectly prepared with the most elegant garnishes.

Portions of each of those tasty offerings also rested upon Mary's plate. Yet every time she attempted to take a bite, her mouth turned dry. Every time she looked at Paul her heart pounded. He had talked smoothly and politely all through the meal as if this were not a clandestine meeting, as if he had not forced her attendance. He had told amusing stories, stories that Mary would have laughed at if every nerve in her body hadn't been stretched taut, waiting in fear of what he might do next. She swallowed hard. "I-I am not hungry."

"Can I not even tempt you . . . ," Paul said.

"No!" Mary said, jumping. "No!"

"With the asparagus in Hollandaise," Paul continued, his tone bland. "It is superb. My chef's particular specialty in fact."

"Oh." Mary looked down in mortification at the untouched green spears strewn upon her plate. "No, no thank you."

"Nor have you touched your wine," Paul said. "Would you prefer a different one? A heavier bodied one, perhaps?"

"No, I would not!"

"I enjoy the lighter bodied ones myself," Paul murmured.

Mary flushed even more deeply. "I do not care f-for either. I do not drink."

Paul gazed at her. His lips tightened. Something flared in his eyes. He wiped his mouth with his napkin and threw it down upon the table. "That is it!"

Mary clutched and wadded hers more tightly. This was the moment. "What is it?"

"It is time," Paul said, rising.

"Time?" Mary wheezed out. "Time f-for what?"

"To ravage you, of course," Paul said, his voice curt. "Is not that what you have been waiting for? Indeed, what you are expecting?"

"No," Mary said, shaking her head.

"Yes, it is. I am the villain, am I not? And thus, must ravage!" Paul appeared to leap at her. "Come, Mary!"

"No!" Mary cried out. Fear exploded within her. She sprung up, fleeing. Only she'd not released her linen napkin. Or what she thought was her linen napkin. Rather it was the unfortunate tablecloth. She heard a clatter, even as an unsuspected weight dragged at her skirts.

"Mon Dieu," Paul shouted.

Confused and alarmed, Mary rotated toward Paul. He no longer attacked her. He was diving toward the toppling candelabra. Mary gasped. She instinctively back pedaled at the fearsome sight. Unfortunately, that combination of movements entangled her further with the yards of damask. She lost any semblance of balance and fell. A worse clattering arose. Bound in her linen cocoon, Mary could feel unidentified objects hitting her, and unknown liquids seeping onto her.

"Mary!" Paul cried. Flat on her back and mummified, Mary opened her eyes, which she discovered she had closed. His image swam before her. He held aloft the rescued candelabra. "Sweet Mother of God!"

Mary closed her eyes. He evidently didn't mean her after all. "Are you all right? Mary, please speak to me! Please!"

Perhaps he did mean her. She opened her eyes. Paul knelt beside her, the candelabra shaking within his hand. His face displayed utter fear. Mary drew in a breath and forced herself to sit up slowly. Splotched linen covered her skirt. Forks, glasses and no longer tasty entrees lay upon her and about her. She blinked back tears. "Oh, dear."

"Do not cry, *cherie,*" Paul said, setting the candelabra down upon the floor. "Forgive me!" He snatched at the tablecloth. Swiped at the dishes. "I only meant to frighten you a little. But not this!"

Mary sat frozen. The only thing that seemed mobile were her tears. They trickled down her cheeks, regardless.

"I am a villain, an utter villain," Paul said, his voice rough. He reached a hand toward her chest. Then he froze, glancing away. *"Mon Dieu."*

Confused, Mary looked down through her tears. Spears of asparagus lay in a perfect design upon her chest. She swore she recognized them. She choked on a sob. "It's my fault. I should have eaten those."

"What?" Paul asked, his hand falling to his side.

A strange, wild giggle escaped Mary. "They wouldn't be there now if I-I had eaten them. W-would they?"

Expressions crossed Paul's face so swiftly, Mary couldn't define them. Then he laughed, a balm to Mary. "You are a delight." He rose and stretched out his hand. "Come, Mary."

The words and tone were different this time. Mary gratefully reached for his hand. "Thank you."

He pulled her up with a sureness of strength that caused Mary to gasp. Everything clinging to her fell away, seeming to disappear. "Are you all right?"

"Y-yes," Mary said. "I am. Now."

"You must sit," Paul said, gently tugging at her hand.

Mary followed willingly as he led her to the sofa. She immediately crumpled down upon its cushions.

Paul sat beside her. Their eyes met. His were dark. "Can you ever forgive me?"

Mary stared at him. One loose, undefined thought rattled through her mind. It was terribly important to her. "You said you wanted to frighten me. Why?"

Paul looked shamefaced. "You were so determined to think me the villain, that I decided to play the role for you. I fear I overdid it."

"I see," Mary said, flushing.

"Which proves I am wicked," Paul said, his face darkening.

Mary's lips twitched. "I-I may have deserved it."

"No." Frowning slightly, Paul leaned over to brush at her hair.

A tingle ran through Mary. "Wh-what is it?"

"Just some . . . sauce," Paul said. He stopped, his expression arrested.

Mary's heart pounded. "Is-is it gone now?"

"No," Paul said, his voice soft. He brushed his hand upon her cheek. Mary held her breath as he then slid it to the curve of her neck. Gazes locked, he leaned slowly over and kissed her. Mary sighed, her eyes fluttering shut. Paul groaned, deepening the kiss. Without thought, Mary leaned toward him. He shifted, enfolding her in strong arms.

Mary was floating. Floating with the sweetest sensations. She heard Paul mutter something, and suddenly she was set adrift. His lips were no longer on hers, his arms no longer about her. She opened her eyes, blinking.

"I am sorry. I should not have done that." Paul stood up quickly and paced away from her. He would not look at her. "You need not come here anymore. I will make certain Josie does not play here."

"No." Mary drew in a deep breath. "I made a promise. I will keep it."

Paul looked at her, startled. "You will?"

Mary smiled. "I would be more wicked than you if I did not live up to our agreement."

"No," Paul said, shaking his head. "You cannot be more wicked. I deceived you."

"How?" Mary asked.

"I had already promised Rothmier I would stop Josie from coming here. Just before you came, in fact."

"You had?" Mary gasped. "Then . . . then . . ."

"I'm sorry," Paul said. "I should not have done it. But you were such the martyr prepared to sacrifice yourself, I could not resist."

"I see." Mary stared at him. She should be angry, but amusement rose within her instead. A giggle escaped her. "I-I was acting like the martyr, wasn't I? So you made me think that . . . oh, that was too bad of you."

"Yes." Paul's eyes twinkled. Then they darkened. "I also wanted to see you again."

Mary smiled. "You did?"

"I did." Paul looked away. "But you do not need to see me anymore. It would not be right."

Rebellion streaked through Mary. She suddenly didn't care to do what was right. She had done that all her life. "No, I wish to see you again."

Paul's gaze returned to her. "You do?"

"Yes, I do."

"Why?" Paul asked, frowning.

Mary flushed. She couldn't say it was because she felt more alive than she ever had. She couldn't say it was because his kiss had done something monumental to her. She forced a smile. "Because I have never had any secrets before, but I think I like them."

Paul's eyes lightened. He chuckled. "Then this will be our secret, *ma belle*. And I promise you, it will not be one you need regret. I-I will not take advantage of you again."

Mary flushed. "Thank you."

Paul grinned. "Perhaps, next Wednesday, then?"

"Yes," Mary said. Excitement coursed through her. And trepidation. She would have a secret.

Alex permitted Betty to lead him up to Cybil's sitting room. The maid had a tendency not to want to look at him. He, himself, was embarrassed about last night. Tonight he was determined to redeem himself with Cybil. Faith, he'd destroyed her salon, brawling with a bruiser as if they were in a tavern. He was normally a man of control, but he had been so disconcerted, so angry at Josie's presence in his mistress's house, he had wanted to kill something. He flushed. Fortunately, Mike had been a man who could hold his own.

Worse, despite his boast to Josie and Mike that he was going to retire with Cybil, he had not. She had been everything that was kind, had even tried to administer to him. He couldn't say why, but he had left her, and none too politely. What the devil was wrong with him?

Alex shook himself. He would make it up to her tonight. He'd been ignoring her too often of late. That could be laid at Josie's door as well. He'd been so busy trying to help the child that he hadn't found time for anyone else. Not even for his own mistress! Thank God that was over with now. The ungrateful chit had told him to stay out of her life, and he would gladly do so. She could very well go her own way, and stumble into every nitwit imbroglio she desired. He'd not care one jot.

He clenched his teeth. That was enough thinking about Josie. He had his own life to live. Last night had already been destroyed by her; tonight wasn't going to be. He carried in his pocket a diamond brooch. That would certainly start the evening out right.

He entered Cybil's sitting room. She lounged upon her settee, dressed in a frilly pink negligee, her blond hair spilling down her shoulders. Alex smiled and strode across the room to sit down beside her. "You look beautiful tonight, my love."

Cybil's full lower lip pouted out. "Do I?"

Alex laughed to himself, but said, "I'm sorry about last night." He drew out the small velvet box. "So sorry that I brought you a present."

"Oh, Alex!" Cybil's eyes lighted. She snatched up the box and opened it. "Oh, Alex, it is beautiful." She quickly dropped it into her lap and reached out her arms. "Thank you."

Alex moved into those open arms and pulled Cybil's body close, kissing her hard. Yes, he could feel a stirring of desire. It wasn't strong, but it was stirring at least. This was what he needed. He must forget about everything else and let passion take over. Cybil moaned. He laughed. "Then, you forgive me?"

"Oh, yes," Cybil said, her hands reaching to push his jacket away. He quickly helped her relieve him of it, tossing it to the floor. "Oh, yes." She expertly untied his cravat and unbuttoned his shirt, slipping her fingers inside to play with his chest hair. "It's been too long."

"Yes," Alex said, drawing in his breath. "I'm sorry Josie interrupted us last night."

"That's all right," Cybil said, leaning over to kiss him even as she undid the rest of his shirt and pulled it from his pantaloons. "I like her."

"You do?" Alex asked, frowning.

"Yes," Cybil murmured. Her lips roved over his chest. Her hand slid down his stomach, and then even farther.

Alex willed himself to respond, but he could not. He was too involved with the confusing thought of his mistress liking Josie. It just wasn't right.

Cybil's hand froze, and she drew back. A frown marred her brow. "What is the matter?"

"Nothing, nothing at all," Alex said. He kissed her quickly. Cybil moaned. "It is just odd that you like Josie."

"Mm," Cybil sighed, pressing into him. "She is eager to learn."

"Forget Josie," Alex said gruffly.

"Yes." Cybil giggled. Her hand roamed intimately once more.

A thought persisted, even as Alex groaned. "What do you mean, eager to learn?"

"Hm?" Cybil breathed, kissing him.

"Eager to learn what?" Alex asked.

"How to be a good mistress," Cybil murmured, performing one of her own special tricks.

Alex stiffened. Unfortunately, in the completely wrong manner. "What in blazes do you mean?"

"What?" Cybil's blue eyes blinked wide.

He disentangled himself from Cybil, a terrible premonition overtaking him. "You talked to Josie, didn't you? You told her how to become a mistress."

"Yes," Cybil said, frowning.

"Blast and damn!" Alex exclaimed.

"You are angry?"

"Of course I'm angry!" Alex shouted. "Good God. Why did you talk to her?"

Cybil blinked. "She said you wouldn't mind. And from what you said last night, I-I didn't think you would either."

"Hang what I said," Alex growled. "You should never have talked to her. Bloody hell!" He sprung up, pacing the room. He must be the most cursed of men. Not only must he suffer Josie, who had no sense of decorum and was surely set upon destruction, but he had to possess an equally buffle-headed mistress who would gladly show her the way. He drew in a ragged breath, attempting to rein in his temper. It was his fault. He hadn't chosen Cybil for her brains, and now he must pay the price. "Very well. Just exactly what did you tell her?"

"Nothing much that I can remember," Cybil said, frowning. "She seemed to know everything she needed to know."

Alex laughed bitterly. "That's what you think."

Cybil looked concerned. "I'm sorry. I was only trying to help. You don't want her masquerading as a man and playing cards, do you?"

"No," Alex said. "But I don't want her to become a mistress either."

"I see," Cybil said. A resigned look entered her eyes. "You aren't going to stay the night, are you?"

Alex sighed. He had sworn he would forget about Josie, but he could not. Just like he could not remain with Cybil tonight. "No. I'm not."

Cybil nodded. "I understand."

Alex gritted his teeth. He wasn't certain if she did or not. Unfortunately, he did. He wasn't going to be able to be with Cybil tonight or any other night in the future. Josie had put paid to that. He strove for a gentle voice. "I think it would be better if we parted, my dear."

"Yes," Cybil said, nodding.

"Yes?" Alex asked, his brow raising.

Cybil laughed, appearing very proud of herself. "I told you I understood."

Alex smiled. "Then we can part as friends?"

"Oh, yes," Cybil said. "That is one of the things I told Josie. You should never fight with a man."

"Perhaps I am glad you talked to her after all." Alex laughed. "However, I do hope you will not talk to her again."

"No." Cybil fluttered her lashes. "I think I'd rather talk to the Duke of Turnbridge. You do know him, do you not?"

Alex grinned. "I promise to make arrangements for your introduction. Needless to say, I will take care of everything until you acquire him . . . I mean another patron.

Also, you will need the necklace to match the brooch I just gave you."

"You are a dear," Cybil said. "I will miss you. Josie is a fortunate girl." Alex frowned at her. She laughed again. "Even if she will never be a mistress."

"And I could have sworn I'd have won," Horace Stanton said, sitting back in the big leather chair, the fire crackling beside him.

"Just bad luck, love," Margaret said, walking toward him with a full glass of port. She sat down upon his lap. Horace wrapped his arms around her full figure and squeezed her. "You couldn't help it," she assured him.

"Guess not," Horace said, relieved. He took the glass of port and drank from it. He shook his head. "Everyone has bad luck once in a while, don't they?"

"That they do," Margaret agreed. "It ain't your fault."

"No," Horace said, brightening even further.

"You just think of the good things you have," Margaret said. "You've got a fine family."

"That I do." Horace turned misty-eyed. "Good wife. Good son. And my girls, each and every one of them sweet girls." He sighed. "It's still too bad about Josie and Rothmier. That was a leveler. Thought he'd save our family. And my poor Josie. What to do?"

"Don't you worry, love." Margaret leaned over and blew gently in his ear. "Your Josie's got a good head on her shoulders."

"Hm, yes." Horace felt the stirrings of desire. "That she does."

"A much better one than me, I'd say," Margaret added, blowing in his ear once more.

"Do you think?" Horace said.

"I know, love," Margaret said. "I talked to her today."

"Hm, what?" Horace asked. He laughed. "Sorry, didn't hear you right. Thought you said you talked to her today."

"I did."

"What! No!" Horace cried. He dropped his glass of port.

"Horace, look what you did," Margaret admonished.

"Y-you talked to Josie?" Horace gurgled.

"I told you that twice, love," Margaret said. "She came ter see me herself."

"B'gads!" Horace shouted. Stunned and frightened, he shot from his chair. Margaret, unsecured, toppled to the floor. "Wh-what did she want?"

"She wanted to know about how to become a mistress." Margaret stood up and dusted herself off.

"No!" Horace shook his head. It was a nightmare. "Not my little Josie."

"Yes, your little Josie," Margaret said. She placed her hands upon her hips. "And she got me to thinking, love. Horace, you don't treat me right or pay me what you ought. I could tell Josie thought so, too."

"She couldn't want to become a mistress," Horace cried. Then he blinked. "She thinks I don't pay you right?"

"She didn't exactly say it. She's a polite soul, she is. But I could tell by the advice she gave me." Margaret's bountiful chest puffed out. "Horace, I'm looking at my retirement years, you know. I can't be wasting them."

"Oh, God," Horace muttered. His daughter knew about his mistress. She had talked to his mistress! She thought he ought to pay his mistress more money! Horace's world careened, the very timbers of his soul hauled out from under him. He stumbled toward the door. "G-got to go."

"No," Margaret said. "You can't leave until we discuss things."

"What?" Horace asked, turning to blink at her in a daze.

"I want you to promise me a diamond necklace before you go," Margaret said. "That's how the high-flyers do it, and I want it, too."

"Yes," Horace said, shaking all the more. "Anything, but got to go."

He turned and half stumbled, half loped from the little house. He hailed a hack and retreated to the last haven he ever expected to have, his club. He broke into a cold sweat at the thought of what his daughter might do. Then he broke into a hot sweat at the thought of what his wife might do.

Horace downed quite a few bottles of port that night, though, unlike his usual self, he did not enjoy the company of any man. In truth, he feared he'd never enjoy the company of any woman again, either. He was completely unmanned.

It was his fault. He was an evil, wicked man. He'd been caught out in his sins by his very own daughter. Because of his sins, his sweet, innocent Josie was even considering becoming a mistress. Lord, what had he done? He laid his head down upon the table and dissolved into the pitiful tears of a man who had lost all his moorings and was three sheets to the wind.

The attendants, well accustomed to Lord Stanton, asked if he wished for them to send him home. He shouted no with such white terror in his eyes, the attendants retreated. Soon everyone retreated, permitting Horace to fall asleep right there. Even in his sleep, he repeated the litany, "Josie, I'm sorry."

Seven

Josie sat alone in the breakfast room. It was far too early for any other Stanton to be awake, let alone dressed and prepared to look at food. Josie was looking at her food. Indeed, she frowned at it in severe concentration. She had expected her full night of sleep would have invigorated her and offered her fresh energy with which to attack her plan of becoming a mistress.

Rather, the full night's sleep had appeared to effect the opposite. Niggling doubts had surfaced to drain her. Did she have enough knowledge to become a mistress? Would she possess the proper talents for it? Cybil had said it was easy, but how did one acquire the proper patron?

She stabbed her fork into her eggs. That was enough of such worrisome doubts. She must simply apply herself. If she had learned anything, she had learned resolve was the answer. She had successfully masqueraded as a man in a gaming den, which many thought impossible. Certainly, becoming a mistress shouldn't be any more outrageous or impossible.

Nor had she known how to play cards at first, until Miss Tellington had taught her. Now she was an excellent player. Learning mistressing would surely be the same way. She sighed. She just wished she didn't feel so unsure and alone in this enterprise.

At that moment, Musgrave entered the room. "Miss

Josie, the Marquis of Rothmier has arrived and wishes a word with you."

"Alex?" Josie asked. Her fork squeaked across the plate. "He is here?"

"Yes, Miss Josie."

"This early?" A tangle of emotions roiled within Josie. The worst one she could define was eagerness. She squelched it. She must remember she was angry with Alex. It was he who had destroyed her one form of income and set her upon this new and unnerving path. He could no longer be involved in her life. Not that he wanted to be. He had made that frightfully clear. Josie set her fork down and rose. She strove for a nonchalance. "Very well. I shall see him."

She attempted a slow walk to the salon, denying her feet the fast dash they truly desired. She had no notion why Alex would come to see her, not after what he had said. However, she promised herself strictly that no matter what he said, it would not affect her. It could not.

Josie entered the salon, that directive firm in her mind, a forced smile of indifference upon her lips. "Good morning, Alex."

"Good morning, Josie," Alex returned, standing.

Josie tried to read his expression, but he wore a proper poker face. Only something in his gaze, something new and undefined, gave her cause to worry. She nodded her head. "You may be seated."

"Thank you." Alex sat down upon the sofa.

"To what do I owe the . . . the honor of your visit?" Josie took up the chair farthest from him. "And so early."

"I wanted to see you before you had a chance to . . . begin your day as it were," Alex said. "Do you have a very active one planned?"

"No," Josie answered, still as cool as she could be. "I was just now deciding what I should do . . . for the day, that is."

"Good," Alex replied, relief crossing his face.

Josie frowned in suspicion. "Why?"

"No reason." Alex shrugged. He studied her a moment. Josie lifted her chin and returned a reserved stare. He sighed and smiled. "Josie, please, I am here to apologize."

Josie lost her reserve. Her mouth dropped open. "You are?"

"Yes, I am," Alex said. "I am sorry for everything. I see now I should not have gone to Paul behind your back. It was . . . er, high-handed and dishonest."

"Yes, it was." Josie flushed. "But . . . but I should not have caused such a scene at Cybil's either."

"I own it is not one I wish to relive." Alex chuckled. His gaze turned solemn. "But I've taken steps to ensure it won't happen again. So may we cry truce and be friends?"

Josie's firm intentions melted away in a warm flood of relief and pleasure. "Yes, yes, I would like that."

"Good." Alex smiled. He glanced away. "I fear I was quite callous in regards to your sincere need to raise funds. I did not take that seriously. I do now."

"You do?" Josie asked, staring.

"Most definitely," Alex said, his lips twitching. Or was that a tick along his jawbone? Either way, he turned the most compelling gaze upon Josie, the kind that always made Josie giddy. "As your friend I should support you. I want to help you. But surely, if we work together, we will accomplish even more."

"Oh, yes," Josie said, dazed. "We could."

"But we must think of what to do first," Alex said. "We need a new plan."

"I have one," Josie confessed. Her heart somersaulted in sudden eagerness. Alex was her friend. He would know exactly how to direct her in becoming a mistress. She wouldn't be alone. Suddenly, becoming a mistress was anything but frightening.

Alex raised his brow, though no surprise showed in his face. "You do. May I ask what it is?"

"Oh, yes, it is . . ." Josie halted. A semblance of her native intelligence regained control. "Well, I think it a very good notion, but I'm not sure you will agree."

"Tell me."

"In fact," Josie said, frowning, "I'm sure you will not agree."

"Josie," Alex laughed. "Didn't we just promise to be friends? Only tell me your plan. I will strive to withhold judgment until I have all the facts. Who knows, you might even convince me."

"Convince you?" That was it! She would convince Alex. Indeed, there could be no better opportunity. He was her friend and the perfect one to practice mistressing upon. She ignored the fact her heart leapt an extra bound at the thought. She drew in a deep breath, stood promptly, walked over to Alex, and just as promptly sat down upon his lap.

Alex stiffened and reared back. "Josie, what are you doing?"

"I am going to convince you," Josie said. She smiled, all her notes from yesterday springing to mind. "Men like a warm armful and . . . a sympathetic ear. Would you like to tell me your troubles?"

Alex shifted slightly. He looked pained. "Not at this precise moment I wouldn't."

"Oh," Josie said, disheartened. She thought quickly. "Then . . . then tell me. What do you like?"

"I beg your pardon?" Alex asked, flushing.

"I want to know your every little taste," Josie said. She imitated Cybil's laugh. "If you know what I mean."

"I may know what you mean," Alex said, his eyes narrowing, "but I want you to tell me."

Josie shifted, settling closer and more comfortably. "I

want to know what you like and don't like. What is your favorite color? Your favorite wine?"

"My favorite wine? Oh, Lord!" Alex exclaimed, rolling his eyes toward the heavens. He shook his head. "Josie, enough. Just tell me. What is your scheme? And don't squirm!"

Josie stopped, though against her will. She rather liked cuddling closer. "Very well. I think I should become a mistress."

Alex seemed to sigh. "Yes, I know."

"You know?" Josie asked, blinking.

"I meant," Alex said, his face alarmed, "I gathered as much from your behavior."

Warmth flooded through Josie. "Then I've convinced you?"

"No!" Alex cried, his voice sounding strained. "I didn't say that."

"Oh," Josie said, disappointed.

"I did say we should discuss all the facts first," Alex said. "Didn't I?"

"Yes." Josie knew Cybil said she shouldn't talk seriously, but Alex seemed a hardened case. "But, Alex, Cybil says I can earn far more money as a mistress than I can masquerading as a man."

"Perhaps," Alex said. "But I don't believe you've considered the drawbacks to the profession."

"Drawbacks?" Josie asked.

"For instance," Alex said, very slowly, "I've just turned Cybil off."

"You have?" Josie squeaked, jumping in his lap.

"I told you to stop squirming," Alex said, gritting his teeth.

"I'm sorry," Josie said. "B-but why did you turn Cybil off?"

"Because I simply felt like it. It was a mere whim!" Alex looked at Josie sternly. "And that should be a warning to you. There is very little security in being a mistress. It is not a stable career. Think, Josie. Do you want that to happen to you?"

"Poor Cybil." Josie shook her head.

"Yes, poor Cybil." Alex's tone was ruthless. "But better her than you."

"Yes," Josie said, meditatively. Josie remembered Cybil saying each time she left a patron, it meant she would find a better one. Somehow, Josie believed her completely. With that thought, another one came hard upon it. Josie gasped and stared at Alex. "Alex, you don't have a mistress anymore."

"I just told you that," Alex said patiently.

"Then could I be your mistress?" Josie exclaimed.

"No!" Alex said, his face dark. "Haven't you listened to a word I've said?"

"I have." She wouldn't like being turned off by Alex, but at the same time she'd rather be his mistress than anyone else's. "And I understand. There is no security. Th-that is one of the drawbacks of the job."

"It is a large drawback."

Josie studied Alex. After Cybil, she could understand why Alex would not consider her for a mistress. Still, she could not give up without a fight. Her heart was caught with the realization that she wouldn't just rather have Alex than anyone else. He was the only one she wanted. Nor did she want him to have any other mistress than herself.

Thinking of Mrs. Cranston's advice, Josie sent up a prayer, leaned over close to Alex's ear and puffed. Alex only blinked. She puffed harder.

"Josie," Alex asked, his tone bewildered, "what are you trying to do now?"

"Nothing," Josie said, blushing. "I was . . . just blowing in your ear. I had heard . . ."

Alex gave her anything but a "patron to mistress" look.

"Just stop that and listen. There's always a chance of children as well."

"Children?" Josie asked. She remembered Cybil talking about them. "Oh, no. I'm not going to have them. I know better."

"You do?" Alex asked.

"Of course," Josie said confidently. "I'm going to have someone like Mike."

Alex stared. "Josie, Mike is a full-grown man."

"Yes," Josie said. "Surely he is by far the better protection. Cybil warned me I would need that." She smiled. "But if I have you as my patron, I don't think I'll need protection."

"Oh, yes, you bloody will," Alex groaned. He all but dumped her off his lap and stood. He strode to the fireplace and ran his hand through his hair. "Josie, what Cybil meant by protection was protecting yourself against having children, bearing them. If you are a man's mistress, you always stand a chance of becoming pregnant and having children."

Josie stared. "But only married people can have children."

"My God, who told you that?" Alex exclaimed.

"Miss Tellington did."

"Just like only single men can have mistresses," Alex said with a sigh. He shook his head. "She knows her cards at least." He raised his brow. "What did your mother tell you?"

"To ask Miss Tellington," Josie said. "That is her job, Mother says."

Alex rolled his eyes. He walked back over and sat down. "Josie, just trust me in regards to this. Miss Tellington was wrong. It makes no difference if you are married or not; if you become a mistress, you can have babies. That is why you should not become a mistress. That is why good, respectable women don't become mistresses. They wait until they are married."

Josie suddenly paled, paled to white. "But . . ."

"What?" Alex asked.

"But th-then," Josie stammered. "Well . . . I've done things mistresses do."

Alex laughed. "No, no. I am confusing you. You can kiss a man, and sit on his lap, and you won't have babies."

"Thank heavens," Josie said. She frowned. "Then what do you do otherwise to . . . ?"

"Never mind," Alex said quickly. He smiled. "I'll tell you sometime, but for right now I'll wait."

"I see."

"But you must promise me," Alex said, "if you have questions, ask me first. For God's sake don't ask anyone else. Anyone at all! Will you promise me that?"

"I promise." Josie was shaken. All that research, and no one had seen fit to inform her of the significant details. Without Alex, she would have made a terrible mistake. The world was a far more confusing place than she had ever realized. She sighed, overwhelmed and frightened suddenly.

"What is it?" Alex asked.

"How am I ever going to be able to save my family," Josie said, "when there is so much I don't understand."

"Come here," Alex said. This time *he* hauled her onto his lap. "Don't be so disheartened. Just because one of your schemes was unwise, there are others. Personally, I think marriage a better notion. That is a surer and safer way."

Hope seeped back into Josie. "You are right. My plan for Mary and the baron is better."

"I didn't mean that," Alex said, sighing. "I think you'll come a cropper with that scheme."

"Why?" Josie asked. "If the baron could only meet Mary . . ."

"Josie," Alex said softly.

"I know he couldn't resist her," Josie continued. "He is the only one we have seen so far who will be right for her. Surely that means she is right for him, too . . . oh, my!" Alex had leaned close and breathed gently on her ear. It was just a whisper really, but Josie felt the tingle shoot straight down to her toes. "A-Alex, what are you doing?"

"Just blowing in your ear," Alex said.

"Oh," Josie said with pleasure.

"Don't worry," Alex said, nuzzling her ear. "This cannot get you in trouble."

"Good," Josie sighed. She squirmed as Alex traced feather-light kisses down the column of her neck. She couldn't help herself. With another sigh she twisted in Alex's arms, seeking his lips with hers.

"Oh, God, no!" her father's voice shouted. "No, my poor little Josie, no!"

Josie, bemused, looked up. Her father stood at the entrance of the room, his clothes disheveled. They looked as if he had slept in them. His eyes held a glazed, wild look.

"Father?"

"Please, my child," Horace said, staggering up to them. He tumbled to his knees. Josie gasped, not from his action, but from the virulent strength of the fumes of brandy wafting to her nose. Horace clasped his hands together. "Don't do this. It's all my fault. All my fault."

"What is your fault?" Josie asked, shaking her head.

"Josie, you must not become a . . . a mistress!" Horace cried. He turned tormented eyes upon Alex. "My little Josie is an innocent . . ."

Alex laughed. "You don't know how innocent. And that may be your fault. But how did you know she was considering becoming a mistress?"

"Oh, dear," Josie gasped. "I never thought . . ."

Horace hung his head. "My mistress told me."

"Faith, she went to your mistress as well?" Alex roared with laughter.

"It ain't funny," Horace cried.

"No," Alex said. "It bloody well floors a man, doesn't it?"

Horace began to tremble. "When Margaret told me. God!"

"Father, I am sorry." Josie couldn't fathom how visiting his mistress had reduced her father to such a state, but she *was* sorry. She'd never meant to hurt him.

"No, no," Horace said, almost tearing at his hair. "I'm sorry. It is my fault. All my fault. Your mother told me I was lax, that I did not show you the proper way." A fervent fire suddenly blazed in his eyes. He crawled to a stance and raised a fist heavenward. "But I will reform."

"R-reform?" Josie asked, wide eyed.

"I swear it," Horace cried. "You, my dear child, will see a new Horace Stanton. One a daughter can be proud of! No more mistresses . . ."

"You turned Mrs. Cranston off?" Josie gasped.

"Yes." Horace flushed. "Was hard to do."

"Oh, Father," Josie said. "It must have been frightfully difficult."

"It was," Horace said, his voice sinking. He shook his head. "She came down heavy. D-Demanded a diamond necklace. I couldn't believe it. She was never like that before. But said she was going to do things right. Had to look to her c-career."

"Did she? How absolutely wonder . . ." Josie halted. Her father was staring at her. "I mean, I am all a-wonder. Just stunned.

Horace's face crumpled. "But I'll do it, bedamn. I'm going to change. You'll see! No more mistresses. No more drinking. I am going to become proper. Set an example for you. Only promise you . . . you won't become a mistress."

"I won't, Father," Josie said, still concerned over his tormented behavior. "I had already decided . . ."

"Josie will promise to follow your example," Alex said quickly. "But you must show her the way."

"Yes, yes," Horace said, nodding his head vehemently. "I will, I will!"

Josie's eyes widened. Alex winked at her. "Thank you, Father."

"Thank God," Horace exclaimed. A flush rose to cover his complexion. "And . . . and no reason to tell your mother? Not about . . . about me past. I'm going to reform."

"Of course I wouldn't tell her," Josie said, mortified.

"G-good, good," Horace said. His gaze sharpened of a sudden. "And you best be getting off Rothmier's lap. That ain't proper."

"Oh, yes." Josie sprung up. "W-we . . ."

"I was just blowing in her ear," Alex said, smiling.

"Blowing in her. . . . B'gads!" Horace cried. He lumbered over to Josie and hugged her close. "Saved you just in time, I did!"

"Yes, Father," Josie said dutifully, her face crushed to his chest.

"Rothmier," Horace said, "y-you stay away from my little girl!"

"Father!" Josie exclaimed, pushing away from him.

"I understand." Alex rose, his face serious. "But if you can find it in your heart to forgive me. I, too, have seen the errors of my ways. I intend to reform as well."

"What?" Josie gasped.

"I've turned my mistress off," Alex said solemnly, "and do not intend to take another one either."

"You have?" Horace asked. "Wasn't you with that high-flyer Cybil . . ."

"Yes," Alex said. "Josie visited her as well."

"Good God!" Horace exclaimed.

"Yes," Alex said. Both men looked at each other, and something passed between them. A look that Josie knew, just on the basis of being a woman, she would never be permitted to understand. "But we all are going to reform. And to prove it, I believe we, both the Rothmier family and the Stanton family, should take their proper place in society."

"They should?" Josie and Horace asked at the same time.

"Yes," Alex said. "I shall have Mother give a ball to that purpose. She will know all the proper people to invite."

"Hm, yes," Horace muttered. His face brightened and he winked. "In that case, you can see my little girl."

"Thank you."

Horace shook his finger. "But don't you blow in her ear."

"I won't," Alex said.

"What?" Josie said, her heart sinking. "Why should . . ."

"And no more sitting on his lap," Horace said, turning a frown upon her.

"But . . ." Josie began.

"She won't," Alex stated, with a sober expression.

"Good, good." Then Horace laughed and rubbed his hands together. "Bedamn, we're all going to reform. That's the ticket!" He chucked Josie on the chin. "You wait and see. Your father's going to be proper and respectable. And so are you! Faith, got to tell your mother." He charged toward the door. "She's been wanting this for years."

He dashed out of the room, leaving Josie staring after him in bewilderment.

Alex chuckled. "I wonder how long that will last."

Josie turned and looked at him. No more sitting on his lap, no more kissing, and he wouldn't blow in her ear either. Josie swallowed hard. She wondered how long that would last as well. Suddenly, reforming wasn't that charming of a prospect. "Why are you doing this?"

Alex grinned. "You want Mary to meet the baron, do you not?"

"Yes," Josie said, rather hesitantly.

"The baron will attend Mother's ball," Alex said. "Your family, quite reformed and respectable, will come. Mary will meet the baron with everyone's support. If you are correct in your beliefs, they will fall in love then and there. Mary will have a secure and sound future."

"I see," Josie said, slightly disconcerted.

"And if your father reforms," Alex said, "your household accounts shall benefit. No large sums will be going out for a mistress."

"But for the necklace," Josie reminded.

"A one-time expenditure," Alex said with a wave of his hand. "He also said he will quit his drinking, which is another costly expenditure."

"Y-yes," Josie said, an even odder feeling overtaking her.

Alex laughed. "Come, Josie. You have performed a great amount today. You should be in high alt."

"I-I am," Josie said weakly. Indeed, it appeared as if some of her schemes were coming to fruition. Yet she couldn't shake the unknown, confused feeling. Perhaps it was because she didn't know exactly how she had effected the success of her schemes.

Alex smiled, this time quite blandly. "And there certainly isn't any reason to consider becoming a mistress. That won't be necessary."

"No, it won't," Josie said. Perhaps it was also because she wasn't sure she was the one in control of all those schemes anymore.

"Are you enjoying yourself?" Alex whispered to Josie as the two of them sat down with both the Stanton family and the Rothmier family at one table. That in itself had been a feat. His mother had tossed both Heartsworn and handkerchiefs in the air, and taken to her bed for two days, before she had come around to promising to throw a ball within only two weeks. She had complained pathetically about what an inordinate brief time she had to prepare. Alex had prevailed. He wasn't going to give Josie any time to veer off on a new, wild money-making scheme. Nor did he depend upon the strength or length of Horace Stanton's reformation.

"Oh, yes," Josie said, her gray eyes alight with pleasure. She was gazing around at the surrounding tables and the opulent buffet line across the room. "Everything is just beautiful."

"Mother has a talent for parties," Alex said dryly. He refrained from commenting that his mother had outdone herself, merely with the hint of the notion there might be a renewed understanding between him and Josie. He shook his head. Indeed, both families, as well as the *ton* itself, recognized that understanding. The only one who didn't was Josie.

"But I feel like I am here under false pretense," Josie whispered.

"You do?" Alex asked, tensing. The words fit in too well with his train of thought.

"The purpose of all this was for Mary to meet the baron," Josie murmured, "and neither are here."

"An unfortunate circumstance," Alex said, feigning sincere regret.

"I am worried about Mary," Josie said. "It has grown of late where she suffers such terrible migraines."

"Some women do," Alex said. "I know Lady Lexing does. That is why she could not attend tonight."

"I suppose it was quite the proper thing to do for the baron to remain home with her," Josie said, her tone diffident.

"But of course." Alex laughed. "Why else would Lady Lexing suffer such a weak constitution? Her and my mother's frailties are very similar. They fall ill for their own reasons."

"It must be frightful to suffer such frail health. But Mary used to never be sick," Josie said. "Indeed, none of our family has ever suffered migraines. When I ask her if she would care for the doctor, Mary begs me not to send for him. She declares it must certainly be a passing thing."

"Josie," Alex said, smiling. "Do forget your sister for the nonce. We will bring her and the baron together later. Rather, why not enjoy yourself?"

Josie looked at him, her gray eyes wide. "I am enjoying myself. Perhaps that is why I am feeling guilty. I always forget to pay attention to what I should when I am with you." A flush covered her face. "I mean . . ."

"No. Do not dare to retract one word." Alex laughed. Josie blushed all the more. A deep satisfaction settled within Alex. She had no guile or flattery. Whatever she said, he knew he could believe her. He grinned. "And why must you always pay attention? To anyone other than me, that is."

Josie's mouth twitched. She giggled and nodded to the table. "We are talking about my family, are we not?"

Alex glanced about the table. A wry smile tipped his lips. Josie clearly scored a point. Horace Stanton was seated next to his mother, deep in conversation. So far, his mother's face had not displayed any form of shock or disapproval. However, even though it was the midnight buffet, for all intents and purposes, the evening was still young.

Louise Stanton sat beside Alex, talking to his sister, Lydia, upon the other side. An empty chair remained reserved next to Lydia. Her distinguished husband had left his seat and plate in an eagerness to meet a late-comer. No doubt it was someone who could do well for his career.

Louise was sincerely discussing fashions and frills, which had Lydia glassy-eyed. Alex nodded in approval. With Louise, there was no chance for the discussion of politics.

Michael, looking so much like his sister, sat beside Josie. He was deep in discussion with Mandy, who sat beside him. Mandy did not appear too interested in the latest horse race, but Alex could count upon Mandy to bear up underneath the strain.

"Everything seems to be well in hand," Alex said, stretching back.

"Yes." He heard Josie draw in her breath. "Perhaps we Stantons can be respectable."

"Yes." Alex grinned. "And perhaps my family can remain off their high ropes for one evening."

"Oh, no!" Josie exclaimed.

"It is not impossible." Alex laughed.

"No!" Josie pointed a shaking finger.

"Damn," Alex muttered. Of all the unforeseen and ridiculous things to happen. Lydia's husband, the Viscount Southwester, was approaching. He escorted none other than Lord Darwood. Josie started to stand. Alex clamped a firm hand upon her. "No, Josie. Just ride it through."

Unfortunately, Alex had a firm grasp upon Josie, but not upon the situation. Michael reacted far more vehemently than Josie when he spied Darwood. He jumped up, skidding his chair back. It toppled to the floor with a resounding crack. "Excuse me. Best bolt. You wouldn't know it, but that man is cracked. He keeps accosting me."

Everyone, including Darwood, looked Michael's way. Darwood's face twisted with rage. "You!"

"Oh, lord," Michael said. "Here we go again."

"I want to talk to you!" Darwood yelled, loping toward him.

"Ain't going to," Michael said. "I didn't the last time and I won't this time."

"You will!" Darwood cried. "You've hit me twice now."

"You're loose a tile," Michael exclaimed. "I never hit you once."

"Oh, dear," Josie moaned. Alex pinched her and she bit her lip.

"You did too," Darwood shouted and charged. Michael shot his arm out. His outspread hand smacked Darwood in the chest, effectively stopping him.

"What's going on!" Horace Stanton roared, jumping up.

"What are you doing?" Baron Southwester cried, arriving late to the scene. "You can't attack Lord Darwood. He's a guest here!"

"A balmy guest," Michael said, holding a windmilling Darwood at bay. "And *he's* attacking me."

"This must not happen," Beatrice Rothmier exclaimed. "Oh, dear, I think I'm going to faint."

"Michael," Louise Stanton commanded, "do let the man go. You are upsetting Lady Rothmier."

"Yes, Mother," Michael said. He promptly drew his hand away and stepped aside. Lord Darwood, who had been driving his entire body weight against that hand, sailed forward. He hit the table before him with such momentum that he jackknifed onto it.

"What do you think you're doing?" Baron Southwester said, closing in on Michael.

"Ain't doing nothing," Michael said, ignoring Lord Darwood, who floundered amongst plates and glasses. "Just ain't going to fight a lunatic."

"My God. Do you know who that is?" Baron Southwester asked.

"I do," Michael said. "A nabob who's dicked in the nob, that's who he is!"

"He is not!" Baron Southwester cried, reddening. "It is you who must be crazy."

"Damn, I'm tired of being called names. And you ain't a lunatic," Michael said. He drew his fist back and popped Southwester in the nose.

Everyone shrieked. Southwester roared. He balled his fist and attempted to hit Michael in the bread basket. Michael sidestepped adroitly. The fist meant for him plowed into the newly risen Lord Darwood, who had just turned around. Lord Darwood groaned, doubling over. The dip plastered to his forehead dripped off.

"That's it!" Michael exclaimed and jerked his arm back for a roundhouse swing. The backward motion sent his elbow cracking into Lord Darwood's face. Lord Darwood cried out, stiffened, and keeled forward.

"My God!" Baron Southwester cried. "Look what you have done!"

"Ain't done nothing!" Michael exclaimed in exasperation. "Everyone's always telling me I'm doing something I ain't."

"He's got a glass jaw," Josie said.

"What do you mean what Michael did?" Horace Stanton cried. "My son wasn't doing nothing. He's innocent. You attacked him!"

"Horace," Louise said, standing. "Remember. You are supposed to be respectable!"

"Respectable?" Horace shouted. *"I'm* being respectable. They ain't!"

"How dare you!" Baron Southwester cried. "Do you know who you are talking to?"

"Everyone's always asking that," Michael said.

"I know who I'm talking to," Horace said, trundling up to him. "Some hoity-toity Tory whose politics don't do twaddle for this country."

"Father!" Josie exclaimed. "I never knew you knew politics."

"Well, I do," Horace said. "Even sober, I know when a man's bad for the country."

"Wig!" Southwester thundered, as if casting out demons.

"Horace," Louise said in an equally dangerous tone as

her husband balled his fist. "Don't you dare hit him. Remember!"

"Blast it! Very well," Horace said. His face was turning decidedly blue, but he dutifully turned away. "Damn Tory."

"Damn Wig," Southwester retorted.

"Bedamn!" Horace stiffened. Walking over to the table, he snatched up a bowl of green beans. He turned and flung them at Southwester, very much as if he was throwing out dirty water.

"Horace!" Louise shrieked.

"I didn't hit him," Horace said, all but grinning.

"Leave," Beatrice Rothmier said in a low, shaky voice. "Now!"

"That I'll be glad to do!" Horace said. "Some fine hospitality this has been!"

"Faith!" Beatrice cried. "I am glad my son rejected your daughter. Thank God our families were never united."

"Oh, Horace," Louise moaned. "How could you?"

Horace glared at Beatrice, shook his head, and reached for the nearest glass of wine. He quaffed it. Then he sputtered. "Watered down, b'gad. Glad my daughter turned down your son! Won't unite with a family who waters down their wine! When your husband was alive he'd never have permitted it. Now he was a man!"

"Well, I never!" Beatrice said.

"That's what he often said, madame," Horace retorted.

"Oh, oh dear," Beatrice moaned. Her hand fluttered to her head. She promptly spiraled to the floor in a dead faint. Alex chuckled, despite himself. For once he had no doubt his mother's faint was for real.

Paul, holding Mary's hand, led her down a darkened path of Vauxhall garden. It had been an evening he would always remember. Mary had apparently never been to

Vauxhall gardens. Her delight in the dinner and the fire-works had been his own delight.

She wore a mask at Paul's insistence. She had said it would not matter, for she knew very few people. Paul demanded, nevertheless. Whether in truth he feared for her discovery, or merely wished to protect her from prying eyes, he would never admit, even to himself. He only knew that if anyone mistook her presence within his company, he would kill them.

"I-I have had a wonderful time. Thank you for bringing me." Mary's brown eyes sparkled like amber jewels beneath her mask.

Paul smiled. Perhaps he fought the unconquerable. Anyone who knew Mary would recognize her because of her eyes. Those beautiful, sweet eyes. And anyone just meeting her surely could not forget her because of those eyes. He forced a laugh. "Thank you for coming. I did not expect you would."

"Why?" Mary asked.

"Ah, was this not the night of the grand ball?" Paul asked.

"Yes," Mary said, her lips twitching. Then she sighed. "Josie was terribly disappointed I did not attend. Those things seem very important to her now."

Paul chuckled. "Our little Josie, becoming the respectable."

Mary smiled. "And I am becoming the opposite."

"No," Paul said, stopping. He squeezed her hand. "You shall always be the respectable, *ma cherie.*"

"Shall I?" Mary asked, her gentle voice holding a surprising tease to it. "Perhaps I am more like my family than you think. Not at all conventional."

Paul laughed, gazing down at her. *"Non.* That they are not. But you, sweet Mary, have a quality. Always shall it be the lady."

"Always?" Mary asked. Her voice was breathless. "Then

I may do this?" She stood on tiptoe and just touched her lips to his. "And still be a lady?"

"Y-yes," Paul said, both confusion and desire cording his muscles. "But you should not."

"I should not even be here," Mary said softly. "But I am."

"Yes, you are," Paul whispered. She did not move, but her eyes asked. That she had even kissed him, shook Paul. To deny her anything else he could not. He groaned and drew her into his arms. She melted into him, her body soft and fragrant, her lips warm with need and acceptance. Paul caught her to him more tightly. He loved this woman. *Mon Dieu,* how he loved her.

That very thought forced him to release her and step back. He laughed, a ragged laugh. "You are becoming a wicked lady, Mary."

She laughed. "Am I?"

He looked at her solemnly. "We cannot do that again."

A flush rose to her face, and she looked down. "I-I know."

She was so lovely, and embarrassed, Paul truly chuckled. "Ah, but there is something we can do that you have missed tonight."

Mary looked up. "What?"

"You have not danced." Paul held out his arms to her.

"I fear I do not dance very well," Mary said, her smile tremulous.

"Ah ha! You were fated to be here tonight."

"I was?" Mary asked.

"Yes. It is much better that I teach you, than for you to have gone to the ball and had some English clod attempt it. Only we French truly know how to dance."

Mary laughed and stepped into his arms. "Do teach me."

Lovers met amongst the dark paths and alcoves of Vauxhall in secret, passionate rendezvous. Paul taught Mary to dance along one of those paths, laughing beneath the star-filled sky, more in love than anyone.

Eight

Josie sat in the parlor, morosely staring into a weak fire. She knew she should bestir herself. It was already well past luncheon and she had done nothing with the day. She simply couldn't seem to collect herself, or forget the past evening.

The Stanton family was in total disgrace. Her father was closeted in the library drinking his finest brandy and forswearing his latest reform. He warned Josie she was never to see Alex again. Her mother was above stairs, still in tears. She had even refused the solace of chocolate.

The only two in the family who appeared unaffected were Michael and Mary. Guilt seared Josie, for they were the ones most affected. Poor Michael had suffered accusations and attacks due to her masquerade. Not that she had known of it until last night. This morning she had attempted to gain the courage to confess to him. However, Michael had seemed so breezy and unconcerned, the words had stuck in her throat.

Then there was poor Mary. When Josie had related the evening's tragedy, Mary had merely laughed. It rather shocked Josie that Mary had found the debacle humorous, rather than scandalous. Of course, Mary could not realize how her family's behavior had destroyed her chances of a wonderful marriage with the Baron Lexing. Josie sighed heavily, blinking back sudden tears.

"In the doldrums, fair Juliet?" Alex's voice asked.

Josie jumped. She peered around, fearing her sanity. Alex, gratefully, stood in the doorway. "Alex! What are you doing here?"

"I've come to see you, of course," Alex said, strolling into the room. "As any good Romeo would."

"But . . . but you . . ." Josie stammered.

"I know," Alex said, sitting down beside her. "I am forbidden to see you. Musgrave informed me at the door. At first we were at swords drawn, I'll admit."

Josie giggled. Musgrave flourishing a sword could only be humorous.

"But then we came to an acceptable agreement. He'd look the other way, and I would find you myself."

"I'm sorry, but Father is in a terrible rant," Josie said. She flushed. "And I'm sure your mother does not wish you to see me either."

"She knows better than to forbid me." Alex chuckled. "First they wanted our union above everything, and now they've turned into the Montagues and Capulets."

"Yes," Josie sighed. "I fear it is no use. We Stantons will never be respectable. We have disgraced ourselves."

"Not according to this morning's *Daily.*"

"What?" Josie exclaimed.

"I thought you might have missed it." Alex chuckled.

"I-I rarely read the papers."

"It is something you must start to do." Alex reached into his jacket and withdrew a sheaf of newsprint. "Now that your family is politically prominent."

"What?" Josie asked, frowning. "You know our family is nothing of the sort. We are many things, but certainly not political or prominent."

"Read," Alex said, handing the page to her. "Or rather, look."

"Oh, my!" Josie gasped as her gaze fell upon the paper. Two cartoons filled the page. The first was a caricature of Lord Darwood sprawled across a dinner table. The artist had taken liberties and stuck an apple in his mouth and sprigged his ears with parsley. Her father, rather than Michael, stood over him, with fork and knife. The caption read, "A Tory Roast!"

The next cartoon to the side showed Baron Southwester wearing a large serving bowl for a hat, with green beans dripping down his shoulders. The lower caption read, "Green beans! A Wig meal, served cold!" A vine wrapped Southwester's lower half and curved over to enwrap a quote, " 'Even sober, I know when a man is bad for the country' . . . Lord Stanton."

"Good gracious," Josie breathed. She looked at Alex in astonishment. "How did this happen?"

"Southwester and Darwood clearly have political enemies. One of which must have been present last night." Alex laughed. "Southwester is retiring to his country seat for the nonce. I wouldn't doubt if Darwood did something of the kind as well."

"Oh, dear," Josie sighed.

"No," Alex said, shaking his head. "You do not understand. Nothing could be better. What happened last night is seen in the realm of politics. Society will not condemn your family; indeed, they may very well laud it."

"But we were anything but respectable," Josie said, still confused.

"Public opinion determines respectability."

Josie flushed. "I do not think your mother will feel the same."

Alex smiled grimly. "No matter how high-in-the-instep my mother is, she is not a fool. She appeared in no better light as hostess to the farce. She will definitely put a brave face upon it."

"Perhaps." Josie looked down. "But she still w-would not wish for a connection between the families."

Alex gazed steadily at her. "Does it matter?"

"I suppose not," Josie said in a small voice. "It is not as if there is one, other than we are friends."

Alex said softly, "Josie, is that all we are?"

Josie looked at him and then looked swiftly down. She pretended to study the cartoon. "Does this mean Mary's chances with the baron aren't ruined?"

"They shouldn't be," Alex said, after a moment.

"Good," Josie said, peeking up. Alex's gaze was patient and quiet upon her. "Now we must devise a different time for them to meet. Perhaps one which is not at a social affair." She brightened. "You know, considering how shy Mary is, it would be even better if we could cause them to meet by chance."

Alex sighed. "I will see what I can arrange."

Josie sprung up. "We must tell Father about this. He is in the library drinking."

"Toppled, has he?" Alex asked wryly.

"Slightly," Josie admitted. "But once he knows about this, it should surely set him back on the right path."

"I have no doubt."

Josie, still unable to look at Alex, hurried from the parlor and across the foyer to the library. She opened the door and dashed into the room. Horace sat sprawled in his large, leather chair. He clutched a bottle to him. He was humming. It sounded like a merry ditty. Josie knew better than to try and define the words.

"Father," Josie said, rushing over to him, "you must look at this."

"Wh-what?" Horace said, raising his head. He smiled beatifically. "Hello, Josie, my girl."

"Look," Josie said again. She shoved the leaflet under Horace's nose.

"What the devil?" Horace exclaimed, his bleary eyes crossing as he attempted to read it.

"We are not in disgrace," Josie said in excitement. "Everyone thinks what you did last night was all right."

"What ho?" Horace exclaimed.

"You are a political lion," Alex said, walking into the room at a more leisurely pace.

Horace growled. "What are you doing here? You are forbidden to see my Josie."

"Father," Josie exclaimed. "Please."

"Mother is going to send around a message of apology this very day," Alex said. "I tender my deepest apologies as well."

"Y-you do?" Horace asked, his face turning a bright red. "Well, hurrumph."

"Father," Josie said. "Do you understand? Everyone is proud of you. Your reforming is making all the difference."

Horace swallowed. "I-it is?"

"Yes." Josie nodded. "And Mother will be happy."

"Sh-she will?" Horace asked.

"Indeed." Alex chuckled. "She could very well be a political hostess if she wished."

"Isn't that famous," Josie said, smiling.

"Er, yes," Horace said, appearing more like a man with the rug pulled out from underneath him than a man in high alts. Sighing, he glanced down at the bottle in his hand. He ran his one hand over it and then passed it to Josie. "Well, best go tell your mother. This is good news. Very good news."

"Isn't this fresh air lovely," Josie said in a bright tone which changed to alarm as her mount snorted and appeared to lunge forward. "My, she is frisky."

Alex, astride a huge black beast who seemed fierce but obeyed Alex far better than her own mount did, laughed. "Josie, Moonbeam is one of the most docile horses in my stables. And, Mary, how do you like Lucy? She should offer you a gentle ride."

Mary, who sat her mount in an extremely cautious manner, and whose expression was that of one sitting on a volcano, said, "Sh-she is fine, thank you."

Alex chuckled again. "I believe both you ladies should ride more."

"Yes," Josie said, forcing an exuberance. "We really should. It is a portion of our education that is lacking. That is why—why we are riding this morning."

Alex chuckled and Josie glared at him. Mary, however, never noticed the interplay. Her gaze was focused upon her horse in extreme unease. Josie sighed. It had seemed such a famous notion when Alex had told Josie he'd discovered the baron's daily schedule, and the one consistency was he rode in the park every morning. It seemed the most perfect of opportunities.

She hadn't counted upon Mary's extreme reluctance to ride early in the morning. It had taken Josie a week to convince Mary to come. Nor had she considered the fact that neither she nor Mary were equestrians. She could only hope when they met up with the baron, Mary wouldn't be so occupied with her mount as to miss her chance to charm him. Not that Mary knew the importance of the matter. Josie had decided not to tell Mary about her impending meeting with her future husband. It might very well cause her to grow shy and nervous. "Besides, the fresh air will be good for you, Mary. Perhaps it will help your migraines."

"What?" Mary asked, finally looking up. A deep flush covered her cheeks. "Oh, yes. Perhaps it will."

Josie smiled and turned her attention to the scenery of the park. A lady rider and her groom were far to their left. Josie scanned past them quickly. They were no concern of hers. Her gaze narrowed, however, when she saw a lone rider in the distance. The rider was at least male, that much she could tell. She grinned as he came closer. It was the baron. Perfect, just perfect.

Without thought, Josie let go of the reins and waved eagerly. "Hello there!"

It was the wrong move. Whether docile Moonbeam reacted to the fact that her reins were free, or that Josie was
almost bellowing, was debatable. Or not. The horse
snorted and actually kicked up her heels. The back ones,
in fact. The left of which shied into gentle Lucy's side.

Gentle Lucy neighed much louder than Josie's original
greeting. She, however, didn't kick up her heels. She dug
them in and tore off at a wild gallop. Mary shrieked and
dropped her reins. Josie could have informed Mary from
past seconds' experience that letting go of her reins was
not a wise equestrian move, but she didn't have a chance.
Docile Moonbeam performed the oddest side step, which
sent Josie sliding to one side, and not to be outdone by
gentle Lucy, dug in her hooves and galloped off in the
opposite direction.

Josie attempted to right herself, gave up, and merely
clung to Moonbeam's hairy neck. Her eyes closed in fear.
She could hear Alex shouting an instruction from behind
her. He was calling for her to grab the something or other.
Since Josie couldn't fathom what else there was to grab
but Moonbeam's neck, she simply hung on all the tighter.
She could also hear Mary's cries farther in the distance.

Josie then heard a new sound: another woman's cry and
horse's snort directly in front of her. She snapped her eyes
open. She wished she hadn't. Docile Moonbeam was
charging down directly upon a lady rider, acting more like
a battering ram than a horse. "Oh, no!"

The strange lady's horse, unidentified as to its docility
or gentleness, reared. In fact, it reared so high and hooved
the air with such dramatic flare, it might very well have
been a performer at Astley's. The lady rider obviously was
not. She flew from the horse. Josie moaned. She dearly
wished to stop and render assistance, but docile Moonbeam rudely galloped past.

Josie closed her eyes again, dreading whatever new object
docile Moonbeam might choose to attack. She never

doubted it would be a tree. However, she heard a thunder of hooves and opened her eyes to see Alex galloping beside her. He leaned over and somehow caught up the reins. It was horse magic. Docile Moonbeam, once again feeling a control on the reins, and a firm control at that, slowed immediately and came to a dead halt . . . docile once again.

"Are you all right?" Alex asked, breathing hard.

"Grab the . . . *reins!*" Josie said. At least that much she now had figured out.

Alex blinked. "I have them. Are you all right?"

"I-I will be." Josie shakily disentangled herself and slid off of Moonbeam's back, who was now enacting a statue. The horse clearly suffered identity problems. Her feet hit solid ground, and she stumbled from the sheer pleasure of it. "Yes, that is better." Then she gasped. "That poor lady!" She teetered around her horse. The lady was on the ground, but at least sitting up, her groom beside her. "Oh, dear."

Josie took off at a run, far preferring her own trustworthy feet to the untrustworthy hooves of docile Moonbeam. She was winded when she arrived. She discovered the lady was in truth just a girl. A very beautiful blonde with blue eyes. Eyes which were filled with pain at the moment. "I am so very sorry," Josie exclaimed, kneeling down. "Do forgive me. My horse . . . I lost control. I am not a very good rider."

"Neither am I, I fear. I should have been able to do something. It is not as if I didn't *see* you coming," the girl said. Her lips twitched and a giggle escaped her. "Oh, I'm sorry."

Josie blinked. Then she laughed. "I'll lay odds I looked ridiculous."

"Well . . . ," the girl said. "It is clear you love your horse."

"No," Josie said. "I hate it."

"I hate mine, too."

Both girls looked at each other and broke into fits of laughter.

"May I join the party?" Alex asked, riding up with docile Moonbeam in tow.

"Oh, Alex," Josie exclaimed. "I'm sorry."

"You are all right then, Miss . . . ?" Alex said.

"Emily, Emily Templeton."

"And I'm Josie. Josie Stanton."

Alex smiled at the two. "And I'm Rothmier. Alex Rothmier. I apologize, Miss Templeton, for embroiling you in our riding expedition."

"Oh, no, it is the most excitement I have had for weeks." A flush immediately rose to Emily's face. "I meant, I-I do not mind."

"As long as you are not hurt," Alex said.

"I am fine," Emily said. "Except for my ankle. That hurts."

"Oh, no!" Josie cried.

"Josie," Mary's voice called out.

Josie looked up and gasped. It was a sight that should have pleased her no end. Mary rode before the Baron Lexing on his horse. His arms were protectively enfolding her. Instead, fear and consternation overwhelmed her. She sprang up quickly. "Are you all right, dear?"

"Yes, but I fear I hurt my foot," Mary said.

"Good God," Alex exclaimed and laughed. The girl on the ground giggled as well.

Baron Lexing frowned. "This is no laughing matter. She could have hurt herself most grievously."

"But I did not," Mary said quickly. "This gentleman saved me."

"He is the Baron Lexing," Josie said without thought. "And I've been—"

"Gerard, I am glad you were able to save Mary from danger," Alex stated. "Things happened rather fast, I fear."

"Yes, it is clear horses cannot be trusted," Josie said. Now that her fear was subsiding, she realized she should make the best of the situation. "I suggest we all repair to

our town house. We can send for our doctor from there."
She turned to the girl on the ground. "That is, if it would
be agreeable with you, Emily."

"Oh, yes," Emily said. "I'd much rather go with you
than . . . er, yes, that would be fine."

Josie considered a moment. "I believe Alex should take
you up before him."

"I am sure that will not be necessary," Emily said, moving
to rise. She gasped, however, and fell back. "Well, perhaps."

"Permit me, Miss Templeton," Alex said, alighting from
his horse. He lifted Emily into his arms. With a grace and
strength that Josie could not help but notice, he once
again mounted his horse.

Only then did Josie realize it was her turn to mount
Moonbeam. She clenched her teeth, walking toward the
creature with determination. "I guess it is my turn."

"Jason," Emily said, "do assist Josie, please."

Josie sighed in relief as Emily's groom came and held
Moonbeam while Josie crawled onto her back. Jason offered her the reins. Josie's bravery deserted her. "You may
keep those if you like."

Jason's eyes widened. "Yes, mum."

Everyone fell silent a moment as Jason led Moonbeam
over to his own mount.

"I have just arrived in town," Emily said then. "What
are the attractions for one to see?"

Josie laughed. "There is Astley's theater if you like."

Everyone laughed, and the procession proceeded.
Emily's question, however, was successful in more ways
than one, for it permitted a steady discussion upon London and its various sights the entire way back to the town
house. Josie was certain she heard Gerard ask Mary if she
enjoyed the opera.

Josie's mind whirled with future plans when they arrived
in front of the Stanton town house. She was just about to
alight, when the front door opened and Michael stepped

out. He halted when he saw the cavalcade. "I say, how was the riding party?"

"We had some excitement, I believe," Alex said.

"Did you?" Michael asked, looking to Alex. He suddenly jerked as if he had been shot. His gaze rested upon Emily. "Hello."

"Hello," Emily replied, her tone soft and breathless.

Josie blinked, for the two then stared at each other in the most intense fashion. "Michael, this is Emily, Emily Templeton. I . . . accidentally ran her down."

"Ran her down?" Michael murmured.

"On my horse, that is," Josie said quickly.

"Ran her down!" Michael exclaimed, starting. He strode down the steps, looking more fierce than Josie had ever seen him. He halted before Emily, gazing at her as if she were the sole one present. "Are you hurt?"

"Only my ankle," Emily whispered.

"Come." Michael reached out his arms. Emily, without a word, fell into them. Michael turned and carried Emily back up the steps. "Musgrave. Fetch Dr. King, man. Be quick about it!"

"I am glad I could be of service," Alex said dryly as the rest of the deserted company stared after the two.

Josie blinked. "Do let us join them."

"Indeed." Gerard dismounted his horse and reached up. "May I be permitted to assist you, Miss Stanton?"

"Certainly." Mary slid down into his arms.

"I'll show you the way," Josie said, tumbling from Moonbeam's side in excitement. She landed hard and felt a stab in her left foot. Clenching her teeth, she determinedly limped ahead, managing to reach the steps and navigate them before Gerard. She entered the town house to discover Musgrave standing in the middle of the foyer, a look of pure confusion upon his face. "Musgrave, are you all right?"

"Yes, Miss Josie," Musgrave said. "Mr. Michael just passed by me with a lady in his arms."

"Yes," Josie said. "That is Emily. We met her while out riding. Did he tell you to fetch Dr. King?"

"Yes, Miss Josie," Musgrave's eyes widened as he viewed Mary and Gerard entering behind. "Miss Mary, not you, too?"

"Yes, Musgrave," Mary said from within Gerard's arms. "But I have only hurt my ankle."

"Where did Michael go?" Josie asked.

"He took the lady to the small salon," Musgrave said.

"He did?" Josie asked, frowning. The small salon was just that, small. Then understanding, or inspiration, struck. She spun. "My Lord Lexing, could you please follow me to the other salon; there is a sofa there as well."

Josie hid her smile of satisfaction when they reached the salon and Gerard placed Mary upon the sofa. She attempted to appear sincere when she said, "If you will excuse me, I must leave now and see about Emily."

Mary's eyes widened. "But, Josie . . ."

"Could you remain with Mary, my lord?" Josie asked Gerard. "Only until I can send someone else."

"Certainly," Gerard said, nodding his head solemnly.

"Good." Josie departed, her mind working feverishly. She found Musgrave once more. "Musgrave, who is at home?"

"I am sorry to say the entire family is out, Miss Josie."

"I'm not," Josie said, sighing in relief.

"It has worked out amazingly, has it not?" Alex asked, walking up from behind.

"Alex," Josie said, starting. She smiled. "I have just left Gerard with Mary. I told them I must see about Emily."

"That you will not." Alex chuckled. "You will be just as de trop there."

"But I couldn't leave Emily alone with Michael," Josie exclaimed.

"If you can leave Mary and Gerard alone together, you can leave Michael and Emily." Alex frowned. "I notice you are limping now as well. Where is there another salon, Musgrave? A small one, I hope?"

Musgrave snorted slightly. "I fear there is only the library sofa left, my lord."

"It will have to do," Alex said, taking up Josie's hand. "Do see the doctor makes his rounds when he arrives, Musgrave."

"Indeed, my lord," Musgrave said, grinning.

"Come," Alex said to Josie, his voice as strong as the one Michael had employed upon Emily. Josie sighed and just as willingly permitted Alex to lead her to the library.

"Are you comfortable?" Michael asked, stepping away from the sofa. He gazed down upon the lovely angel he had just placed there. His arms felt empty. He wished he could still hold her.

"Yes, I am," Emily said, looking up at him with wide, blue eyes

Michael coughed. "Frightfully sorry. About Josie running you down, that is. I don't know why she wanted to ride a horse anyways. She never has before."

"No, I understand," Emily said. She flushed. "I-I was out riding when I shouldn't have either."

"You shouldn't do that," Michael said, frowning. "It's very dangerous if you don't know what you are about. I love horses myself, but I know what I am doing."

"I am sure you do," Emily Templeton said, her eyes filled with admiration.

Michael flushed and looked desperately around. A chair was what he needed. He walked over to a chair and fell into it. Only thing was, now Emily seemed too far away from him. "Why haven't I seen you before?"

"I've only been in London for four months," Emily said.

"Four months?" Michael shook his head. "I should have seen you then. Or heard of you at least. Men must be falling all over you."

"No, no," Emily said, blushing. "I-I live with my Aunt Pennington, and . . . and she is a recluse. She doesn't like society much. Or anybody else, for that matter."

"She must like you," Michael said. "Who wouldn't?"

"No, she doesn't," Emily said. "But she doesn't dislike me either. She just doesn't care either way."

"Oh," Michael frowned.

"And my guardian is a busy man and . . . and has no time for me."

"I can't believe that," Michael said, scooting his chair slightly closer.

"He's left town as well." Emily frowned. "That is something Aunt Pennington will not explain."

"Left under a cloud, did he?" Michael asked, reasonably.

"I-I don't know," Emily said. "It is something to do with another man. He calls him his nemesis."

"Hm, I don't know what that means," Michael said. "My sisters would."

Emily sighed. "He is very eccentric, I fear."

"Every family has them," Michael sympathized. "We don't have a one in our family. But most do."

"He doesn't believe a young girl should be introduced to society early," Emily persisted.

"He don't?" Michael exclaimed. "That is odd."

"But . . . but how will I ever learn anything if . . . if I never go anywhere, or . . . or see anyone?" Emily asked.

"True." Michael nodded. He just had to walk his chair a little closer. "Look what happens. You was out riding when you shouldn't have. It was dangerous because you didn't know how."

"Yes," Emily said, looking down.

"You can't do that again," Michael said sternly. "You want to go riding, I'll take you riding. I will teach you. But I don't want you to go without me. I won't have anyone run you down again. Not even Josie."

"All right," Emily said, very simply.

Michael broke into a wide grin, holding out his hand. "It's a deal then."

"A deal." Emily put her hand in his. She flushed and looked down. "I've been here four months and I still haven't seen London."

"Can't have that." Michael clasped her hand more tightly. It was so tiny in his. "You must know London. If you don't, you will get lost all the time. That is dangerous."

"Not if you are with me."

"That's right," Michael said. "I know all the rigs. I've been on the town all my life. I'll steer you clear."

"Then my guardian cannot worry," Emily said, smiling. "He thinks just because I am an heiress, I am in danger."

"An heiress!" Michael exclaimed. He dropped her hand quickly.

"Y-you don't like that?" Emily asked, her eyes showing fear.

"Er," Michael gurgled, rising. "Don't know. I never met one before."

"I'm not a very large heiress," Emily said quickly. "Not really. I'm—I'm only a medium heiress."

"Still," Michael said. "Y-you shouldn't meet me. I'm . . . well, I'm all to pieces."

"I-I don't care," Emily said. Her lip began to tremble.

"But you are supposed to," Michael said.

"Why?" Emily asked. A tear formed in her eye. "If I like you when you don't have money, I don't see why you shouldn't like me when I do have money." The tear trick-led down. "I think that is . . . is frightfully mean."

"Don't cry!" Michael exclaimed, rushing over to her. "Don't. I didn't mean to be mean."

"I-I suppose you won't take me riding," Emily said. "And I'll be in danger all the time."

"No!" Unable to speak from the emotions overcoming him, Michael grabbed hold of Emily and kissed her, kissed her with the fervor of what he could not explain. He pulled back, glaring at Emily. "You won't go riding without me. I won't have you in danger."

Emily leaned toward him. "And you like me even if . . . if I am an heiress."

"Yes," Michael groaned. Her lips were far too close and he kissed her again. This time she melted into him, making a sound like a kitten purring. Michael tore himself away and sprung up. "But . . . but we can't do any more of that. Said I'd steer you clear. You . . . we . . . can't be doing that. Not until we get to know each other better. Well, truth. We ain't supposed to do that until we're engaged or something."

Emily smiled. "But we will get to know each other better, won't we?"

Michael gave up. He smiled inanely back. "Bound to. I've got a lot to show you. Got to teach you, after all."

"Are you comfortable, Miss Stanton?" Gerard asked, standing stiffly.

"Yes, indeed," Mary said. A lovely flush rose to her face, and she looked down.

He coughed. "I . . . the circumstances are peculiar, I own. But I would not feel right in leaving you here unattended."

"No," Mary said. "I thank you. And I must thank you again for saving me."

Gerard stared at Mary. Her eyes were of the gentlest

brown. Her modesty, even under such taxing duress, was everything proper. "You have been very brave."

"Oh, no," Mary said, smiling. "You were brave, considering how my horse galloped down upon you. If you hadn't caught it, I shudder to think what would have happened. I-I only wish I could have maintained my seat. But—but I am not a proficient rider." She laughed. "I warned Josie, but she was determined we go riding this morning."

Gerard shook his head. "You . . . you are nothing like your sister."

"No," Mary said, looking down. "Josie is fearless."

"I suppose you could say that." In truth, Gerard thought Josie brash and forward. "Yet there is nothing wrong with a woman who is not so. The feminine persuasion was not meant to be forced to face the dangerous things in life. We men are meant to protect them from such."

Mary's eyes widened. It appeared she wished to speak. Then she lowered her lashes. "Perhaps. But riding is not generally considered a danger of life."

"It is still a strenuous exercise," Gerard said seriously.

They fell silent a moment. Mary smiled weakly. "I-I suppose Josie is detained. I do hope Miss Templeton is all right."

"I am sure she is," Gerard said. "Please, do not concern yourself."

"The rest of the family must be out," Mary said. "Now that I think of it, Mother was going shopping this morning."

Gerard stiffened. He was rather grateful not to meet the rest of her family. He had heard of the debacle at Lady Rothmier's. Evidently they were as brash as Josie. It amazed him Mary was so different. She was the jewel, glimmering in a family of quartz. "I fear I have not had the opportunity to meet the rest of your family. I was to meet them at Lady Rothmier's ball, but was unable to attend."

"I was unable to as well," Mary said. She laughed.

"Though I heard about it. I must say I am glad I was not present." An odd, sweet smile curved her lips. "I fear our family and food are a dangerous combination."

A warmth welled within Gerard. How nobly she protected her family, and how painful it must be for her. "It is fortunate you did not attend."

Mary looked down. "I . . . I had the migraine that night, I fear."

"Just like my mother." Gerard nodded. "She suffers them as well."

"Does she?" Mary asked. A look of relief crossed her face. "Do tell me about her."

"She is a very brave woman, as you are," Gerard said, finally taking up a seat, discreetly across the room. "She suffers much, but always attempts to overcome it."

"Indeed?" Mary asked.

"Indeed." Gerard nodded. He did his best to take Mary's mind off her pain, regaling her with the best stories he could think of about his mother. The time passed swiftly, and he was surprised when Musgrave entered with a bluff man, who was the doctor.

He rose and bowed. "I shall leave you. Would it be permissible for me to call upon you again? T-to make sure you are well?"

"Yes," Mary said. "Though I am sure it is nothing. The pain has receded already."

She was such a brave woman. "I shall call, then."

"Certainly," Mary said, flushing. "And . . . and thank you for saving me."

Gerard nodded solemnly and took his leave. Mary's gentle brown eyes remained in front of him. He had saved her today. His heart pounded. Perhaps he would be permitted to save her in a far more important way. He had found the woman of his dreams.

* * *

"Now sit down and put your foot up upon the sofa," Alex ordered in a stern voice.

"Yes, Alex," Josie said, obeying him.

He smiled. "Since this is your father's library, I don't doubt there must be liquor somewhere present."

"Yes." Josie pointed to a cabinet on the far side of the wall. "Over there."

"Ah," Alex said and crossed over to open it up. "Yes, brandy." Josie's eyes widened as he proceeded to set two tumblers out and pour from the decanter.

Alex carried the glasses over to her, holding one out. "Here."

"I don't need a drink," Josie said, blinking.

"Well, I do," Alex said, shoving the one glass into her hand, and then sipping from his own.

"Why?" Josie asked, frowning.

"I'm not sure," Alex said wryly. "Either it is from the fact that both you and Mary could have been seriously hurt this morning, or from the stunning thought that this scheme of yours may very well work."

"Do you think so?" Josie asked, clutching her glass.

"I do," Alex said. "When a man saves a woman it always affects him. It has something to do with our protective instinct. Or perhaps it is the danger itself."

"Oh," Josie said consideringly. "Then this really worked."

"Yes," Alex said, laughing. "Take a sip. It can be considered medicinal."

"I don't think I'm truly hurt," Josie said, determined to be honest.

"Then make it a toast." Alex grinned. "You may have succeeded in bringing Mary and Gerard together."

"I will drink to that," Josie said, returning the grin. She lifted her glass and sipped from it. "My."

"Yes, my." Alex chuckled. "You may have succeeded

more than expected. I would say Michael was very attracted to Miss Templeton.''

"He *was* acting oddly.'' Josie frowned.

"That happens to men sometimes,'' Alex said, taking another sip.

"But we do not know anything about Emily,'' Josie said, worried.

"You can't control everything, Josie,'' Alex leaned over and deliberately set his glass down upon the table. He returned to stand over Josie with a direct look. "Which ankle did you hurt?''

"The left one.''

"Very well.'' He moved to her feet. Lifting them up, he sat down and rested them upon his lap.

"Alex!'' Josie exclaimed, completely shocked.

"I only wish to examine your ankle. The doctor is going to be one busy man when he arrives.'' Alex very discreetly shifted the hem of her dress and slid her left slipper off. Josie started as he put his hand upon her foot. "Does this hurt?''

It did anything but hurt. "N-no.''

"Good,'' Alex said. He began to rub her stockinged foot. Josie flushed deeply. "Alex?''

"Yes?'' Alex asked, grinning.

"This . . . this cannot be proper,'' Josie stammered.

"No,'' Alex said. "But then, Josie, you are anything but proper, and neither am I.''

"But . . . but,'' Josie sighed. "We are supposed to be reforming.''

"We are,'' Alex said. He laughed. "It stuns me how much I am reforming. But we must take it slowly, as not to, er, traumatize ourselves.''

Josie, in truth, felt slightly traumatized. Just from the pleasure. Then a frightened thought crossed her mind and she sat up. "Alex?''

"Yes?''

"This . . . this isn't . . . ?" She halted.

"Isn't what?" Alex asked.

Josie flushed. "Something a . . . a mistress does?"

"No," Alex said. "You may relax."

"Thank heaven," Josie sighed, leaning back.

The oddest smile tipped Alex's lips. "This is something married people do."

"Truly?" Josie asked. An envious, yearning pang shot through her.

"It is."

"I see," Josie said, slightly woebegone.

Alex silently set her left foot down and slipped the right slipper off. "If Mary, miracle of miracles, weds Gerard, will you be satisfied?"

"What do you mean?" Josie asked, attempting to ignore the tingles as Alex began massaging her foot.

"Your father is reforming, and has cut his 'expenses,' " Alex said. "And if Mary weds the baron, she will be settled. Do you think you might be able to accept that your family is well on its way to a secure future."

Josie bit her lip. "Perhaps."

"Then it would be time for you to consider your own future," Alex said. "Would it not?"

Josie's heart pounded. "Yes."

"And marriage?" Alex asked softly. "Your marriage?"

Josie's breath caught in her throat. He was so very close to her secret dream. She could only nod her head, hoping the rest of her dream did not show in her eyes too much.

The door opened at that moment. Musgrave and Dr. King entered.

Musgrave stiffened. "Forgive me."

"It is all right," Alex said, smiling and not batting an eye. "I was only examining Josie's foot to see if I could determine its injury."

"Dr. King," Josie said, flushing. She quickly sat up and shifted her legs from Alex's lap. "H-how is Mary?"

"Her left ankle is sprained," Dr. King said, entering and leveling an accusing stare upon Alex. "Nothing more."

"And . . . and how is Emily?" Josie continued, turning a bright red.

"You mean the pretty blonde with your brother?" Dr. King asked with a huff.

"Yes." Josie nodded.

"She'll be fine," Dr. King said. "Her ankle is sprained, too. The right one," he added in a professional tone. He stood before Josie and raised a brow as he looked at Alex. "May I?"

"You are the doctor," Alex said. "I was only trying to help."

"I can see that," Dr. King said, bending down. He quickly ran his hands over Josie's ankles. It didn't feel anything like when Alex had done so. He straightened. "Hmph. Just what I expected."

"What is it?" Josie asked.

"Neither of your ankles are hurt," Dr. King said.

"Miracle of miracles," Alex said, shaking his head. "She has been saved."

"That remains to be seen," Dr. King said, casting him a stern eye. He turned and walked toward the door, outrage in every step. He halted beside Musgrave. "You called me out for this? You don't need a doctor, man, just a bloody chaperone."

Musgrave coughed, but presented a serious face. "Yes, sir."

"I'll send my bill," Dr. King growled and stormed from the room. Musgrave, a twinkle in his eye, turned and dutifully followed the good doctor.

"I fear you have lost your physician, Josie," Alex said. He laughed and placed an arm about her shoulders. "That leaves you to my care, does it not?"

Josie flushed. She knew she should object, but could not find it in herself to do so. She never had liked Dr. King.

Nine

Mary entered the town house, packages of lace beneath her arm. She halted. Miss Tellington, Josie and Rachel were all crowded at the library door. Rachel employed her official position, kneeling and peeking through the keyhole. Josie and Pansy stood above, ears pressed to the wood. A dreadful premonition filled Mary.

"What is happening?" she whispered as she crossed the foyer floor.

"Mary!" Josie exclaimed. She turned, her eyes brilliant. She waved vehemently. "Gerard has finally come!"

"For what?" Mary asked, slowing.

"He is asking Father's permission to propose to you," Josie said, holding out her hand.

"He is?" Mary asked, grasping Josie's hand tightly. "I-I do not believe it."

"He is." Rachel giggled. "You should see him. He's poker stiff."

"And you should hear him," Pansy added. "It has taken him all of twenty minutes to come to the point. He's said 'highest regard' at least five times."

"And 'deep respect' ten," Josie said, nodding her head.

"But . . . but how can he pr-ropose?" Mary asked, stunned. "We've only just met."

"It's been three weeks," Josie said with a grin, ". . . and two days to be exact."

"Has it?"Mary asked, blinking.

Josie laughed. "I think you bowled him over the very first day."

"He's in l-o-o-v-e," Rachel drawled out, making a face. "Yech!"

Mary bit her lip. She wouldn't have said it in the same manner, but with her heart wrenching as it did, she could enter fully into the sentiment. The wrong man was in the library asking for her hand.

"I just knew he'd be smitten with you," Josie said. "That is why . . ."

"Why what?" Mary asked.

Josie flushed. "I guess I can tell you now. I set up the riding expedition knowing he would be there. I-I had made sure to find you just the right man."

Mary bit back a groan. "You did?"

"Yes," Josie said. "He's everything respectable. He'll be a perfect husband."

"And he doesn't have wooden teeth," Pansy exclaimed.

"And he has a chin," Josie said, nodding her head in satisfaction.

"And he has money!" Rachel said. "Not as much as Alex, but he has money."

Mary's heart sank. "Yes."

"Oh, no," Rachel exclaimed. "Father is walking toward him."

"Is he castaway?" Mary asked hopefully.

"Sober as a judge. He's shaking Gerard's hand now, oh . . . oh . . . ," Rachel said, tumbling back. "They are coming!"

"Everyone to the salon," Josie whispered. The ladies rushed across the foyer and dashed into the salon. Rachel giggled as each took up her seat. Mary tried to appear unaware as Horace Stanton entered the room.

"Good, good," Horace said, nodding. "Fortunate you are all here. I have some excellent news!" He walked over to Mary and took up her hand. A sheen of sweat dappled his brow. "The Baron Lexing has asked for your hand in marriage, Mary."

"He has?" Mary attempted surprise.

He patted her hand. "You've saved us, my dear."

"I am pl-pleased," Mary stammered.

"This is wonderful!" Josie exclaimed. "Oh, Mary. It is a dream come true."

Horace shook his head. "And here I'd thought of Canton for you."

"You remember?" Mary gasped. She flushed. "I-I mean, you did?"

"Yes, rather silly, ain't it?" He laughed. "Now that you've got such a fine young man as the baron asking for your hand. It's like a . . . a miracle."

"Y-yes," Mary said, a numbness chilling her.

"It was simply meant to be," Josie said, beaming with obvious love and pride. She looked at Horace. "D-did you talk of settlements?"

"No, no. The baron is sending his solicitor round." Horace flushed. "Er, thought that best. Truth, your young man will keep me on my toes. Very respectable fellow. But we are becoming respectable now, ain't we?"

"Yes," Mary lied. She could not say her heart was set upon a gamester.

"He's coming to propose to you at nine o'clock tomorrow," Horace said. He coughed. "You—you ain't going to surprise us like little Josie did, are you?" Something flashed in Horace's eyes. It shimmered like hope, but surely must be fear.

"N-no, Father," Mary whispered.

"Good, good," Horace said. "Well, best find Louise. She'll be happy, I'm sure. Blast, forgot. She's out at a charity meeting. Raising funds for savages or something."

"What ho," Michael's voice said. Everyone turned. "Here you all are."

"Michael," Josie cried, standing. "Gerard has asked Father for Mary's hand! Isn't that famous!"

"B'gad, already?" Michael exclaimed.

"Yes, it is shocking . . . I mean, surprising, isn't it?" Mary said.

"No, it isn't," Josie said, her tone stout. "It's been three weeks and two days. And he's courted Mary assiduously."

Mary stared at Josie. Surely she exaggerated. It was true, Gerard called upon her daily, but that was in concern for her health. He had taken her riding mishap more deeply to heart than she. They had gone to the theater and opera together, but he was an aficionado of the arts and held a season box. He had also introduced her to his mother, but that was because . . . Mary gasped. That was because Gerard *had* been courting her! She simply hadn't realized it.

"Er . . . suppose he has," Michael said, his face showing the same astonishment that Mary felt. He grinned at her. "Well, makes no difference. Shows he's got a brain in his bone box. Knows to snatch you up before anyone else does."

"Thank you, "Mary said, looking down.

"I'd say this calls for a celebration," Michael said, rubbing his hands together.

"Michael, you aren't . . . ?" Josie stopped. She flushed. "You will not celebrate overly much, will you?"

"By Zeus, see if I don't." Michael grinned. "I was planning to take Emily to that museum she waited to see, but I think I'll take her for ices, what? I told her she didn't want to go look at things from dead people, mighty morbid is what I say. She'll like ices better."

"Yes." Josie laughed. "Don't draw the bustle too much."

Michael winked "Can't. You get a bellyache if you eat too many of those ices."

"Ices?" Horace Stanton frowned. "No, by Jove. We must have a better celebration." He looked to Mary, reddening. "Take my daughter out when she's still my daughter."

"I'll always b-be your daughter," Mary said, choking.

Horace coughed and blinked. "Glad to hear it. But you'll be a baroness soon and will have many responsibilities. Move in those higher circles and all."

"I'll always be your daughter," Mary repeated numbly.

"Of course she will," Josie said, confusion on her face. "And I think it will be wonderful to celebrate tonight. What shall we do?"

"Anything our little Mary wants!" Horace stated.

Mary bit her lip. What she wanted was to run, to escape. She wanted Paul. Her heart caught suddenly. "I—I would like for us to go to Vauxhall tonight. Would . . . could we do that?"

"Excellent!" Horace exclaimed.

"Oh, yes," Josie said, her eyes bright. "Alex and I were attending a musical tonight. I must tell him of the change of plans."

"By Jupiter," Michael said. "Wait until Emily hears she's going to Vauxhall! Best go tell her now. She'll need to think what she's to wear. She sets store in those things. Has to tell her aunt, too."

"I'll be about making the arrangements," Horace said, beaming. "By God, this will be a party. Have some fun, we will!"

Mary sat quietly as her family hastened away to do their errands. When they were all gone she rose slowly, trembling. She had a message to send as well.

"A toast to Mary and her future as a baroness," Horace said, standing up. He lifted a glass of champagne.

"Yes," Josie said, in a glow of pride and excitement.

"Indeed," Alex added, his eyes brilliant upon Josie's.

"Horace," Louise stated in a different tone.

Horace, who was just then about to drink his champagne, coughed. "Er, will only have a sip, of course."

A large boom rent the air.

"Oh!" Emily squeaked, almost jumping into Michael's lap.

Michael grinned, placing a protective arm about her. "The fireworks are beginning."

"Fireworks?" Emily asked, her eyes wide.

"Wait till you see them." Michael laughed. "They are something to like. But best hurry!"

"Yes," Mary said. She rose so swiftly, she knocked over her glass of champagne.

"Mary!" Josie exclaimed. "Are you all right?"

"Yes," Mary assured, snatching up a napkin and blotting at the tablecloth. "Only, w-we do not wish to miss the fireworks, do we?"

"But what about the toast?" Horace asked, his glass still raised, a look of disappointment on his face.

"Horace," Louise scolded, "do let the children go on to the fireworks."

"Yes, yes," Horace said, clutching his glass. "You children run along. I'll just have my one sip."

Alex winked at Josie as everyone rose, and she giggled. The throng departed, Michael expounding to Emily about the munificence of the fireworks. Emily's eyes were growing wider by the moment. Josie turned to whisper to Mary about the change in Michael, only to discover Mary walking away from them.

"Mary," Josie called. "Where are you going?"

Mary stopped and turned. "I—I, er, I thought we might go through the gardens to the fireworks."

"We don't have time for that," Michael said, frowning.

"Gardens?" Emily asked.

"Yes," Mary said. "They are very lovely. Especially tonight, I-I would think."

"Can we?" Emily asked, almost hopping in excitement.

"But the fireworks," Michael objected.

"I'd like to see them both," Emily said.

"Guess we have time," Michael stated.

"Certainly we do," Alex said. Josie peeked at him. His gaze was so full of devilment, she chuckled.

The group as a whole turned to follow Mary. Rather than looking pleased, Mary looked disappointed. Josie frowned a moment. Then understanding dawned. She remembered the night before she received Alex's proposal. It had been nerve-wracking. Mary must be suffering the same jitters. Of course, Mary was not facing the pain of knowing she must reject Gerard's offer. She could accept the man of her dreams without guilt or a moment's hesitation. A silent sigh escaped Josie. How wonderful it would have been to accept Alex's proposal like that. She started then, flushing. That was a dangerous line of thought.

Forcing a smile, Josie directed her attention back to reality. She discovered Michael, Emily and Mary had progressed much farther along the path than she had expected while she'd wool-gathered. Only Alex remained beside her, matching her slow pace. She glanced at him, surprised and embarrassed. He lifted his finger to his lips. Confused, she focused upon the conversation drifting back to them.

"Now, you can only go through these gardens with me," Michael was saying to Emily.

"Truly?" Emily asked.

"Vauxhall's a dandy place," Michael said. "But all sorts come here. And they don't always . . . er, behave as they ought."

"They don't?" Emily asked.

"No," Michael said. "Too many dark paths, you see. Too many places to hide."

"Hide?" Emily asked, wide-eyed. "Why would they want to hide?"

"I don't know," Michael said, his tone strained. "Something about all the trees and bushes is what I think."

Alex took hold of Josie's arm, and suddenly dragged her

to the left. Josie muffled an exclamation as they stumbled into an alcove.

"Alex," Josie said, "what are you doing?"

"It has something to do with all the trees and bushes, I think," Alex said, his face devilish. He laughed. "I didn't know your brother was so knowledgeable."

A heat flushed through Josie. "He . . . he is very protective of Emily, isn't he?"

"Yes," Alex said in a solemn voice. "And she listens to him. Far better than a certain lady I know listens to me."

"I-I haven't done anything lately you would dislike," Josie said.

"No, you haven't." Alex clasped her hand and drew her over to a bench, which was conveniently placed in the alcove. It wasn't Michael, apparently, who was knowledgeable. Alex sat down, and Josie prepared to settle next to him.

"No," Alex said. He pulled her onto his lap instead.

"Alex!" Josie exclaimed.

"Be quiet," Alex said. "Why don't you listen to me like Emily listens to Michael?"

"I-I do," Josie said. "Well, sometimes I do. But—but this isn't proper."

"I know." Alex laughed. "But now your plan is accomplished, I believe we have earned the right to relax our respectability, just for the moment, of course."

A laugh escaped Josie. It felt wonderful to be held in Alex's arms again. "It is wonderful isn't it . . . I mean, Mary wedding Gerard?"

"Yes." Alex chuckled. "One Stanton marriage has been successfully arranged. But what of the next one?"

Josie started slightly. She looked away. "You mean Michael?"

"We can talk about him for a moment, if you wish. I would say he and Emily will make a perfect couple as well."

"Yes," Josie sighed. "But I wish we knew more about Emily and her situation."

"Her situation?" Alex frowned.

"She is an heiress, you know."

Alex frowned. "Josie, you must desist in being a snob."

"Snob?" Josie asked, stunned. "I am not a snob."

"Yes, you are," Alex said. "You hold it against anyone who has a fortune."

"I do not," Josie said, flushing. "I-I only worry about Emily's family and if they will accept Michael. All we know about is her aunt, who is a recluse . . ."

Alex leaned forward and gently blew in her ear.

"A-and who never cares what Emily does, as . . . as long as she need not exert herself."

"She will accept your family all the faster," Alex whispered, nuzzling her ear.

Josie shivered. "Yes, but what about her, ahm . . ."

"Her what?" Alex murmured.

"Her?" Josie blinked. "I don't know."

"We've talked enough about Michael," Alex said, grinning. He leaned over and placed his lips upon hers. Josie groaned and immediately wrapped her arms about his shoulders. She kissed him back with all her might.

Alex drew back, chuckling. "Very well. Now it is time to be proper."

"Now?" Josie blinked.

Alex lifted her off his lap, forcing her to stand. "Yes. I only wished to give you another incentive, when I see you tomorrow."

"You are going to see me tomorrow?" Josie asked, bemused.

"I am." Alex nodded. "And I promise to be very proper. I believe if Gerard is permitted to make a proposal, I should be able to do so as well."

Josie's heart caught. "Proposal?"

"Yes," Alex said, grinning. "Remember. I said proper. I will not be asking you to become my mistress."

"Oh," Josie breathed. She was afraid to say anything else.

Alex laughed. "I hope for a more formal response than that, Josie. But that is for tomorrow. We must be proper. Must we not?"

He took Josie by the hand and led her from the alcove. Josie's heart felt like bursting. Only moments before she had been dreaming of being able to accept Alex's proposal without guilt or a moment's hesitation. Her dream was about to come true.

"But as long as you are with me," Michael said, "you won't have to fear."

"I won't," Emily said. She giggled.

Michael looked down at her. "What is funny about that?"

"We are alone," Emily said.

Michael looked about, startled. Mary, Josie and Alex were noticeably absent. Or now they were. "Where'd they go?"

"I don't know," Emily said, her brow wrinkling. "I just looked back and they were gone."

"I'll be hanged."

"Maybe they are hiding."

"Not all three of them together," Michael said. He flushed. "I mean Alex might take Josie off. He's a bit of a rake. But not with Mary. He ain't that much of a rake. And Mary's soon to be engaged."

"It . . . it is surprising, isn't it?" Emily said, a slight flush to her cheeks.

"No, it ain't," Michael said. "They just fell behind. That's all. It's easy on these paths. I was just telling you that."

"No," Emily said. "I was talking about the baron proposing to Mary. They've only known each other as long as we have known each other."

"B'gad, you are right," Michael said, blinking. "We met on the same day."

"Yes," Emily said, studying the ground. "Three weeks and two days."

"True," Michael said, his voice cracking. "True."

"Th-that is a very short time," Emily said, the sweetest flush painting her cheeks, "for a man t-to decide he l-loves a girl."

Michael gazed at Emily. His heart flooded with an uncontrollable warmth. "No, it isn't."

"It isn't?" Emily asked, her blue eyes rising in wonderment.

"No, it isn't," Michael said. It must have been all those trees and bushes. Or maybe it was the moonlight shining down upon her golden hair, creating a halo. Or perhaps it was what had been growing and building in his heart from the very beginning. "I fell in love with you the moment I saw you."

"So did I," Emily said, sighing.

Michael blinked. "What did you say?"

Emily looked down. "I-I fell in love with you, too. The very moment I saw you."

"By Jove!" Michael shouted with happiness. "You didn't?"

Emily nodded and laughed. "I did."

"You did?" Michael exclaimed. Bursting with joy, he picked Emily up and swung her around. "You love me."

"I do," Emily giggled.

"You love me!" Michael said again. He gave her a smacking kiss. Then he blinked and she blinked. Slowly he set her down, but could not release her. He bent and kissed her again, long and tenderly. Emily sighed and wrapped her arms about him.

Shaken to the core, Michael drew back. He flushed. "Sorry. Got over . . . er, excited there. I shouldn't have done that."

"But I want you to," Emily said.

Michael frowned. "I told you, we can't do that sort of thing unless we are going to be married or something. It ain't proper."

Emily looked down. "You mean like the baron and Mary?"

"Exactly," Michael said sternly. "That is, after he proposes and she accepts."

Emily cuddled up to him. "And then they can do this?"

"Y-yes," Michael said, his nerves stretched.

"After he proposes?" Emily asked, her head against his shoulder.

"Y-yes," Michael stammered. "And she accepts."

"I would," Emily said. Her voice was a muffled whisper.

"You would?" Michael asked. He frowned. She would accept the baron? Michael's heart exploded. Never. He'd never allow her to accept the baron, or anyone else. She loved him. "No, you ain't going to marry anyone but me!"

Emily lifted her head. In fact, she lifted it so swiftly, it clipped Michael on the chin. "But that is what I meant."

"What?" Michael asked. His jaw stung. "I thought you said . . ." He halted in confusion. Yet love can help a person to make gigantic leaps. "You mean you will marry me?"

"Yes," Emily said, nodding. "I will marry you!"

"You will?" Michael asked.

"Yes," Emily said. "Yes."

"But . . ." Michael asked. "Are you sure?"

"I am." Fright entered Emily's eyes. "But are you?"

"Yes," Michael said, then frowned. "But who do I ask?"

Emily blinked. "Why, you ask me. Or asked me."

"No," Michael said, shaking his head. "I have to ask

permission from somebody in your family. That would be your guardian, I guess."

"He's not in town," Emily said. She smiled happily. "But you can ask my aunt."

Michael gulped. "Will she see me?"

Emily giggled. "I'll make her see you."

Michael grinned. "I love you. You are going to marry me."

"I am going to marry you." Emily nodded with eagerness. She reached up and drew his head down. They kissed each other and then stood clinging to each other.

"When can I see her?" Michael asked desperately.

"She is always home," Emily said. "Tomorrow should be a good time."

"Yes," Michael said, squeezing his intended one more time, before setting her from him. He coughed. "I guess we ought to see the fireworks now."

"Must we?" Emily asked.

Michael grinned. "We should. When we are engaged, we'll come back."

Emily giggled and slipped her hand into his. "Good. I like this."

"So do I," Michael said. He'd never been in the petticoat line before, but with Emily, he thought of things he never had in the past.

Mary walked behind Emily and Michael, her mind in turmoil. She must somehow break away. She cast a nervous glance back. Her eyes widened. Josie and Alex were no longer behind them. She looked back to Emily and Michael. Michael was still expounding upon the lack of decorum in the gardens of Vauxhall. Mary would have found it humorous if her heart wasn't thumping so loudly.

She slipped quietly into a shadow and waited. Then she hastened through the gardens. Pray God, Paul was there.

When she came to the place she remembered so well, her soul sighed. Paul sat upon the stone bench.

He smiled the smile that had taken Mary's heart. "Hello, sweet secret. I was charmed to receive your message." Then he frowned, his eyes darkening. "What is it? What is the matter?"

Mary drew in her breath, walking over to sit down beside him. She wanted to lean into him, to hold him close. Rather, she clasped her hands tightly in her lap. "The baron has . . . asked for my hand in marriage."

Paul stiffened. "I see."

"H-he talked to Father this afternoon," Mary said, her mouth drying up. "I-I am to receive him tomorrow."

Paul remained silent. Mary gazed at him, her heart in her eyes. He smiled, a twisted smile. "Then this is the last of our secret."

"No," Mary said. "I-I do not want that."

Paul stiffened. He shook his head. "I suppose I deserved that. But I have been honorable with you. Do not ask me to see you after you are engaged. I could not."

"I am not engaged yet. I-I do not want to marry the baron," Mary said lowly. She trembled. "I want to marry you."

"You do," Paul said. His voice was not surprised. Rather it was odd, almost tired.

"Yes." Mary nodded. She attempted a smile. "I love you."

"No!" Paul exclaimed. He sprung up and strode away from her. "No, do not say that. Do not speak."

"You do not love me?" Mary asked. Paul spun, his gaze fierce. In that fierceness, Mary saw her answer. "You do love me!"

"Yes! No!"

He was so different from his normal, suave self, Mary laughed.

"It does not matter," Paul said.

The laughter died. Pain knifed through Mary. "It does not matter?"

"We cannot marry."

"Why not?" Mary asked.

"What kind of life could I offer you?" Paul asked, his voice stern.

Mary blinked. "I do not care what kind of life you can offer me. I want to be with you."

"No," Paul said, his hand slashing through the air. "You, sweet Mary, can never be a madame of a gaming hell."

"But . . ." Mary shook her head numbly.

"I cannot do that to you," Paul said, rushing over to her. He knelt before her and clasped her hands. How odd, Mary thought. It was the position a man took when he proposed. Paul was not proposing. "You, sweet Mary, are too fine. You deserve better. A respectable man. A respectable life."

"No." Mary tore her hands from his, anger flaring within her. "Everyone says that. But I am not respectable. I am as much of a Stanton as my sister, or my brother or my father. I do not want to marry the baron. I do not want that life." Tears welled in her eyes. "You taught me that."

"I know," Paul said. His laugh was bitter. "But I was wrong."

"You were not wrong."

"I was." Paul's eyes darkened. "For me, I have chosen this life. It is what I want. But . . . but now, I cannot see you living this life. I cannot permit it. You deserve better. Wed the baron. He will give you what I cannot."

"I see," Mary said, her lip trembling. "Y-you say you love me, but tell me to marry another man."

"Yes, because I do love you," Paul said, his voice hoarse. He stood. "I-I have been fooling myself. And you. I would never permit a wife of mine in a gaming hell."

Mary rose, her heart breaking. "Y-you cannot love me."

He looked away. "I wish I did not, *cherie*."

Mary saw her one chance. "Then kiss me goodbye."

Paul's gaze returned to her, tormented. He stepped back. "No."

"You . . . started our secret with a kiss," Mary said softly. "Will you not end it with one?"

"No." Paul shook his head vehemently. "I will not."

"Very well," Mary said, fighting back the tears. He would not permit her a life in a gambling hell. Mary choked. It did not matter. She had gambled everything that was important tonight. "I fold."

She silently left Paul, her secret and her life. She walked down a path she had once danced upon, and never would again.

Ten

Josie sat in the library with the rest of her family. Except for Mary, of course, who was closeted with Gerard. Pansy forcibly held an excited Rachel in her seat upon the settee. Horace sat in his large leather chair, rolling and unrolling a newspaper. Michael alternately stood and then paced before the fireplace. Louise sat beside Josie. She was setting stitches to a sampler which espoused cleanliness and godliness. It was for one of her newly acquired philanthropic societies and was destined for those poor savages in India or Africa. Louise had never been a seamstress, and godliness read more like dogliness, but Josie gave her mother credit for the effort.

"How long do you think it will take?" Rachel asked, squirming.

"We don't know," Pansy said.

"Will it take as long as it took Josie and Alex, do you think?" Rachel asked.

"Lord, I hope not," Horace muttered. He cast Josie a sheepish look. "Sorry, me dear."

"That is all right," Josie said. Only now could she understand how her family had felt waiting for Alex and her that first time. She smiled. This outcome was sure to be better. And this afternoon, perhaps, she could make amends for the torments she had put her family through the first time she had rejected Alex. She held that marvelous secret close to her heart. She would not steal any of Mary's excitement away. She sighed in bliss. Life for the Stantons had turned around wondrously.

"I think you should let me go see about them," Rachel said.

"No!" Pansy exclaimed. She coughed. "No."

"Course not," Horace said. "Ain't no time to interrupt them."

"I wasn't going to interrupt them. I was just going to—" Rachel received Pansy's elbow in her side. "Never mind." She leaned forward. "Do you think they are kissing?"

"Rachel!" Louise exclaimed. "For shame. You should not think about that, let alone ask such a question."

Michael laughed. Louise cast him a frown. His grin lacked repentance. "I can't help but wonder. I mean, he's so proper." He sobered, looking at Horace. "I would like to know. How . . . how did Gerard ask for your permission to marry her, sir."

"What?" Horace asked. "Why do you want to know?"

Michael flushed. "Just curious. What did he say to you exactly? Any special thing a man should say to—to whoever he's asking for . . . em . . . I mean, a lady's hand?"

"Oh . . . ," Horace said, blinking. "Can't remember what he said."

"He said . . ." Josie bit her lip. She ignored Pansy's warning grimace and leaned forward with a show of interest. "Yes, Father, what did Gerard say?"

"Don't know," Horace said, tapping his rolled-up newspaper on the arm rest. "S'truth, was too nervous to listen."

"Did he say he held Mary in high regard?" Josie asked, her eyes innocent.

"Hm, yes, yes," Horace said, nodding. "That was it."

"High regard?" Michael asked, blinking.

"And deep respect," Rachel said. She flushed. "Did he say that, Father?"

"Did at that," Horace said. "In fact, he said it quite a few times."

"Deep respect," Michael said, frowning. He repeated it as if memorizing it. "What else? H-he didn't say love or anything like that."

Rachel giggled, and Horace bent a stern eye upon her. She choked into silence. "No, didn't say anything about love. I guess it's bad form if you want to be proper. No, he talked regard and respect and then settlements."

"I say," Michael muttered, turning pale.

At that moment the door opened. The family as one fell quiet as Mary entered. She appeared as pale as Michael had just gone.

"Well? What happened," Josie asked, bravely breaking the silence.

"H-he proposed," Mary said in a quiet voice, "and . . . and I accepted."

"Congratulations!" Josie cried. She sprung up and rushed over to clasp Mary's hands. "I am so excited for you."

"Yes," Michael said, cracking into a grin. "Congratulations."

"Th-thank you." Mary's voice was but a whisper.

Josie frowned. Mary's hands felt as cold as ice. "Do you feel well?"

"Yes, of course." Mary pulled her hands away swiftly.

Michael coughed. "I must leave now. Got an appointment. Only wanted to hear the news. Glad for you, sis. Gives me courage, blast if it don't."

"Must you go?" Josie asked as Michael sauntered across the room, appearing suspicious rather than nonchalant.

"Must." He winked. "But I might have some good news myself, later."

Josie raised her brow, then giggled. "So might I. What is yours?"

Michael colored. "Won't tell yet."

He halted when he came close to Mary. He hugged her soundly. "I wish you the best of luck. I know you will have it. No one can say Gerard ain't a good man." He drew back, frowning. "You cold, Mary?"

"N-no."

"You are shaking."

"It-it must be from excitement."

"I can understand that." Michael laughed. "Think I'm shaking myself. I'd better go."

Michael departed. Josie stared after him, diverted. What surprise could he possibly have for them?

"This is wonderful!" Louise exclaimed. "Did you and dear Gerard discuss the wedding date, Mary? We all must have new wardrobes, of course . . ."

"Did he kiss you?" Rachel asked.

"Hush, Rachel, I told you not to speak of that," Louise said. "We must pay particular attention to your wedding dress, Mary. Something refined. Seed pearls, perhaps?"

"And your honeymoon," Josie exclaimed eagerly. "Where would you like to go?"

"Why can't I know if he kissed her, Mama?" Rachel asked.

"It ain't respectable, that's why," Horace said. "Well, it's a firm thing. I'll tell me solicitor to take care of it."

"And the engagement party!" Louise cried. "We must have it here. No, I shall ask the dear baroness what she wishes. Her circle is far more elite."

"Heh. Even Prinny might come," Horace said, nodding to Mary. "That will be a feather in your cap, what?"

"Why isn't it respectable?" Rachel complained. "I want to know if he kissed her."

"Quiet!" Louise and Horace said at the same time.

"Sorry," Rachel apologized, her tone sullen. "I only wondered, that's all."

All eyes turned to Mary. She visibly trembled. A tear rolled down her cheek. "No, we did not discuss the wedding date. I don't care what kind of wedding dress I have, or . . . or who has the engagement party, or . . . or if the prince comes." A wracking sob tore from her. "And yes, he kissed me!" She spun and turned and ran from the room.

"Guess I shouldn't have asked," Rachel said into the stunned silence.

"I-I have the highest regard f-for Emily," Michael said, standing straight at attention. His cravat had turned into a damp, strangling snake about his throat. The dark-haired woman who sat before him, taking tea, rattled him. Emily's Aunt Pennington could only be considered a Tartar. Her manner was not aggressive, though. Rather, the opposite. She possessed a totally dispassionate air, studying a person as if they were nothing more than a toiling ant, there to amuse. Or be swatted. That was the nerve-wracking rub.

"The highest regard. Pleasant." Aunt Pennington nodded. "Anything else?"

"And . . . and . . ." Michael choked. "A deep respect."

"Ah," Aunt Pennington said. "Not just a respect. But a deep respect."

"Yes," Michael said. Sweat trickled down his cheek. "A deep respect. Very deep, mind you."

"And that is it?" Aunt Pennington asked.

"Y-yes, ma'am."

"I see." Her mouth moved as if she were swirling his words around and tasting them for flavor.

"So . . . so," Michael broke. "Could I please marry Emily, ma'am. Please."

Aunt Pennington cracked a smile. Hope flared in Michael. Surely her smiling was a good sign. "You're after Emily's money, aren't you, boy?"

"No!" Michael yelped.

"Lay odds you are," Aunt Pennington retorted.

"No," Michael sighed. "Truth be said, I wish she didn't have it."

"Do you?" Aunt Pennington asked. A dark brow flared up.

Michael flushed. "No. I didn't mean that exactly. I do want her to have it. I want Emily to have everything, everything in the world. But . . . but I told her when I met her sh-she shouldn't see me."

"Did you?" Aunt Pennington asked. "A novel approach."

"I don't know about novel," Michael said, turning even redder. "But I ain't a slow-top. Emily shouldn't have met me. I . . . well, I ain't plump in the pocket."

"Under the hatches, are you?"

"Yes. It runs in the family. W-we Stantons don't know how to manage money, I fear."

"You saying you're spendthrifts?" Aunt Pennington asked.

"Afraid so," Michael answered. "That's the sorry fact. I told Emily that. Only, it made her cry."

"Did it?" Aunt Pennington asked.

"Yes," Michael said. "She told me I was mean not to like her just because she had money. I never meant to be mean. Not to Emily. I hated to see her cry."

"So you continued to see her," Aunt Pennington said.

"Yes," Michael confessed, shame-faced. "I couldn't help myself. I fell in love with her the moment I saw her."

Aunt Pennington hooted a laugh. Actually hooted!

Michael frowned. "Did I say something funny?"

"No, you clunch," Aunt Pennington said. "Why didn't you say that in the first place? Rather than that pudding-hearted regards and respect twaddle?"

Michael stared at her. A slow, bemused grin crossed his lips. "I-I-I w-was told it wasn't proper. I wanted to do my darn . . . er, best I could to be proper."

"Proper, bah," Aunt Pennington said. "I don't give a

tinker's damn for that. And I warn you, if you want proper, you're ogling the wrong girl. Emily is just barely genteel."

"No," Michael said, frowning sternly. "I won't let you say that, ma'am. Emily ain't always up to snuff, but she's a lady. Just . . . just got to take care of her. She's too innocent by far. Lands in the suds if you don't watch her."

"I didn't mean that," Aunt Pennington said, her tone impatient. "I mean her money still smells of the shop."

Michael frowned, perplexed. "Never thought money had a smell, ma'am. I'll sniff it the next time, if you like."

Aunt Pennington laughed. "You have my blessing, my boy, for what it is worth. Marry Emily."

"Thank you, ma'am," Michael said, sighing. "Thank you."

"Don't thank me," Aunt Pennington said. "I'm not the one you have to please. It's Emily's guardian who's the piper that plays the tune. If he don't approve, Emily can whistle her fortune away to the winds. Emily's father was old-fashioned that way. Gothic, I say. Never trusted a woman to know what she wanted. He gave his partner, Joseph, complete control over whom Emily could marry, or not marry. A shame, really. Emily's rich enough to buy an abbey, but can't choose her own husband. Not without Joseph's permission."

Michael choked and broke into a spate of coughs.

Aunt Pennington frowned. "Are you all right?"

Michael swallowed. "You're roasting me. Emily . . . she can't really buy an abbey . . . can she?"

"She could." Aunt Pennington nodded. "Not that she'd be totty-headed enough to want one. She's got more sense than to want a drafty old thing like that. Haunted most the time. It is bad enough to have to try and rub along with the living, let alone the dead."

"But . . . but she told me she only had a small . . . or medium fortune," Michael said, paling.

Aunt Pennington's brow rose. She laughed. "She told you that? I said she had sense."

"B'gads," Michael said. "I-I hope her guardian likes me."

"We'll soon find out," Aunt Pennington said. "He's late as usual."

"B-but he's out of town," Michael objected.

"No. He came back last night. The man's a here-and-therian. Never tells me when he's coming or going." She frowned. "Or, I suppose he does. I just never listen to him. He's a dead bore. Always too dramatic for my tastes."

A knock sounded upon the door, and Aunt Pennington's butler entered. "Madame, Lord Darwood has arrived."

"Darwood!" Michael exclaimed. "B'gad!"

"Bring him here, Tartlon," Aunt Pennington said, waving an accepting hand.

"Darwood!" Michael repeated.

"Yes," Aunt Pennington said. "Do you know him, then?"

"No." Michael shook his head vigorously. "He claims I do. But I swear, I don't. I must be going. He's a crazy man."

"I agree. But you can't go," Aunt Pennington said. "Not if you want to ask for Emily's hand."

"But . . ." Michael bit off his plea as Lord Darwood entered the room.

Darwood spied Michael straight away. His face twisted. "My nemesis! God! Why? Why are you here!"

"I told you. Always too dramatic," Aunt Pennington said, shaking her head. "Joseph, this is Michael Stanton."

Darwood charged at Michael. "You demon!"

"Zounds!" Michael exclaimed. He jumped behind the sofa. Lord Darwood, his eyes wild, ran toward Michael. He attempted to surmount the sofa in his path, rather than circumventing it. He did not succeed. Its high, scalloped back in cherry wood caught him up, rather painfully at that.

"I guess you know each other, then," Aunt Pennington observed.

Darwood howled. Michael, unable to see such agony, gave Joseph a helpful push backward. Then, his survival instincts high, he dashed over for the cover of a sturdy chair.

Darwood, keening slightly, righted himself. Blue in the face and wheezing, he nevertheless followed Michael in a hunched walk.

"Joseph, do stop," Aunt Pennington said. "Michael has come here to ask for Emily's hand in marriage."

"Never!" Darwood choked out. "Never will I permit it!"

"Now, Joseph," Aunt Pennington said, "you haven't heard the boy out."

"Make a fool of me, will you!" Darwood cried, staring mad-eyed at Michael.

"You're doing fine on your own, I think," Aunt Pennington said, her tone tart.

"Now who's laughing?" Darwood jeered. He made a wild rush toward Michael, but halted this time before he and the furniture could clash. "You'll never have Emily's hand. Now come and fight me!"

"I w-won't," Michael stammered. "I don't go out with lunatics. I told you that!"

Darwood growled, clenching his fist. He swung at Michael. With a sturdy chair between, the punch fell abysmally short.

"Very well, if you aren't going to listen to him, Joseph," Aunt Pennington said, setting her tea down and standing, "this interview is over." She walked directly up to Darwood, who was winding up for another roundhouse swing. Her arm shot out in a no-nonsense, swift jab to Darwood's jaw.

"The devil," Michael breathed in astonishment. It wasn't from the fact Darwood instantly stiffened and toppled over. He had seen that before. He just hadn't seen a lady deliver the blow before.

Aunt Pennington turned toward him, flexing and un-flexing her fingers. "He has a glass jaw, you know? It's about the only thing I like in the man."

"Mary?" Josie whispered, hesitantly entering Mary's bedroom. She hadn't knocked. Instinct warned her she would not be received willingly.

Mary lay across the bed, sobbing. She sat up. She refused to look at Josie. "Yes?"

"You aren't happy," Josie said, stating the obvious. It was her only clue to follow. "Why?"

"Oh, Josie," Mary said. "I-I cannot tell you."

"Yes, you can." Josie walked over and sat down beside the red-eyed, trembling Mary. "You can tell me anything."

"I cannot." Mary shook her head.

"Please," Josie pleaded. "It cannot be worse than anything I've done."

Mary fell into Josie's arms. "I-I do not want to marry Gerard."

"You don't?" Josie asked. Shock waves coursed through her. "I . . . I thought he was perfect for you."

"I do not love him," Mary whispered.

"W-was it when he kissed you?" Josie asked.

"I-I felt nothing," Mary said. "Nothing."

Josie blinked. She couldn't imagine it. Alex's kiss always made her feel everything. How absolutely . . . lonely it would be to kiss a man and feel nothing. "Nothing?"

"Nothing," Mary whispered. "Oh, Josie. I love Paul."

Josie frowned, utterly lost. "Paul? Who is Paul?"

"Paul Desuex."

"You cannot love him," Josie objected. "Y-you only met him once."

"No," Mary sniffed. "I-I never wanted to tell you this. B-but when I learned you were playing at his place, I-I visited him to ask him t-to stop you." Her eyes pleaded.

"Forgive me, Josie, I was afraid for you. I thought Paul was dangerous. Only I fell in love with him, and have been secretly meeting him since."

Josie stared. Her sister, Mary, the only respectable Stanton, had been slipping out and meeting an owner of a gaming den. Impossible! She was supposed to wed Gerard. Gerard, whom the light had shone down upon. That light dispersed in a shattering thought. "It is my fault. You would never have met Paul if it were not for me."

"No," Mary said. Her chin lifted. "And I am not sorry. I at least knew love once."

"You cannot wed Gerard," Josie said, shaken. Knight or not, if his kiss did nothing, it was wrong.

"I will," Mary said softly. She looked away. "P-Paul will not marry me. A gaming hell is not respectable. H-he says I-I deserve better. If he will not marry me, I do not care what I do. If it will save the family, I-I will marry Gerard."

"But Mary . . ." Josie began.

"Josie, please! I-I do not wish to talk about it anymore."

"I-I am sorry." Josie rose in a daze. What had she done to her sister's life? She left Mary's room, meandering down the hall, as if drunk. She halted. Michael approached her. His step and gaze appeared similar to hers.

"What happened?" Josie asked numbly.

"I d-don't want to talk about it." Michael grimaced.

"You can tell me," Josie said, squaring her shoulders.

"I-I went to ask for Emily's hand," Michael said. "I wanted to surprise you all."

Josie's heart dived low. "You were not accepted?"

"No," Michael said. He shook his head. "Lay you odds you can't guess who her guardian is."

"No." At this moment she couldn't guess anything, even her own name.

"It's that Darwood fellow." Michael laughed.

Josie stared. Then swayed. "Oh, no."

"Josie?" Michael rushed up and grabbed her. "You all right?"

"Yes," Josie said. "I . . . I just need to sit."

"Good idea," Michael said, his voice shaky. He promptly sat, dragging Josie down with him.

She sighed, looking at Michael. "It is all my fault."

"Ain't your fault," Michael said. "It can't be helped. Emily's got a dicked-in-the-nob guardian. Queer how it goes. But there you have it."

"No," Josie whispered. "You do not understand. I . . . I am the one who hit him. He thought you were me. Or I was you."

Michael stared and shook his head. "You feeling all right?"

"I-I masqueraded as you one night," Josie admitted, blushing. "You had lost so much at Paul's that I decided to go there and win it back. Only, only I beat Darwood, and he objected, and . . ."

"You hit him!" Michael exclaimed.

"I didn't mean to," Josie said. "It just happened."

"I know how it goes," Michael commiserated, staring off into space.

"He has a glass jaw," Josie and Michael said together.

Michael laughed. Josie peered at him. "Y-you aren't angry with me?"

"No," Michael said. "I must be the lunatic, but I would have loved to see you pretending to be me." He sobered. "And it ain't your fault. I don't think old Darwood would have accepted me anyhow. Do you know Emily can buy an abbey if she wants?"

Josie gasped. "No. Can she?"

"She can," Michael said, sighing. "If old Darwood approves, but he don't. I . . . I want Emily to have her abbey."

"I'm sorry," Josie whispered.

"No," Michael said. "Only . . . only I don't think I can stay here. I've been thinking on my way home. I sh-should join the military. I've said it before. It's more important now. There is nothing else I want to do."

"D-do you truly wish that?" Josie asked.

"I do," Michael said. "But I don't have the ready."

"But if you did?" Josie asked.

"I would," Michael said solemnly.

Josie rose slowly. "I'm sorry, Michael."

She left him sitting in the hall. She wandered down the stairs. As she passed the library, she noticed her father, sitting alone. Suddenly, the little girl in her wanted to run to her father. She entered. "Father?"

Horace glanced up. His eyes watered. "Hello, my girl."

Josie sighed. She moved swiftly to sit upon a chair next to him. "What is wrong? You can tell me."

"I shouldn't," Horace said.

"No," Josie said, "you should."

Her mind slowly struggled out of the fog as she listened to her father. Everything was her fault. She had thought her family better off because of her efforts. Yet her schemes had destroyed their happiness. She had contrived to force her family to become what they were not, merely so she could wed Alex. The stark, honest thought showed itself.

Her father continued to talk, and Josie nodded, and nodded some more. She must make restitution. She must help her family out of the morass she herself had thrown them into by her schemes and ploys.

The final scheme came to her. She knew how to help her family mitigate the damages she had caused. It was pathetic, she knew, on her part, but it would also involve Alex. She could not marry him, but perhaps, if he agreed, she could still be in his life.

The thought of a man kissing her and her feeling nothing rose once again. She shivered. She loved Alex. No other man's kisses would do.

* * *

"Good afternoon, Musgrave," Alex said, grinning at the butler when he opened the door. He wore his best attire. A ring rested in his pocket. He stifled a laugh. He was cold sober, and not only willing, but eager to propose to Josephine Stanton. Life had indeed changed. "Is Josie at home?"

"She is waiting for you, my lord."

"Excellent," Alex said, laughing. He followed Musgrave to the library. He entered to discover Josie sitting upon the settee. He impatiently waited for Musgrave to depart and strode up to her, grinning. "Good afternoon, Miss Josephine Stanton."

"Good afternoon, Alex," Josie said. She glanced up and glanced down, her expression almost frightened.

Alex smiled. "Josie, I know I said I would be proper, but not if it makes you uncomfortable."

"No." Josie sprung up and scurried to the other side of the room.

Alex stiffened. An unwelcome premonition invaded him. "Josie. Don't you dare."

She peeked at him. "D-dare what?"

"Don't you dare tell me you are going to do me the honor of rejecting me."

"I must," Josie said, her voice low.

"Fiend seize it!" Alex exclaimed. He strode up to her and clasped her shoulders. "Why? What is your excuse this time?"

"It is not an excuse." Tears drenched her gray eyes. "But nothing has changed. Not really."

Alex bit back a groan. Things *had* changed. He loved Josie. Wisdom told him it would be useless to tell her at this moment. "Why do you say that?"

"Alex, I-I have destroyed my family!" Josie cried. She twisted from his arms, hastening away.

"Destroyed your family?" Alex barked a laugh. "That would be a well nigh impossible thing to do."

"It is all my fault. I thought I was helping. I-I wanted so much for . . ." She halted. "I have been terribly selfish."

"Selfish?" Alex asked. "Faith, you are anything but that. Everything you've done is for your infernal family. You never do anything for yourself."

"No," Josie whispered. "That is not true. I wanted my family to be settled and rich, so that I could . . ."

"Could what?" Alex asked. His heart jumped.

"I-I cannot say it."

"Yes, you can," Alex demanded roughly. "Say it!"

She shook her head, looking away. "Mary accepted the baron this morning."

"Yes," Alex said impatiently. "That is good."

"It is not," Josie said. "She loves Paul Desuex."

"What?" Alex exclaimed, stunned.

"She met him because of me," Josie said, a catch in her voice. "She has been secretly meeting him and loves him. He will not marry her. He says she deserves better."

Alex shook his head. "Good lord."

"And . . . and Michael asked f-for Emily's hand this morning."

"I don't think I want to hear this."

"He was rejected," Josie said. "Emily's guardian is Lord Darwood."

"Impossible," Alex said. It was like arriving late upon the last scene of a bad play, a very bad play.

"It is all my fault," Josie bemoaned. "Michael thought Darwood merely crazy. But . . . Darwood has complete control over Emily's fortune. She can buy an abbey, you know?"

"Can she?"

"Michael wants to join the military. He cannot remain in London where Emily is."

"Oh, God," Alex muttered. "What next?"

"And I have destroyed Father's life, too," Josie said. "H-he is miserable."

Alex clapped his hand to his forehead. "I should not have asked."

"He's been trying to reform just for me," Josie said, tears welling up. "He doesn't like politics, or charities, or . . . or respectable connections. And the baron scares him."

"Famous," Alex said. "Just famous."

"I cannot marry you," Josie said, her voice choked. "I'll never be able to marry you."

"Josie." Anger fought with pity inside Alex. "What does this all matter? Just marry me for God's sake. We will work these issues out." He laughed, slightly embarrassed. "After all, with your family it will take a lifetime."

"I know you are saying that to be kind," Josie said, her voice watery.

"Kind?" Alex groaned.

"You do not need to do so." Josie drew in her breath. "But . . . but c-could I be your mistress?"

Alex stared at her. "I offer you my hand and name. You reject me. But you are willing to become my mistress. Damn you, Josie!"

"If . . . if I become your mistress," Josie said quickly, "it will disgrace the family. Th-the baron is very respectable. He would withdraw his offer, wouldn't he? If Mary will not withdraw, Gerard must be made to do so. And . . . and Father will not feel forced to be respectable, once I am not."

"And Michael?" Alex asked, his anger rising.

"He will need a set of colors," Josie said. "They are expensive."

"So you will sacrifice yourself for your family," Alex growled. "I wish to God you would do the same for me."

"I-I must fix what I have done," Josie said, her chin trembling. "I must make restitution."

"If that is the way you want it," Alex said, gritting his teeth. "Then so be it. I will take you as my mistress."

"Y-you will?" Josie asked. He heard the breathless catch in her voice.

"Since that is the only way you will accept me, yes," he said viciously.

Josie cringed back. Fear traced through her eyes. Then the determination, that odd courage, he'd seen before replaced it. She straightened. "H-how do we do this?"

Alex's anger evaporated, became a mere mist. He could not help but love the infuriating, impossible girl. Yet what the devil was he going to do with her? Inspiration struck. He knew very well what he would do. It matched any scheme Josie had devised. He hid an evil grin. "As my mistress, you are to do whatever I say."

"Yes?" Josie asked hesitantly.

"I am sending you to my hunting lodge."

"What?" Josie exclaimed.

"I want you all to myself for a while, sweetings," Alex said, strolling up to her.

"But . . ."

"No, arguments," Alex said. "Cybil told you that a mistress doesn't fight with her patron, didn't she?"

"Yes," Josie said, blinking. "But if I leave . . . how . . . ?"

"No arguments," Alex repeated firmly. "A good mistress does what she is told."

"But . . ."

"Josie," Alex said sternly. "Do you want to become my mistress or not? Do you want to make restitution, or not?"

"I-I do."

"Very well," Alex said. "You will leave tomorrow morning. You may take Miss Tellington as a companion, if you wish. Mistresses always have a lady friend when they travel, you know?"

"Pansy may come?" Josie asked. Patent relief crossed her face.

"Yes. But she is the only one you are to let into your

confidences. You are not to tell the rest of the family any-thing."

"N-not tell them?" Josie gasped.

"I will do that for you," Alex said. Faith, wouldn't he just! "I do not intend to give them a chance to change your mind. You have committed to becoming my mistress, and I won't have you back out."

"I-I wouldn't d-do that," Josie stammered.

"It makes no difference," Alex said. "This is the way it is to be if you are to become my mistress."

"I-I see," Josie said, her cheeks flaring deep red.

Alex could feel her resolution weakening. He was playing it too heavily. He hauled her into his arms and kissed her swiftly. Desire torched through him, and he felt it the min-ute it caught through Josie. He pulled back. They gasped in equal measure. Josie looked up at him with passion-filled eyes.

Alex cleared his throat. He feared for his own resolution. "I will pay you well. Even more than I did Cybil. It . . . it shall only be a few days before I join you."

"Join me?" Josie asked, blinking. "You are not . . . ?"

"I have to tell your family, do I not?" Alex said. "And I have a few other . . . business affairs I must attend to first."

"I see," Josie said. Confusion and despondency replaced the passion in her eyes.

"I . . . I will send money along," Alex said quickly. "You and Pansy can . . . shop. Buy new wardrobes. As my mis-tress I-I want you well turned out. And why not decorate the house, I mean lodge." He sighed. That should keep her safely occupied.

"What?" Josie asked, her eyes widening.

Alex forced a smile. "Make it into our very own little love nest, why don't you?"

"V-very well."

She looked so bewildered, Alex wanted to reach out for her. Instead he clenched his fists and smiled. "Do not fear,

Josie. We shall have wonderful times together. Only you must go to the lodge. Shop and decorate to your heart's content. I will join you for our new, illicit life together as soon as I can."

Eleven

"I don't think he knows you are a fallen woman," Pansy whispered as Alex's coachman closed the door upon them. Dawn had not even touched the sky with her light fingers yet. "He is acting very polite."

Josie clutched the heavy envelope the coachman had given her with his master's compliments. It rattled her all the more that Alex had not even seen fit to see her off. However, she had received her instructions, and as a good mistress she must learn to follow his wishes. "Y-yes, he is."

Pansy all but bounced upon the opposite seat. Her brown eyes glittered in the dim light as she looked at the envelope. "Do see what is in it!"

She opened the envelope with shaky fingers, then gasped. It was thick with fifty-pound notes.

"Well?" Pansy asked. Josie could only open and close her mouth. Not a squeak would come forth. Pansy reached over and took the envelope. She delved into it, her fingers riffling through it faster than if she held a deck of cards. "My stars. The wages of sin do pay well."

"Pansy!" Josie wailed.

"I am sorry." Pansy giggled. "Only, I've never held such an amount in my hands before."

"H-he said to buy clothes," Josie said, dazed. "And . . . and decorate the lodge . . . I mean, our love nest."

"There is more than enough for that."

"It . . . it could go toward Michael's commission," Josie murmured.

"No, it won't," Pansy said, clutching the envelope to her chest. "If Alex said to buy clothes and decorate your love nest, then that is what you will do. It's play and pay."

Josie's lips trembled. "But . . . but what if I am not good at it? Wh-what if I-I make an awful mistress?"

"You won't," Pansy said, her tone stout. "W-we'll figure out how to go on."

"I-I want to be good," Josie whispered. "I love him."

"Yes, dear." Pansy nodded.

Josie blinked. It was the first time she had ever said it to anyone. Perhaps because now her course was set, it did not seem so frightful. "Y-you know?"

"Of course," Pansy said. "And if he asked you to marry him again, he loves you, too."

"I-I couldn't marry him," Josie said. "Not with the family, and . . . and everything."

Pansy shook her head. "I don't know, dear, but if this is what he thinks is meant for clothes and decorating, he might be able to support it. Even your mother could not outrun the carpenter with this."

"Yes, she could."

Pansy giggled. "Very well. Perhaps. But you couldn't. I believe you would be a frugal wife. Wouldn't that balance out the accounts?"

Josie blinked. She had not considered it. She bit her lip. It was wishful thinking. There were sixteen pages in the ledger book. Though perhaps it was down to fifteen at this point. Besides, it would not settle all the other issues, the ones that were all her fault. "No, Pansy, this is the only way."

Pansy sighed. "Then you must play the cards the way they were dealt. My father always said that." She frowned. "He also said losing your virtue wouldn't pay."

"I know."

"Just think," Pansy said. "To be paid all this merely for your company."

Josie flushed. "There is more to it than what you thought Pansy."

"There is?" Pansy asked. Her tone was actually eager. "Do tell me!"

"I-I cannot," Josie said. "I-I do not know everything, but the things I do know . . . I-I like. And Alex told me he would explain the rest later."

"No doubt," Pansy said, nodding. "And you do have all the advice from th-those other professional ladies, don't you?"

"Yes," Josie said, "I do."

"Very well. That should help." A starry-eyed look crossed Pansy's face. "And then we'll . . . we'll use our imaginations."

Suddenly Josie did not feel so scared. If Pansy could look at the matter with such a positive view, so could she. She would make Alex the best possible mistress ever!

Alex watched astride his horse from a distance. He saw Josie and Miss Tellington enter the carriage and his driver start his team. He knew it would take but a few hours for Josie to reach the small manor of his. If all went well, he would join her tomorrow night. He disliked leaving her even two days alone, but it could not be helped. He had a list of tasks he must perform first. He thought a moment. It could be considered extremely early, or very late, according to how one looked at it. He smiled grimly. He didn't particularly care. He knew the first person he wanted to visit.

Paul threw down a card upon the table. He played with the last stragglers of the evening, the true, addicted gamesters. He was losing. It did not matter. He had already lost the most important thing. He felt, rather than saw, someone step beside him. He glanced up. An instinctive tension corded his muscles. "Hello, Rothmier."

"Hello, Desuex." Alex's gaze was firm. "Would you care to dismiss yourself from the game for a private conversation, or would you rather discuss it in front of these gentlemen?"

Paul flushed. There should be no connection, but when he saw Alex, he could only think of Mary. He rose swiftly and bowed to the men. "If you will excuse me. I have already folded. Please continue without me." He looked at Alex. "Follow me." He led Alex through the main room and into his private one, then turned, raising a brow. "What is the private matter you wish to discuss?"

"This," Alex said. He walked up and landed Paul a blow to his jaw.

Paul's head snapped back. Fighting the pain, Paul focused his gaze upon Alex. "That is the second time, my friend."

"The first was for Josie," Alex said, shrugging. "This one is for Mary."

Paul sucked in his breath. "Sh-she told you?"

"No, Josie told me," Alex said. "Mary told Josie."

"Of course."

"If you care to know," Alex said, "Mary has accepted Lexing."

"You do not hold any punch back, do you?" Paul asked in a wry tone. He moved slowly to sit upon a chair.

"You act surprised." Alex laughed and took up the chair across the table from Paul. "You shouldn't be. You are dealing with the Stanton ladies. They will do much for their family. Especially if you offer them no other choice."

Paul flushed. "There is no other choice."

"Is there not?" Alex asked softly. "Weren't you the one

who declared Josie had a right to come to this gaming hell? That she should not marry a fortune, but make it?"

"Yes," Paul said. "But Mary is different."

"No, she isn't."

Paul jumped up, his fist clenched.

"Do not!" Alex ordered, his eyes shooting sparks. "I will forgive you this once, but only this once. Only because I believe you now understand how I felt when Josie played here."

Paul started. A bitter laugh escaped him and he sat back down. "God, but I do."

"You and I are very much the hypocrites, are we not?" Alex said, smiling. "Whatever life we choose, the women we love must not live the same."

"I-I cannot have Mary here."

Alex shrugged. "That is your decision. I can only tell you Josie has asked to become my mistress."

"What?" Paul started up again.

"Sit," Alex stated.

Paul noticed the particularly fierce look in his eye. Paul sat.

"She intends to disgrace herself, to make the baron break the engagement. She doesn't think he will wed Mary, not when there is a whore in the family. I would imagine she has the right of it."

"*Mon Dieu,*" Paul breathed.

"Yes," Alex said. "Since you will not stop Mary, Josie will. Or at least try to do so."

Paul glared at him. "Y-you will not do this to Josie. She is an innocent. Sh-she does not deserve this."

"And does Mary truly deserve a life with the baron?" Alex retorted.

"It would be better than a life with a gambler in a gaming hell."

"Truly?" Alex asked. He shook his head. "I will tell you now. I will willingly change my ways for Josie. I have lived enough of that kind of life. I do not want Josie to do so. Truth be told, I fear it matters more to me than Josie. She will accept me either way. It is I who will not." He raised a brow. "I believe you feel the same about Mary."

Paul's fists clenched. Yet they relaxed and he sighed. "I may. But you have more to offer Josie than I do Mary."

"Do I?" Alex asked. "I have a title. The Stantons appear to be frightfully democratic about that. It does not matter to them. I have a reputation. But as you said, Josie is an innocent. She does not understand the full import of that. My slate will always be clean with her. I have a fortune. That has been to my disadvantage. Now, what more do I have to offer than you?"

Paul stared. "When you put it that way, not much."

Alex nodded and stood. "Very well. I would far prefer to have you as my brother-in-law than the baron. But then, I would prefer to have Josie as my wife rather than as my mistress." He rose. "I would say both ladies are well worth winning."

"Yes," Paul said. The love he fought so hard entered into his heart. No, it was not the love he had fought, only his past. He laughed. "Beware, Rothmier, I have as much to offer as you do."

Alex smiled. "I believe I just said that."

Paul chuckled. Rothmier didn't understand. He did have as much to offer. Only now he had the love to make him go back and claim it.

Horace sat down to his breakfast at ten o'clock. It was indeed early for him, but these days it seemed he could not sleep, nor was there a reason to do so. Louise had already risen and would be at some breakfast or other to support workhouse orphans.

He stared at his eggs. It used to be he would never even look at food at this time. However, he was becoming respectable, and respectable meant staring at runny yokes and whites early in the morning.

A commotion was heard, and Alex Rothmier entered the room. Horace brightened. Company was acceptable. Far more acceptable than eggs. "Hello, Rothmier."

"Hello, Lord Stanton." Alex moved and took up a chair beside Horace.

"Care for some eggs?" Horace asked hopefully. "You can have mine."

"No, I've already broken fast." Alex leaned back in his chair. He raised a brow. "Do you know where Josie is?"

"Josie?" Horace asked. He blinked. "I suppose she is in her bed."

"No," Alex said. "At the moment she is traveling to my Meldon manor. Of course, she thinks it is my hunting lodge."

"Hunting lodge?" Horace asked, frowning. "Josie don't hunt. Why would she do that?"

"Because she is going to become my mistress."

Horace started up. "No, bedamn. She will not!" He slammed his fist down. It hit runny egg, and splashed below, cracking bone china. Horace jerked his hand back in shock. He shook it. "She promised me. If I reformed . . ."

"Have you reformed?" Alex asked, picking up a napkin and leaning over to offer it to him.

"Confound it, I have," Horace said, snatching it from him.

"Or are you only pretending?" Alex asked. "And are miserable because of it?"

Horace flushed. "I might have said that. But . . . everyone else is happy. Mary is going to wed the baron. Louise is in fine fettle. She likes being a politician's wife. And Josie, well, I thought Josie was happy."

"No, Josie only wants you to be happy," Alex said. "But I think it only right that she is happy as well."

"Being your mistress won't make her happy," Horace

said, scrubbing at congealing egg furiously. Fiend seize it! It hadn't done that on the plate; why now on his hand?

"It will not make me happy either," Alex countered.

Horace froze. "What?"

"I want Josie as my wife. She will not marry me, because she fears you and the family will batten on me."

"B'gads," Horace breathed.

"It was she who rejected me the first time," Alex said. A bitter smile twisted his lips. "At that time I proposed under duress. Family duty. Josie, in her own fashion, rejected me because of family duty. I will warn you right now, if Josie and I wed, it will have nothing to do with either family. And nothing to do with duty."

"Fine. Fine. I understand that," Horace said, frustrated. "But if you want to marry her, why are you going to make her your mistress? That's what *I* don't understand."

Alex sighed. "Josie believes if she becomes my mistress you will no longer feel obligated to be respectable. It is known as all bets are off."

"Bedamn," Horace murmured. His head hurt, and that without a drink.

"And all bets *are* off," Alex said, rising. "I intend to wed Josie if I can. I will make a settlement with you when the time occurs. I will not promise to pay all your debts. I made that mistake the first time."

"I-I don't know what to s-say," Horace stammered.

"You need not say anything," Alex replied. "As for whether you remain reformed or not is your choice. But certainly do not do it for Josie's sake. She's loved you either way. Personally, I think respectability a dead bore."

"Damn, that's why I wanted you as my son-in-law," Horace hooted. Then he sighed. "Instead, I got that baron fellow."

"That may change yet. But it will depend upon what the people involved really wish to do." His gaze turned razor sharp. "Just like it depends upon you to do what you wish."

Horace stared at Alex. He suddenly felt a lightness, as if a ton of bricks had dropped from his shoulders. "Hm. I think I want a drink. One, mind you. I want my head clear. I sort of like that. Then I'm talking to Louise. I ain't a politician, never will be. I know what's good for the country, but I want to share it with those who care. And they ain't in office. And I'm damn tired of Louise's savages, and workhouse orphans, and nose-in-the-air ladies. I never see her anymore. And I want to." He flushed. "Always have. She's my wife."

Alex chuckled. "I understand. I want Josie as my wife, myself."

"Huzzah!" Horace cried, shaking his fist.

"But I'll take her as my mistress if it is the only way she'll have me," Alex added.

Horace's face fell. "Bedamn!"

"As I said. All bets are off!" Alex cracked a grin and walked toward the door. When he reached the portal, he halted and turned. "Do you know where Michael is, perchance?"

"No, I would have thought he was in his bed. But I thought Josie was there as well." Then Horace gasped. "Is Mary in her bed?"

Alex chuckled. "From what I gather, she is. She is engaged to the baron after all."

It was late afternoon. Michael forced a grin and lifted his brandy toward his best friend. "Here's to . . . to whatever it might be."

"S'true," Winston said. He bolted his glass back and looked at Michael. "Glad to see you again. Y-you ain't been around lately."

"No," Michael said. He sipped from his brandy. "Just didn't feel like it."

Winston nodded, very much like an owl at midnight. "I

understand. But you almost missed it. Old Keliegh's hunt-ers are going on the block at Tattersall's. He gambled his family seat away Friday last. Put a bullet through his head. You know those hunters. Finest in the land. You should try for them. They will go cheap."

Michael shivered for some reason. "Can't do it. I'm . . . going into the military."

Winston, just then lifting his brandy glass, started. His glass slipped through his hands. "What?" he exclaimed. Whether it was from the news or from the brandy dripping over his unmentionables was undetermined. "You? In the military?"

"Hello, Michael," Alex Rothmier said, seeming to ap-pear from out of nowhere.

Michael set his own glass down. "Hello, Alex."

"Would you mind if I had a word with you?" Alex said. He looked at Winston. A brow shot up as his gaze turned to the man's lap. "Accident, St. James?"

"Yes," Winston sprung up. His brandy tumbler tumbled to the ground. "Got to . . . to go clean this."

"Good man," Alex said in an indifferent tone as he took up Winston's hastily departed seat.

"Want a brandy?" Michael asked.

"No," Alex said, grinning. "I would say I need one, but I do not intend to have one as of yet." He turned a piercing gaze upon Michael. "Josie told me about you and Dar-wood. She believes it is all her fault."

Michael flushed. "No. I was . . . was shocked to find out what she had done. And, well, thought old Darwood just off his beam. It sort of makes sense now." He frowned. "But it ain't of no importance. I don't think the bed-lamite—er, man—would have permitted me to marry Emily anyways. I-I ain't good enough for her. She can buy an abbey, you know?"

"It clearly runs in your family," Alex said in a whimsical tone.

"What does?"

"A snobbery against the rich."

"Emily said that." Michael sighed. "B-but, it ain't no use. I'm under the hatches, and she—she's got a fortune . . . if she don't marry me."

"Does she want that fortune?" Alex asked. "Or does she want you?"

"I didn't ask," Michael said, flushing. "I just told her aunt to tell Emily goodbye."

"That also runs in your family," Alex said, shaking his head. "You always believe you know what is best for the other person."

Indignation rose in Michael. "I am many things. I ain't the wisest man. But . . . but I do know I don't want Emily to lose an abbey 'cause of me. I want her to have everything."

Alex studied Michael with a sharp intelligence that shone within his eyes. It was the kind of intelligence Michael had learned to respect, and defer toward. "Darwood is a politician with a reputation. My advice to you is to marry Emily out of hand. I do not know Emily's background completely, but since I do not, she is not of the highest *ton*. She may be an heiress, but her money was made. It—"

Michael gasped. "It smells of the shop?"

"Precisely." Alex nodded. "Darwood has already been embarrassed by you. The *ton* will not be pleased if you give the Stanton title to an upstart. However, they will side with you if you marry Emily in the teeth of Darwood's disapproval."

"I-I don't understand," Michael said, frowning.

"The Stantons have a reputation," Alex said. "But you are of the *ton*. They will choose to support you over Darwood."

"Do you think so?" Michael asked.

"I will supply the funds," Alex said, "if you wish to go to the border. I will also use all my power to make Darwood accept the marriage. I assure you, when I choose, I have the power."

Michael frowned. "I must think about this. I don't want anyone to think my Emily ain't good enough. She can buy an abbey. That's more than I can do. And . . . I never meant Darwood to look like a fool. I thought he was cracked in his top loft, but once Josie explained it, I can understand. He got the wrong man . . . er, woman that is."

Alex shrugged. "It is your choice. Joining the military can be a short life. Whereas you could have a long one with Emily, if you choose."

Michael choked. It was simply the offer between hell and heaven. He looked down. "I will think about it. But . . . but I don't need you to pay for anything. I will pay myself if I go to the border."

Alex rose. "Very well. But I will tell you now. Josie has offered to become my mistress in order to raise the funds for you to have a set of colors."

"What?!" Michael shouted, springing up.

"She feels responsible for what has happened with you and Darwood."

"That . . . that ain't right," Michael said. "She was only trying to help."

"I am glad you understand that," Alex said. "And do not concern yourself. I have sent her to a small estate of mine. I want her as my wife, not my mistress. I believe I can tell you this, because I now know what love is."

Michael, despite himself, grinned. "I thought you two were good for each other. It is a shame you and she didn't make a go of it the first time."

"Indeed?" Alex asked, raising a brow. "None of this would have happened otherwise. And I would have married Josie out of duty, not love."

"B'gads," Michael said. He fell into his chair. "I d-didn't think of that."

Alex bowed. "Neither had I. I hope to call you brother sometime."

Michael grinned. "So do I."

"I am obligated to remain in town until tomorrow afternoon," Alex said. "Then I will join Josie at Meldon where I hope to settle our affairs. Until then, I will be a your disposal."

"I've got to think about this," Michael murmured. "It' a tricky thing, when you love. You've got to think abou more than one thing."

Alex's smile twisted. "Do you? I am now inclined to believe there should only be one thing. And that is love.' He laughed wryly. "How the mighty have fallen."

He turned and wended his way through the tables. Michael shook his head. He loved Emily. Only he wanted her to have everything. He sighed. Josie had shocked him with her gumption and ingenuity. He was her twin. He was male. Surely he should think of something. He must. His Emily depended upon it.

Winston at that moment returned and sat down. He looked embarrassed. "Er, I can't remember. Did you say you were off to join the military?"

"No," Michael said. "I changed my mind. I haven' thought it all through, but I am going to marry an heiress."

"What?" Winston yelped.

"She's beautiful," Michael said stoutly. "And the catch of the season. Only, she's been under wraps."

"You sly dog." Winston cracked a grin. "Stole a march on us, did you?"

"I did at that." Michael grinned. "And you can tell everyone you know. I might have to fight for her, but I will."

Twelve

"When do you think he will come?" Josie asked, pacing the parlor. Her ruby red dress rustled about her. She could barely breathe. It was nerves. That or the merry-widow corset which had been created for a woman even slimmer than she. Josie hadn't thought that possible until today.

"When did he say he would come?" Pansy asked, her voice barely slurred. Her hair no longer held even the pretense of confinement. It fell about her shoulders in wild disarray. She lifted a glass of wine. "Do have a drink, dear. It will calm your nerves."

"No, thank you." Josie took another revolution, side-stepping a huge, gilded cage, two lovebirds nestled next to each other and asleep. It had seemed a marvelous notion at the time to buy them so they could hang in the entryway. Yet their perpetual, raucous squawking had caused both Josie and Pansy to reconsider the idea, as well as the logic of their name. In truth, the fowl sounded far more fractious than loving. "H-he didn't say exactly when."

Pansy sighed, sipping from her wine. "Well, we have tried. If he does not come until tomorrow, everything will be prepared."

Josie looked at Pansy in gratitude. "I do not think I

could have done it without you, Pansy. I would have had no notion on how to go about it."

"I think I enjoyed it." Pansy burped and then giggled. "Of course, having all that money to spend made it quite simple."

"True," Josie said, finally settling into a chair. "I never knew one could buy other ladies' clothes if you promised to pay double the amount."

"It was fortunate we found Mrs. Landry." Pansy lowered her voice. "Of French descent. That makes the difference. She knew exactly what you wanted."

"Yes." Josie flushed. Of the few seamstresses they had found in the small town, most had acted shocked at any request Josie or Pansy had tendered past sturdy, wholesome cotton, linen and bombazine.

Only when they discovered Mrs. Landry had things taken the turn for the better. She supplied the apparel for a Mrs. Barrette and her young ladies. Though Mrs. Landry could only sell Josie the ruby dress and what she called a "peignoir" (that was when Pansy divined she was French), she promised upon the morrow to have a full wardrobe sent round, if it took her all evening to take in and tuck. The ruby dress and peignoir had been commissioned for a "Jasmine," obviously one of Mrs. Barrette's daughters. "How fortunate she directed us to Mr. Niven for the decorating of the house."

"Yes. Such a charming, inventive man." Pansy nodded, sipping from her wine.

"We bought a frightful amount from him," Josie said. She finally went and picked up the glass from the table. One sip could not hurt.

"Hmm." Pansy peered around, rather owlishly. "It is a shame he can't start until the next week. Only look. It is so very masculine and . . . and far too proper. It doesn't look anything like a love nest. But, if it is a hunting lodge as well, it stands to reason. At least there are no heads on the wall."

"Heads!" Josie exclaimed. "I hope not!"

"Of animals," Pansy said. "Deer, elk, rabbits, field mice. Whatever men shoot. My father was no sportsman."

"Neither is mine," Josie admitted. Stalking out the wine cellar had been the only hunting he was accustomed to performing.

"Mr. Niven has set us up right and tight." Pansy nodded vigorously.

Josie frowned slightly. Her eyes skittered to a tall statue set close to the fire. Mr. Niven had said it was fashioned after an original classic. At least there was a strategically placed fig leaf. "I do wonder if your, er . . . Mr. David is not too much."

"This is a love nest," Pansy said, sighing. "He is perfect."

Josie giggled. The few sips of wine assisted her. "You should not have stolen Mr. David from Mrs. Barrette. Mr. Niven swore the lady had been waiting for his delivery for three months."

"Mr. David is artwork," Pansy said, waving her glass expansively. "I have always wanted to bid exorbitantly upon artwork, just like the rich. And why should that Mrs. Barrette have my David for her garden? Artwork should not be put out to the elements."

"True," Josie said, settling down more comfortably in her chair. Indeed, she slouched, shifting to avoid the punishing whalebone of the merry widow. "But he *is* stone."

"I wish he were not," Pansy sighed.

"Hm," Josie sighed. She gazed at the fire. "We accomplished much, didn't we, Pansy?"

"That we did."

"I hope Alex likes it all," Josie said. Her lids refused to remain open.

"I am sure he will like it. No, love it." Pansy reached for the wine bottle. "I know I do." She received no answer. Glancing over groggily, she noticed Josie fast asleep. She shrugged and poured herself another glass.

* * *

Alex let himself into Meldon with his own latchkey. Granted, it had taken him a time to discover the correct key. Meldon was the smallest of his holdings, and he had only thought of it on the spur of the moment. Far too tired, and unwilling to wake the household, he had sent his coachman to the stables and carried the coach lantern with him.

Waiting upon a special license had taken much longer than he expected. Worse, dealing with the local reverend had been a trial of patience and perseverance. He believed perseverance had won out. He rather thought the little man had only agreed to perform the ceremony tomorrow because Alex had forced him to remain discussing the matter well past the good reverend's bedtime.

He entered the small hall, lantern raised, and promptly rammed into a coat rack. It clattered to the wooden floor. His wince changed to an entire cringe as an obscene squawking arose. Bewildered, he followed the strident sound into the small sitting room off the foyer. He halted.

The faintest fire fought to stay alive in the fireplace. Its meager glow was obstructed by a stone statue. Alex peered at it. It looked to be the statue of David, only David sported a fig leaf. Either the artist was terribly confused on his classics, or merely a true Englishman. Not far from the statue, almost in the middle of the room, was a huge, gilded cage. Two lovebirds flapped against its bars, the dreadful source of the squawking.

Upon the settee close by, her hair straggling about her shoulders, Miss Tellington rested. She clutched a glass of wine in her hand. Josie was in the other chair. She didn't sit, but rather was curled up, sleeping soundly. She wore the most brilliant of ruby dresses. The tight, plunging bodice displayed more of her charms than Alex, tired and uncontrolled, could bear to look at.

"Hello," Pansy said. She struggled up. The glass in her hand flew. It crashed and splashed into the gilded cage. For a moment there was a cessation of noise as the lovebirds fluffed and preened wine-splattered wings. Pansy meandered over to them. "Ah, poor things. Can birdies drink?"

"I don't know," Alex said, entering the room. He focused upon the gilded bird cage. It was far wiser than to watch the gentle rise and fall of Josie's chest. "What are they doing here?"

"We bought them," Pansy said, giggling. "Thought they would be perfect for a love nest. We were going to hang them in the entryway."

The birds immediately let up a squawk. More like a howl, if translated into tipsy bird.

"Watch birds. How novel," Alex said.

Pansy stared at them. "They are lovebirds. Though they do not sound like it."

Alex swiftly looked toward Josie. Despite the commotion, she did not wake.

"Should I awaken her?" Pansy asked, stumbling around the cage. She winked broadly, the kind of salacious wink Alex had never expected to receive from a governess. "She's been waiting for you."

Alex glanced at Josie. His sexual desire faded, replaced with a soft tenderness. "No, let her sleep." He walked quietly over, though it seemed totally unnecessary. The birds squawked to wake the dead. He bent and lifted Josie into his arms.

"Ah," Pansy sighed. "And the strong hero picked up his love and carried her away . . ."

Alex turned. "Pansy . . ."

"Yes."

"Be quiet," Alex said. "And show me Josie's room."

"Oh, dear, yes," Pansy said. She bolted forward. Alex followed her, gladly leaving the unloving birds behind.

Josie felt a mere featherweight in his arms as he carried her upstairs. Pansy was rambling on about how surprised he would be on the morrow. Alex didn't listen. Holding Josie, warm and innocently sleeping in his arms, drew his attention, his heart.

As they reached the room, Pansy giggled. "Here it is."

"Thank you."

"But . . ." Pansy halted. She frowned, swaying on her feet. "Oh, dear, I'm not sure I know what I'm supposed to do."

Alex smiled. Evidently Pansy's lifelong instincts as a governess warred with her new role. "It is all right. You may leave."

"V-very well . . . if you say so." Sighing, Pansy turned to weave down the hall. Only she swung about. "I-I love Josie."

"I know you do," Alex said gently. "So do I."

"Good," Pansy said. "Because . . . because . . ."

"I will take care of her, Pansy."

"Please do," Pansy said. "I-I have tried. And . . . and I don't regret it."

"Go to sleep, Pansy," Alex said, smiling.

"I will." Pansy turned and continued her serpentine path.

Alone at last, Alex carried the sleeping Josie into her room. She stirred when he laid her down upon the bed. "Alex?"

"I'm here," Alex said softly.

Her eyes opened, sleepy and dazed. "I waited. I shall . . ."

"Go to sleep."

"I want to be a good mistress," Josie murmured. Her lashes fluttered. "Sh-shouldn't I be awake?"

"You can be a good mistress in the morning," Alex said. "Just sleep now."

"Yes," Josie sighed. Her lids fluttered shut.

Alex rose and quietly retired to his own room.

* * *

When Josie awoke the next morning, she sat up slowly and stared down at herself. She wore the ruby red dress, which was crinkled, its skirts twisted up. She gasped. A hazy memory of Alex laying her down upon the bed floated back to her. His words sifted through her sleep-laden brain. "You can be a good mistress in the morning."

"Oh, dear." She must have been a terrible mistress last night. She had tried to wait up for him. He had arrived and carried her to her bed, and she had slept through it.

She scrambled from her bed and dashed over to the bureau. Alex surely expected her to make amends this morning. Josie swiftly changed out of the ruby dress into the peignoir. It was not as transparent as Cybil's had been, but it was still thin and very flowing and fluttery. Josie sighed. Any woman let loose of an overly tight whale-boned corset would sigh, of course.

Josie glanced at her hair in the mirror. She refused to look farther. The rest made her embarrassed and nervous in a tense, unknown manner. She attempted to arrange her hair, then let her golden strands fall. Cybil's hair had been a halo the night Josie had seen her. Josie's only looked unkempt and wild. She turned from the mirror, grimacing.

She scampered downstairs, feeling far too drafty. She feared the housekeeper agreed. Upon sight of her, Mrs. Haversham, who carried a rasher of bacon at the moment, dropped it. "My stars!"

Josie flushed. It was *not* as transparent as Cybil's after all. "Is Alex . . . I mean, Lord Rothmier, arisen?"

"H-he will," the housekeeper said. She flushed and glanced down at the bacon now greasing the wooden floor. "He—he is breaking his fast in the breakfast room."

"Th-thank you." Josie hastened past the ogling house-keeper and pelted into the breakfast room. She drew in a steadying breath. Alex sat at the table, reading his newspaper. The butler was just then pouring his tea.

"Hello," Josie squeaked.

The butler looked up first. Or saw her first. He promptly dropped the teapot. "Blimey!"

Josie frowned. Mistresses surely didn't eat much if every servant about them tossed any available food down upon sight of them.

Alex's gaze darkened as he looked at her. "That will be all, B-Biddle."

"Er, St-tubbings, my lord," the butler said, his gaze glued to Josie.

"Whatever," Alex murmured.

"Yes, wh-whatever," the butler stammered. He bowed and, gaze diverted, hastened toward Josie and then past her. A loud thud occurred when he missed the door opening and ran into the frame. "Excuse me. Terribly sorry."

Josie wondered if the apology was meant for them, or for the door frame. She forced the question from her mind and smiled brightly at Alex, as if nothing were unusual. "Good morning, Alex."

She attempted to float gracefully toward him, hoping her peignoir fluttered appropriately. She promptly sat upon his lap. It was a tight squeeze, since he was drawn up to the breakfast table. Worse, when she looked down, she saw the broken teapot and spilt tea. Against such odds, she bent and blew in Alex's ear. "I've been waiting for you."

"Er, yes," Alex said.

"I-I am sorry I was asleep last night."

"It was late."

"I meant to be awake," Josie said, cuddling close. She leaned over to kiss Alex.

He turned his head and scooted his chair back. "Josie, we must talk, and talk seriously."

"Hm?" Josie murmured. She managed to shy a kiss upon his cheek.

"Yes. And stop that. You are not listening. Or, I-I'm not listening," Alex muttered as Josie's lips found his.

"Madame!" Stubbing's voice shrieked from outside the breakfast room.

"Where is that conniving slut?" a deep female voice roared. "No one tries to move into Belinda Barrette's territory." A woman stormed into the room. She wore the brightest yellow-and-green-striped silk dress. Her face was thunderous. She turned a slitted gaze upon Josie. "You Josie?"

"I-I am," Josie stammered.

"I'm going to tear your hair out, vixen," Belinda Barrette said. She was a deep-chested, full-figured, extremely tall woman. Josie never doubted the woman's word. Especially since Belinda charged down upon her with fingers splayed out like talons. Josie shouted and tumbled from Alex's lap.

"Hold!" Alex commanded. He stood and bravely stepped into the path of Belinda's onslaught. His bulk far outstripped hers and gave the woman pause. "What is this about?"

"I ain't going to let you and your fancy piece move into this here town; it's my territory," she said, putting her hands to her hips. "There's only one house here and that is mine."

"I-I wasn't trying to move into town," Josie said. "I don't want any territory."

"Oh, no?" Belinda asked. "You stole my girls' dresses right out from under my nose. Mrs. Landry confessed the whole." Her gaze narrowed and she nodded. "I commissioned that one there for Jasmine."

"But . . ." Josie stammered.

"And you've been to Mr. Niven," Belinda said. "He told

me about your *gold* room, and your *purple* room, and your *pink* room."

"Oh, good God," Alex muttered.

"And you stole my statue, too!" Mrs. Barrette said, shaking her finger. "So don't tell me you aren't trying to set up a house. I wasn't born yesterday."

"Josie is not going to be a madame, madame," Alex said.

"No," Josie squeaked. "I'm a mistress."

"Oh, so you are?" Belinda Barrette said narrowly. "No girl works on her own rounds here. Causes problems, it does. Gives my girls hoity-toity notions of independence."

"She's not going to be a mistress either," Alex said in a firm voice.

"She's not?" Belinda glared at him.

"I'm not?" Josie asked.

Alex looked at her, his eyes dark. "She's going to be my wife."

"She is?" Belinda asked. "You ain't bamming me?"

"I . . . I cannot b-be your wife," Josie said.

"Yes, you can." Alex walked over to Josie, gazing down at her with a fierceness. "I've tolerated as much as I can, Josie. I will never take you as a mistress. I want you as my wife." He hauled her into his arms and kissed Josie ruthlessly. So ruthlessly that when he drew back, Josie clung to him limply. "Marry me, Josie. I love you."

"That man can kiss, missy," Belinda said. "Best tie him down as fast as you can."

"B-but my family," Josie said weakly. "They . . . they . . ."

"I don't give a damn about your family," Alex growled. He kissed her deeply again. He drew back. "And if you marry me, it better be because *you* want to marry me. Not because of the family, or duty, or any other crazy scheme you've thought of, but because you want to marry *me.*"

"I . . . I do want to marry you," Josie sighed. "But . . ."

"No, Josie," Alex said, holding her close. "No buts. You are going to marry me for better or worse, richer or poorer.

Whether your family battens on me or not. Whether my family faints and wails. You will come first with me, and no one else will. And I want to come first with you."

"I-I . . ." Josie felt as if she were going to faint.

"Tough little nut, ain't she?" Belinda said. "Kiss her again. She's about to crack."

Alex chuckled, and before Josie mustered a word, Alex kissed her again. This time when he drew back, he was forced to hold her up. Josie gazed at him. Nothing else *did* matter. "Yes, Alex, yes. I-I love you so much."

"Well, there now," Belinda Barrette remarked. "Glad I don't have to tear your hair out. I hate being fractious before breakfast."

"Thank you," Josie stammered. "I-I will have everything sent back."

"Ha," Belinda said, heading toward the door. "Won't be no use. Mrs. Landry has taken them all in. Only one they'd fit would be Jasmine. And that hussy doesn't need any more clothes. But you can send me my statue. It is a classic piece of art, you know? Will spiff up my place!"

"She will," Alex promised, his tone vehement. "I assure you."

Mrs. Barrette halted a moment as a short, little man entered with Stubbings. "Hallo, Reverend Jenson."

"Good day, Mrs. Barrette," Reverend Jenson said, appearing nervous.

"Don't fret yourself," Mrs. Barrette said, laughing loudly. "My business here is done. You're just in time to start yours." She turned and winked at Josie. "I'm glad you ain't going to be competition."

"Yes," Josie said. She cringed into Alex, staring at the reverend.

"Reverend Jenson," Alex said, taking his jacket off and swiftly placing it around Josie. "You are early."

"A-am I?" Reverend Jenson asked, twitching. It was clear he thought he was too late. "I-I am sorry. I only arrived early t-to discuss the wedding service." He turned a bright red, looking down. "Pleased to meet you, miss."

Josie stared up at Alex. "Wedding service?"

Alex grimaced. "I wanted to explain it all before this. I have a special license, and I thought if you would marry me, we could do so now. Without waiting on anyone. Without your family, or my family. Just the two of us."

"The way it should be," Josie said, nodding. "I-I would like that. Like that very much."

"Oh, dear," a voice said from the door. Pansy, white and pale, walked slowly into the room.

"Pansy!" Josie exclaimed.

"Oh-h," Pansy moaned.

"Alex and I are going to be married."

Pansy halted but a moment on her slow, cautious trek toward the breakfast table. "I am so glad, dear. I do not think I can survive you being a mistress, after all."

Josie giggled. "Will you stand up for me?"

"Certainly, dear," Pansy said in a vague voice. She crumpled into a chair. "Just let me sit down first."

Alex laughed. He looked at Reverend Jenson. "Reverend, if you would follow Stubbings to the parlor. We have a few things to sort out and then we will be ready."

"Y-yes, I understand," Reverend Jenson said. He quivered and appeared all too eager to escape.

Alex grinned down at Josie. "Perhaps a change of dress might be in order?"

Josie gasped. "Oh, dear, yes! But what am I to wear?"

Alex winked. "The ruby dress I saw you in last night would be nice."

Josie flushed. "Y-you liked it, then?"

"Yes," Alex said. "I'm glad you promised to marry me now. I was worried how long I could resist you."

"Hello!" a voice called out.

Josie and Alex turned. Horace and Louise Stanton stood within the doorway, both laden with boxes.

"These were being delivered," Horace Stanton said, grinning. It was clear he was a bit on the go, but not anywhere near castaway. "Decided we'd bring them in. Louise has that butler of yours busy taking her trunks up."

"Father, Mother!" Josie exclaimed. "What are you doing here?"

"Are we too late?" Louise asked, wafting into the room.

"F-for what?" Josie asked, blinking.

"You haven't become . . ." Louise flushed. "Well, you now."

"A fallen woman," Pansy sighed.

"We would have been here earlier," Horace said, "only Louise had to pack. Had a tough time keeping it from Mary and Rachel. We didn't want them to know about it. Got on the road and . . ."

"We got lost," Louise said. She giggled, sounding like a schoolgirl.

"Got confused," Horace said. "We went to your hunting lodge first. I didn't think. It stuck in my memory. I forgot you said you wasn't there." He beamed. "But . . . we had a famous time."

"It was like a second honeymoon," Louise said, flushing.

Horace coughed. "We plan to do it more often. Taking off. Leaving the world behind. Louise has promised to leave her savages and orphans behind, and I, er . . . well, you know I've left everything else behind, too."

"What is in here?" Louise asked, rattling the box she held. "It is a dress box."

"Now, down to business," Horace said, frowning. "I am here to talk you out of being a mistress . . ."

"Oh, my," Louise said when she opened the box. She slammed it shut. "Scandalous!" She bit her lip. "But quite lovely."

"Heh?" Horace asked, coming up to stand behind his wife.

"No, Mother," Josie said. "Please do not show . . ."

Louise opened the box again. Horace's face lit up. "Be damn, but ain't that something. You'd look good in that Louise."

Louise flushed. "Horace, not in front of Josie."

"Well, since it's Josie's," Horace said, "I don't see an reason to act niffy-naffy."

"Indeed." Alex laughed, strolling over. "May I be per mitted to see it?"

Louise slammed the box shut. "Most certainly not."

"Even if it is going to be for Josie's honeymoon?" Ale> asked.

"Honeymoon?" Horace barked.

"Yes." Alex nodded. "Josie has resigned from her caree as mistress, and has promised to be my wife. The reverend is waiting in the other room."

"By Jove, you've done it, me boy," Horace cried. He reached out and hugged Alex. "Glad to have you as m son-in-law, finally. After all these years."

"Yes," Alex said.

"If you will excuse me," Josie stammered, burrowing into her coat. "I-I believe I will change."

"We will be in the parlor, waiting." Alex winked at her "The ruby dress, remember? Just because you are not go ing to be my mistress, there is no reason the dress shoulc be wasted."

Josie sucked in her breath and nodded. She scurried past her parents. She had difficulty making it up the stairs Boxes and trunks crowded the path. Her mother never could travel light.

"Miss Stanton," Stubbings said, coming out of a room panting. "W-will this be all right for my lord and lady?"

"Yes. And please ask Mrs. Haversham to serve wine, o any liquor," Josie said. She grinned. "My father is here."

"Yes, ma'am," Stubbings said, bowing. He turned and stumbled into a trunk. The box on top of it fell, spilling

ıt a cherry pink and black merry widow. Stubbings stared
it, gurgling.

"Oh, dear, th-that should go in my room," Josie said.
t is part of my . . . my wedding trousseau."

"Yes, ma'am." Stubbings nodded. "I congratulate Lord
ıthmier."

Josie's eyes widened, and she giggled. "Thank you, Stub-
ngs."

He picked up the corset, studying it. "Should I check the
her boxes, t-to ensure which room to place them in?"

"Oh, dear, yes," Josie said. "If you would not mind?"

"Not at all," Stubbings said.

Josie grinned. Stubbings was proving to be a very con-
ıentious servant. She rushed into her room and changed
viftly into the ruby dress. She stared at herself in the mir-
ır for a moment. She certainly didn't look like a bride.
ıe grinned. She didn't care. Alex liked the dress and she
as going to marry him.

She rushed down the stairs and dashed into the parlor.
ıe halted, gasping.

Everyone in the room gasped back, including three new
ıhabitants. Michael, Emily and an unknown lady had
owded into the parlor.

"Josie!" Michael sprung up and dashed over, hugging
er. "Just heard the good news. I'm glad you are marrying
lex, and not being . . . er, can't say it in front of Emily."
le grinned. "She ain't a married lady . . . yet!"

Josie blinked. "Yet?"

"Michael and I are going to be married," Emily said,
ıshing up to her.

"You are? But how . . . ," Josie gabbled.

"Well, it took some time convincing Lord Darwood,"
lichael said. "That's what took us so long."

The unknown lady snorted. "He's hard-headed, that
ıe. It is fortunate he's also soft-jawed."

Michael grinned. "Josie, this is Aunt Pennington."

Josie stared at the lady. Finally, to meet the recluse. "I am pleased to meet you."

"Pleased to meet you, too. I like your wedding dress, Aunt Pennington said. She nodded to the statue. "And him, too. I'm glad to know Emily's marrying into a fami of eccentrics."

Josie flushed. "He isn't mine."

"Oh, just visiting for the ceremony?" Aunt Pennington asked, a glint in her eyes.

"You could say that," Alex said, taking off the new jacke he had donned. He went and wrapped it about Davi "Now he is properly attired."

Josie blushed, and turned her gaze back to Michae "Y-you and Emily are truly going to be married?"

"Yes," Michael said. "Didn't even have to run off to th border like Alex told me to do."

"You told him that?" Josie stared at Alex.

"I did," Alex said. "I thought it would be better tha him running off to war. But it sounds as if Michael h upon a different scheme."

Michael flushed. "I wanted to see if I couldn't talk Da wood around first. Alex showed me the way. I don't hav any money, but am of the *ton*. Still, I had a hard time (it. He didn't want to listen to me—too busy swinging me—but Emily took care of that."

Emily giggled. "I hit him in the jaw."

"He was out for a while," Michael said. "He seemed little more reasonable when he came round and saw ho it was going. So I hit him again. I had to wait almost a afternoon to talk to him again."

"Stubborn man," Aunt Pennington said.

"I thought I had him ready to agree, only Aunt Per nington decided to hit him."

"It was my turn," Aunt Pennington said.

Michael grinned. "She's got one devilish left. I gues you could say, Darwood had to sleep on it then. So did l

That's when the notion struck me. I made a compromise early this morning with him. That's why I'm here. I want Alex to be my second in a duel."

"What!" Josie cried.

"It ain't going to be a duel to the death, or anything," Michael said. "It's all set up proper. Darwood was still sticking at being a laughingstock. I told him if I could marry Emily, I'd go out with him. Let him best me. Show the world he ain't a laughingstock."

"Wasn't that wonderful of him?" Emily asked.

"Well, he's going to be family. I don't want him embarrassed all the time, what? Gave him his choice. We're going to use foils. Darwood says he knows how. He'll pink me in the arm. Be the man of the hour. We'll bury the hatchet. I'll marry Emily. I've promised never to hit him again, stay out of politics, and name my first son after him."

Josie broke out laughing. "I had never thought . . ." A sudden warmth flooded through her, and she peeked at Alex.

He grinned. "He took care of it all rather handily, did he not? Certainly no need to worry about him."

"No," Josie admitted.

Suddenly the sounds of a commotion outside the parlor were heard. Josie turned around.

"Hello, is anybody here?" Rachel's young voice called out. She appeared at the doorway. "Jupiter, you are. Wait!" She disappeared.

Everyone waited. Then Mary entered. She rushed up to Josie. "Oh, dear, Paul told me what you were going to do for me. Please say—"

"No," Josie stammered. "I am going to marry Alex, instead."

Mary laughed. "And I'm going to marry Paul instead."

"Who's Paul?" Horace exclaimed.

"He's a gambler," Josie stated.

"Hmmm," Horace said. "Sounds better than that baron, already."

Mary turned toward the door. "Bring him in here, Mike."

Mike entered. He carried Paul over his shoulder like a sack of grain. Rachel followed behind, holding Paul's head to keep it from bobbing.

"Heavens!" Josie exclaimed. "Wh-what is the matter with him?"

"He's sleeping," Mike said. He whistled. "That's some sort of dress, Miss Josie."

"Thank you, it is my wedding dress," Josie said, grinning.

"Put him . . ." Mary began. She looked around. The parlor was already crowded. "Oh, dear."

"H-he may have my seat," Reverend Jenson jumped up. He stumbled over the lovebird's cage at his feet. They squawked loudly.

"Please, not again," Pansy murmured from the corner where she huddled.

"Thank you, gov," Mike said. He lumbered over and half sat, half laid Paul down upon the settee. "He's out for the count, he is."

"He's been to France and back," Mary said, her voice full of pride.

"France?" Josie asked, frowning.

"Yes," Mary said. A beautiful smile crossed her lips. "Josie, do you know who Paul is?"

"Of course I do," Josie said. "You only met him because of me."

"No," Mary said, her brown eyes twinkling. "He's not just a gambler."

"He's a Captain Sharp." Michael nodded sagely.

"No," Mary said, grinning. "He's the Marquis de la Tor."

"Impossible!" Josie gasped.

"Faith," Alex said, laughing. "He told me he had as much to offer as I did."

"He and his family had a falling out years ago," Mary

aid. "He left them, swearing never to return. Only he did, or me. He said I was too respectable to be a madame in a gambling den, and since he couldn't live without me, he would have to become a marquis again."

Rachel giggled. "He said when he arrived in France, he went straight to his family, told them he would take his title back, toasted them, and left. He was in a hurry to return here."

"Rachel!" Mary gasped. "How did you know that?"

Rachel flushed. "Well, there wasn't anyone to stop me." She grinned and all but crowed. "And he did kiss her!"

Everyone laughed and looked to the sleeping Paul, who promptly emitted a snore.

Alex chuckled. "I don't mean to interrupt, old man, but I have my own lady I would like to wed." He looked to Josie. His brow quirked up. "Are you ready?"

"Yes." Josie nodded. She wended her way through the crowded room to finally clasp his hand.

Alex turned to the reverend, who was now jammed into the corner. "Reverend, will you do us the honor?"

"Er, yes," Reverend Jenson said. He reached into the confines and drew out his book. More shifting occurred as he tried to forge closer to Josie and Alex.

"You are beautiful," Alex whispered into Josie's ear. He grinned. "Are you sure you still wish to be married in that dress? We are in the midst of very august company now. We have an heiress and a French marquis present."

"Yes," Josie said, gazing up at him with all the love she felt. "You like the dress. That is what matters to me." She giggled. "They *are* only family, after all."

About the Author

Cindy Holbrook lives with her family in Fort Walton Beach, FL. She is the author of ten Zebra Regency romances, including *My Lady's Servant, The Country Gentleman, The Actress and the Marquis, Lord Sayer's Ghost, A Rake's Reform, Covington's Folly, A Daring Deception, Lady Megan's Masquerade*, and *A Suitable Connection*. Cindy's newest Regency romance will be published in June, 1999. Cindy loves hearing from her readers, and you may write to her c/o Zebra Books. Please include a self-addressed, stamped envelope if you wish a response.

BOOK YOUR PLACE ON OUR WEBSITE AND MAKE THE READING CONNECTION!

We've created a customized website just for our very special readers, where you can get the inside scoop on everything that's going on with Zebra, Pinnacle and Kensington books.

When you come online, you'll have the exciting opportunity to:

- View covers of upcoming books
- Read sample chapters
- Learn about our future publishing schedule (listed by publication month *and author*)
- Find out when your favorite authors will be visiting a city near you
- Search for and order backlist books from our online catalog
- Check out author bios and background information
- Send e-mail to your favorite authors
- Meet the Kensington staff online
- Join us in weekly chats with authors, readers and other guests
- Get writing guidelines
- AND MUCH MORE!

**Visit our website at
http://www.zebrabooks.com**

ROMANCE FROM JO BEVERLY

DANGEROUS JOY   (0-8217-5129-8, $5.99)

FORBIDDEN   (0-8217-4488-7, $4.99)

THE SHATTERED ROSE   (0-8217-5310-X, $5.99)

TEMPTING FORTUNE   (0-8217-4858-0, $4.99)

ROMANCE FROM FERN MICHAELS

DEAR EMILY   (0-8217-4952-8, $5.99)

WISH LIST   (0-8217-5228-6, $6.99)

AND IN HARDCOVER:

VEGAS RICH   (1-57566-057-1, $25.00)